What reviews

"...Well-written, fast paced historical novel by a most talented author. The book was rich in historical detail" -The Road to Romance

"...an incredibly well-written, easy to read, impossible to put down, chronicle of one young lady's journey through the years of the Civil War. Kudos to the author, Ms. Connolly!" - The Romance Studio

"A story of bitterness, healing, forgiveness and romance, FLAME FROM WITHIN provides a glimpse of Civil War life in the south, while offering hope in the face of loss and hurt. Worth the read, Connolly's novel is entertaining and encouraging."- Author's Choice Reviews

"...engaging, well written and entertaining. The author's extensive research into the war between North and South shone through the entire story. The inspirational aspects were not overdone, but instead were threaded seamlessly throughout the story as it unfolded." -Coffee Time Romance

"Flame from Within had wonderfully vivid descriptions of the old south and terrific characterizations. Thoroughly enjoyed the story of this Civil War Epic. A real keeper!" -Terry Spear, Author, Winning the Highlander's Heart

Flame From Within

Shirley Kiger Connolly

Vintage Romance Publishing
Ladson, South Carolina
www.vrpublishing.com

3

ISBN: 978-0-9793327-1-5

PUBLISHED BY VINTAGE ROMANCE PUBLISHING, LLC
www.vrpublishing.com

To Patti Walters (my forever friend)

Cries of battle – shattered hearts
Torn jagged 'cross the grain
Left flames of hate and wills to die
Mingled with great pain.

'Twould take one's cry for healing
and a mend of such a breach,
For Him who knew the perfect way –
This lady love to reach.

'Twould take a faithful warrior
Armed with kindness, love, and peace,
To show a hope worth living for;
Not life-thought dwelt on cease.

He could take compassion
On one scarred and broken life,
Restore the anguished wretched soul
Endured with fear 'n strife.

Thus forward came his chosen one –
He'd single out to break
A stubborn will; a rebel's soul,
For love and saving sake.

Could now the cruel flame ebb away,
To embers set to fade?
When lady love, with open heart
To die no longer prayed.

Shirley Kiger Connolly

The crucible for silver and the furnace for gold,
But the Lord tests the heart.
Proverbs 17:3 NIV

Chapter One

August 1864
Vicksburg, Mississippi

Aimée Lebrún leaned forward and checked out her open window again, half in anticipation half in dread. Her future appeared no better now than it had a moment earlier.

They were still there.

"Aren't we about to the harbor, Elijah?" She called up to the driver. "I've simply got to get out of this thing." She leaned back in and sighed.

Her head thumped harder. She pressed two fingers to her temple. No doubt it had to be the insufferable heat.

"Don't you worry none, Miss Lady Ma'am. She's just up ahead," old Elijah Johnston called down as the carriage neared the loading dock.

Aimée could hear him twist around uncomfortably in the squeaky seat above her. "It's about time. It's stifling down here."

"Yes, Miss Aimée. I's hot too and weary to the bone."

Did the leathery patches on the old man's face and arms still show the after-effects of yesterday's stale heat? She couldn't help but wonder. She, he, and Lulu, her maidservant had been out in the elements it seemed, forever.

Aimée had also noticed earlier the poor old man's britches were full of sticky wetness and smelled bad, too.

She leaned her head out the window once again. Where was that boat? There wasn't much time.

The breaking dawn had turned a dirty-brownish hue, almost hazy after the prior night's sodden rain...much too sultry for that time of morning in late August in Southern Mississippi.

"Talk to me, Elijah," she hollered up again. "Tell me when you see it. It must be there...somewhere."

"You knows I will, Miss Lady Ma'am. I'm searchin' hard as I can."

Aimée rocked back and forth as she felt the driver pull her horse, Smoke, to a jerking stop.

With the stamping of Smoke's hooves and his nervous whinnies, the thinning gray steed finally settled down but not before his hoof-beats caught the attention of the harbor crowd.

Staring out beyond the Vicksburg waterfront, Aimée could not see a familiar Confederate ship anywhere. Instead, only several armored gunboats scarred with shrapnel were nestled against the port in organized fashion, huffing and puffing, to be of service at a moment's call if ordered.

She had to believe what she'd been searching for was out in that harbor. "Elijah! I think I see her. See that one riverboat looking out of place and lost? I'm sure that's it—the *St. Honorine.*"

He squinted his eyes. "Yas'm, Miss Aimée, there her is," he replied, "I sees your boat, too. I's just been rubbin' my eyes so's I can see good."

"Then let's get going."

"But wait, Miss Lady Ma'am. Oh, My! Does you see what else I sees? I'm thinking you better sit tight!"

"What is it Elijah?" she asked.

"It's one of them boys in blue, and he's headed this way."

With a side-long glance, Aimée gave a shudder as she watched the soldier saunter over to seize the horse's bridle.

He cocked his head sideways and peered in.

"Hey there! Where'd you folks get this carriage and horse? Don't you know all means of transportation has been cut off to most of you southerners and belongs to the Union? None of you don't look like no Union soldiers to me."

Aimée didn't like the way the gruff-sounding blue-clad private talked when he turned to stare first at her then up at her driver.

"Are you directing your attention to me soldier?" she asked.

After his brief glance back in the window, she watched as the soldier turned back and ordered her driver down from the top, motioning for him to open the carriage door.

"You heard the man, Elijah," she returned. "Go ahead and come down."

Aimée continued watching out the window as old Elijah eased his worn-out body off the side and stepped down onto the soggy ground. He reached up for his old hand-carved cane then rested his hip against the side of the carriage.

"I's awful sorry, Miss Lady Ma'am," he rasped as he peeked in. "I don't wants to have to tell you to get out if you don't want to."

She nodded and gave him a half smile. "You did what you could."

Pulling back, he unlatched the passenger door. He gave a nod as he watched as she stepped out onto the street and gave him her hand with her maidservant following behind.

Once on the ground, she blinked then focused her gaze downward, refusing to make eye contact with the private.

Following Aimée's smug motion, in unison, the others pulled together with her and turned to face the harbor, standing as stiff as soldiers in a fresh pile of horse dung.

After getting a whiff of the foul spreading odor, the scrawny private pinched his nose and pulled back. He attempted to make way for Aimée to step up onto the boardwalk to get out of the foul-smelling waste.

Instead, she clenched her jaw and swiveled, turning her back on him. When she eventually turned around, she noted he was not only studying her from head to toe but Lulu as well.

Poor thing, now she too is a victim of this man's glare.

A huge ache filled Aimée's heart, but her expression hardened the more she watched him.

"Hey, girl! I thought you'd be something sweet to for my beady eyes to look at! Not only ain't you that, she ain't neither! Why that thing ain't nothing more than a haggard slave!"

He was far from being finished.

"Let me see here," the soldier mumbled, walking around both her and Lulu, while rubbing his whiskered chin. "You sure don't seem nothing like them Southern Belles I hears about back at the barracks."

No doubt about that, soldier. Like other young and ignorant Yankees she'd come in contact with lately, he was making her blood curl.

His barracks talk had to have been heightened by the women they encountered during their momentary triumphs at the plantations they frequented. Their conversations most likely drifted toward tales of boastful conquests at a most degrading level.

Even now she could not stand the illicit look this one gave her. Aimée knew she didn't look like much more than her servant right now. 'Twas true. It wasn't her fault.

Bare of foot and ankle, all she wore was a singed and stained yellowed muslin dress, tattered in several places, caked with mud.

She wanted desperately to plug her ears from the dim-witted man's talk. He just would not be silent.

"…though it's hard to say what might be behind the dirt and grime," he rambled on, picking a small clod of dirt off her arm. The private shrugged his shoulders and then eyed her more closely from head to toe.

"I can just about see 'neath that clingy rag you're wearin' on your back," he said, laughing. "One might wonder, 'cept for that bidding shape, if you's even worth the time or effort I'm spendin' here talkin' at you."

His eyes narrowed and hardened. "That is, 'less, of course you have something to offer me...for later in the evening...after you clean yourself up a bit."

Aimée found it difficult not to turn and glare at the soldier. Maybe if she answered, he would cease.

"The carriage and stallion belong to me. If you want them, Private, you might as well take them, but you'll not have me!

Her snap came out swift, cross, and sharp. When she finished talking, she turned her head to avoid having to face the man any longer than necessary.

Her back stiffened, as unwelcome bitterness crept up her neck. No matter what her Papa tried to teach her about kindness to others, there was no help for the hostility in her heart for all the male population dressed in the deepest of blue now. She refused to allow it to go away.

Taking another corner glance at the private as he reached up to scratch his whiskers, she noticed he was about to speak again. Her lips thinned as she waited.

"Beggin' your pardon, ma'am, maybe I coulda' been more careful with my tongue when I was speaking out like that," he spoke again.

Looking half-humbled, he slowly licked the leftover grime off his upper teeth. "Sides, you should probably be celebrating, ain't that right? I hear your fellow Johnnie Rebs are being paroled right and left. Now ain't that exciting news for you folks?"

Moseying in closer, the private reached up and pinched her cheek. He cleared what looked like stale chaw out of the corner of his lip and spewed it out.

Aimee swallowed, nearly choking as the spittle fell on the ground directly in front of her right foot.

"Hows about you and me, just the two of us..."

Just as she noticed he was about to finish his proposition, his face suddenly drained of color, his words hanging like icicles in thick air.

Her first impulse was to reach up and strike the begrimed soldier hard across his face. His intentions, after all, were less than honorable. She also knew she was being treated like poor-white-trash or worse...if there was such a thing.

Maybe the man figured he had good reason to insult her by her appearance, but she was not about to stand for his crude talk, not today...not any day.

Fighting the urge, Aimée clasped her hands together tightly and remained silent as she glanced up and caught sight of the approaching captain,

The closer the higher-ranking officer headed toward her, the more memories of her burned home came to mind.

With stiff dignity, she forced back her tears. She didn't want to have to think about it all...not again. On any other day, perhaps, when thoughts of the critical war were not on her mind, she might have been more apt to notice the color of the handsome officer's deep-set hazel-hued eyes. Once they caught and held hers, they never left.

It was something she normally enjoyed, looking at the eyes of men from a distance...and knowing they looked at her. But the way he seemed to be boring through her filled Aimée with a sudden icy contempt. Her eyes narrowed suspiciously.

On this morning especially, the look in the captain's eyes only frightened her. Would she forever have these fears growing inside her that were difficult to explain even to herself?

Strikingly handsome or not, the officer was an enemy from the North—a Yankee—a soldier. It was the Union Army who had destroyed her home, most of her family. Thanks to him and the soldiers he commanded, she no longer had anything to live for. Too many experiences from her past remained etched in her mind, as if they had happened only yesterday. And yet her father had always said she should be nice to them.

Well, Papa was now dead.

Seeing nothing but a great mass of blue surrounding her, she shut her eyes and sent up a silent plea to whoever might listen. Perhaps if she prayed, the men in arms standing around would disperse...somehow. She and her companions could then board the tired riverboat before it pushed off the docks. Aimée might finally get out of Mississippi.

She simply had to get to her sister's in New Orleans. What other choice did she have? There was always Tante Fran's. But she would have to go to her sister's to find out how to even get there. Her anxious mind fluttered at what was to come. Even going to Florette's frightened her now, particularly knowing about her sister's questionable reputation.

Besides, Florette doesn't even know me anymore. If Papa were alive he would tell me what to do. He always made things so much easier for me.

When her eyes blinked open, she was disappointed to see the long-legged, flat-stomached officer still standing there. To her surprise, however, with great zest, he suddenly commanded the private back to his post with the promise of a reprimand if he left it again.

Her mouth dropped open as she watched the young private respond with a muttered, "Yes, sir, Captain Jordan, sir."

In the next moment, he slumped off into the crowd, his shoulders bent like that of a spoiled child. His commanding officer further rebuked him for being disrespectful to a woman.

She glanced back at the captain, amazed.

"How can I be of assistance to you, ma'am?" he then asked in a deep but gentle voice.

"You can't...and you won't, not if I have anything to say about it," she said.

"Ma'am?"

She pointed across the harbor towards the battle-scarred sidewinder. "We intend to board that riverboat over there if we can get past your vulgar-minded and foul-mouthed men!"

Nodding in its direction, she continued. "That's all that matters to me. I don't need assistance from the likes of any of you *Billy Yanks.*"

He peered beyond her and back. "You've signed your oath to the Union, I presume," the ramrod-straight soldier stated, lifting a brow. "It's necessary, you know; otherwise I cannot allow you to leave the area."

"I signed your absurd oath! If it truly meant something, maybe I could believe in it…sir!"

He nodded slowly. A momentary look of discomfort crossed his face as he asked the next question. "Excuse me…ma'am. I am assuming you know *St. Honorine* is primarily used for Federal shipping, mind you, and elsewise as a hospital ship. Only a small number of civilians from here in Vicksburg will be taken. And even if you have a destination in mind, it would cost you some heavy coin."

Aimée stood stiffly as he searched her over from head to toe. "Are you able to pay for the ticket?"

"I beg your pardon?"

As the captain surveyed her, his mouth curved in a lopsided grin. "There's also the chance you could run into some danger on the trip…what with the war and all…ma'am."

Aimée frowned. "In what worse danger can I be now? Take a peek around you, Yankee. You've already destroyed my town and all whom I dearly love, one by one. Is there anything worse I can experience?"

She went on. "I doubt you are truly worried about me in the least. Isn't that right…Yankee?"

Thumbing behind her, she drew attention to her last link to home. "As I told your underling before, the stallion and my papa's carriage should cover ample fare for the ride. It may appear rough now, but it can be cleaned up with a little lye and water."

He leaned around her for a closer observation. "You're absolutely right, ma'am."

Aimée chewed on her lower lip. "I promise you, officer, the horse is of good breeding. He won't let you down...if you can bring yourself to learn to treat him kindly."

"Well, I—"

After pulling Lulu and Elijah in closer by her side, she finished. "These are my friends, and they shall accompany me. Did you want to try to challenge me on that too...sir?"

* * * *

Captain Jordan drew his brows together as he watched and listened to the blue-eyed young woman speak. It took greater effort to contain the slight smile stealing across his face over the girl's rough appearance.

There was no doubt in his mind she would become the brunt of many a joke on the boat by the primary occupants—lonely young men

He'd hoped to save her from embarrassment or from having to beg, but his attempt to make excuses for her would fall only on deaf ears. He caught himself scrutinizing her further.

As he continued observing the girl, he noticed she stood only a few hands high. Though she appeared more than amply proportioned in the correct places with her waif-like stature, she didn't look as if she weighed much more than a large bale of hay.

She could not have been more than around ten and eight, if that. No less than a couple of years older than Annabelle, his kid sister.

In spite of her humble appearance, she seemed not the least bit bashful. She'd certainly made that known to the world during what he'd heard of her discussion with his private a few minutes earlier.

He cleared his throat. "Listen, ma'am, I don't care who you bring with you. It wasn't my idea to have a war."

"Nor mine, Captain, but I've no choice in the matter, do I?"

"Ma'am?"

"Excuse me." She was visibly trembling.

"You see…"A warning voice whispered in his head. *Leave the poor girl alone.* "Never mind. I will be on my way then, if you don't mind."

With a slight gesture, Palmer lifted his chin and clicked his boots together, touching the edge of his wide brimmed hat in a salute with his fingers. "We'll pick up the horse and carriage later, and I'll inform the captain of *St. Honorine* you will be boarding."

Without waiting for her acknowledgment, he made an about face and walked off to where a couple of other Union officers up ahead stood and waited for him.

Stopping, he turned and stared over the pedestrians in the harbor to get another glimpse at the barefooted girl still standing in the dung with her two traveling companions. His heart stirred within him.

"God speed to you, young redheaded miss," he murmured. "Who knows, perhaps someday, God willing, we can meet under more favorable circumstances."

If he could have had his way, he would have been anywhere but where he was that day, like back in Virginia at Pencil Ridge working cattle with his Pop or helping out with the hay harvest.

Home would always be Virginia where he and Annabelle spent all their summers until their dad died, and they were constrained to move with the relatives up to Ohio. Life had never been the same since then.

Palmer knew the facts. If he and his cousin, PJ, had *not* been in Ohio the year the war began, neither would have found themselves fighting for the Union. Both their lives had radically altered and had played a large hand in how Palmer had ended up in Vicksburg that August morning.

He heaved a sigh and stared back at the girl again. There was no way this victim of the war would know about all that, much less care. It would do no good to return and tell her now.

One of the other officers shifted his weight on the other foot. "You coming or not, captain?"

He swung back. "I'm here. Hold up."

The three officers soon fell into step, making their way towards the *St. Honorine*. Palmer made his way up the gangplank. When he glanced back one more time, the girl he'd searched for earlier had disappeared completely from his view

* * * *

Excitement mixed with apprehension poured through Aimée as she previewed the area while stepping out of the dung. "I can't believe we're here at last! Can you, Lulu?"

"We's here all right, Miss Aimée."

"Lemme' just get your trunks on that big boat, Miss Lady," Elijah suggested, wiggling his hat in his hand. "Tain't far—n' tain't no trouble."

She glimpsed up at the old man and acknowledged with a half smile and a nod. As she watched the busy dock, she shook her head. "It's hard to imagine I'm finally here."

She peered down at her tarnished dress, worn ragged from continued wear, reminded once again of where she'd spent the last few months.

Faded marks of a doused fire still lingered along the hemline of her crumpled skirt, her crinoline singed along its border. Even after all the times she'd scrubbed her clothes and herself in the river, in no time at all, she became caked again from head to toe with stale mud, soot, and encrusted clay. Did it matter anymore?

These days, she found she didn't care about much of anything…anything or anyone, except for her friends, Lulu and even Elijah. She reached over to take Lulu's hand.

Thank goodness for Lulu calling out like she did! Why, if she hadn't screamed out that night from the burning veranda, I

*might never have found her, and she would've burned with all
the rest, and I...I....*

Aimée visualized the scene again, as she had many
times before—how she'd run up the burning steps of her
mama's porch and grabbed the hysterical servant.

It had all happened fast. Like flashes of lightening,
the two of them had rolled (it seemed forever) off the
veranda and onto the once beautiful lawn.

Parts of Aimée's boots had begun melting like stale
wax, until the flames caught the hem of her dress and
raced up the fabric, almost setting her aflame. The fire
wasted no time in leaving a large scar on the backside of
her right leg. In truth, it was a miracle she and Lulu were
alive. Yet she'd been too late for the rest of the family.

"Sometimes I still wonder if it was all worth it."

"I knows, Miss Aimée."

Since that night, neither woman had eaten a
complete day's meal nor slept a full night. She couldn't
even recall when she'd taken her last real bath, aside
from her occasional dips in the shallows of the muddy
Mississippi. Those she'd forced upon herself had brought
little refreshment to her grungy body.

Yes, she was grateful she at least still had her friends.
It was inevitable the time would eventually come to
leave Vicksburg. Was there anything left there that could
make her want to stay? This was her home, all she'd ever
known. Another look around convinced her otherwise.

"How's your feets doin' this day, Miss Aimée?" the
servant asked, causing a break in the stilted silence
hanging in the thick air. Her maidservant had not spoken
much in days.

"They'll be fine, honey." She gave a warm smile as
she gazed into her tired eyes.

"I sure wish you'd took my shoes stead of going
without none on your toes," Lulu said faintly. "It still
don't seem right and proper I still has something for my
feets, and you don't got none. I never liked these much,"
she mumbled on, looking down. "These here is them
store bought'ns you gemme' Christmas for last."

Aimée snatched her hand away and tried to hide her tears. "Stop it now."

"Miss Aimée, you is thinkin' about your mammy and pappy again, I can tell. I seen that look before!" She closed her eyes.

"And stop with that praying, too. Open back up, Lulu. I know good and well what you're doing."

With a quick jerk, Aimée watched her servant kick off her flimsy shoes and toss them into a stale, waterlogged pile of leftover horse dung. She stood and stared at them with a frown on her face.

Hearing the splatter, Aimée wiped her tears with her dirty sleeve. "Pick up those shoes and put those back on right now. You know you love those shoes, Lulu Jean. I told you before, I'll be fine. There are plenty more slippers and boots in my trunks. I want you to take your mind off me and my poor lost soul and start watching for Elijah, you hear?"

Lulu pouted and bent down to get them. "Yas'm, I hears you."

Aimée's lip quivered as the two of them went back to searching for the old man. If only Elijah would hurry back, she might be on her way. She had to get to a place where she could close her mind to her memories.

Turning one last time to gaze at her papa's black carriage, no longer shiny after months of storage in the underground cave, she ran her once dove-soft fingers along the carvings etched in the side.

Leaning her head against its surface, she took a deep breath. Would her dreadful memories ever leave her? Right now, without any happiness or heartsease it appeared that would be impossible. Surely, life could get no more out of kilter than it was right now.

Aimée, sick of weeping and sick of thinking about the past, was also sick of dreading what was to come. The only thing keeping her sane was looking around the busy dock and seeing her situation was not at all isolated. Although she felt completely alone, she saw by the look on the faces of hundreds of others there were many more who hated life right now as much as she did.

Lulu's nudge on her shoulder brought her back to the present. When she opened her eyes, to her relief, Elijah came into view.

"Come on, honey," she said with a hurry. "Let's get going. We certainly can't stay here any longer."

Chapter Two

Aimée gazed over at the hired hand, who was limping back towards the carriage. Her tears streamed down her cheeks.

"Miss Lady Ma'am?" Elijah questioned. "I come to tell you—"

"I...I'm sorry." Aimée wiped her eyes with her sleeve. "It all came back again. I declare, I—I cannot seem to get it out of my mind."

"It's okay, Miss Aimée. Your trunks, they is on the big boat, now. You gonna be okay now. Is there enethin' else you be wantin'? Them fellas back yonder, they's needin' some more roustabouts to help with s'plies. I could do that, if you'ns don't mind."

"Certainly, Elijah. I only wish I was able to compensate you like Papa did for all you've done to help me these last few months! If it weren't for you, my trunks would be long gone, and I probably would not be standing here alive."

He grinned wide, showing her his yellowed teeth. "Them houses down in that dirt...they was somethin'!"

"I don't know how you did it."

"It weren't hard. I just took me a shovel and burrowed down deep like in them hills over by the riverbank lak your pappy told me. Din't tell nobody else.

Nobody knowed about *our* secret place by the time them soldiers done come neither." He grinned again.

"'Twas the best of the best, thanks to you!" said Aimée.

"Your pappy, he and them others, they smelled trouble for weeks."

"Yes, they did," she answered again. Aimée remembered how her papa had insisted she go on ahead with some of the other neighbors to hide in those underground caves.

Why did he have to stay back with the rest of the family? Why did young Christopher, her brother, have to take ill?

"I didn't want to go alone."

She shook her head. Most of the servants at *Shadow Grove* had stayed back, loading up trunks with clothing and the family silver, china, and other heirlooms. It was what her mother had wanted.

Ruby Lebrún was funny that way. She had been anxious to get everything stored safely in one of the barns for Elijah to come and move them down with Aimée later.

"Papa had promised he would bring them to join us, Elijah, but they never came."

"It were hard times, Miss Lady Ma'am."

After five days, when no one showed up to the underground caves, Aimée could not stand being alone any longer. On the fifth night, she had found her way back to the house, only to be sent off again.

"Please," her mother had begged, "Go back; be safe. You must protect our silver, Aimée darling. We'll join you very soon. We must get rid of little Christopher's scarlet fever before we can move him out of the house, darlin'. You know how poorly he's been."

"Papa, must I?" Aimée remembered crying, hoping her father would allow her stay at the house until her baby brother improved.

But he too had remained firm. "Go now, my princess. We'll be along. Everything will be okay before you know it."

Those were the last words she would ever hear him speak. His words still rang in her ears.

When nearly another week had passed, and there were still no signs of the family, she and Elijah had waited until dusk before riding out through the neighbor's small cherry orchard.

As if sensing his rider's needs, Smoke walked gingerly, holding back his usual whinnies and grunts as they traveled along the darkened path.

Over the final hill, they had seen it all as they had watched the skies, which had already ignited, and the smoke shooting above the tree line. When they had reached the front drive, the blazes had left the barns and moved to attack the house with full force.

By the time Aimée, in her shock, had seen Lulu crawling out towards the edge of the burning veranda and heard her terrifying screams, she knew she had returned to *Shadow Grove* too late.

"We done the best we could."

She knew Elijah was right.

"Your mammy and pappy, well, I just couldna' ask for nicer boss folks. I means..." He stopped to blow his nose on a rag. "Your pappy, he allus' took good care of us, huh, Lulu?" Elijah looked over at the maidservant.

Aimée gazed over at her servant's huge brown eyes and dirt-stained cheeks as she nodded.

"He amanceepated us long before Mr. Lincum made that proclamation legal-like. I just wish there was somethin' more I could do to help *you*, Miss Lady Ma'am.!" The old man squinted.

"You've done more than enough, Elijah."

There was a tug on Aimée's arm. "Miss Aimée, didn't you heared the sound of the whistle? You doesn't wants to miss the boat does you?"

She turned. "Was that ours, Lulu?"

You wants to get to New Orleans to see your big sistuh. They's about to leave us behind!"

"Oh, my! We must be quick!"

* * * *

The landsman bent down to take up the gangplank, as Aimée lifted her torn skirts and ran as fast as her bare feet could carry her across the planked jetty. Tears blinded her eyes. It was impossible to overlook the throbbing from her splinters and bruises even after weeks and months of walking around bare of foot.

Lulu and Elijah remained fast at her heels.

"Please, Sir, please stop!" she called out. "I declare, please wait a minute!"

The landsman gazed out and saw the three running towards him, almost breathless in their pursuit by the time they reached the edge of the landing.

"Don't know if there's room or no," he drawled out slowly, leaning over the side to spit out some juices from his wad of tobacco.

After setting the gangplank back down, he curled his left eyebrow and lip in harmony and added, "But I'm guessin' if you wants a ride, we could find a spot for ye. Got any coin?"

Blinking back a fresh spray of fishy smelling water, Aimée pointed back to her horse and carriage.

The man showed a satisfied scrutiny then moved aside to make room for the three to climb aboard the already overcrowded sidewinder. No sooner than the passengers were on deck and off the makeshift bridge, the gangplank lifted again.

With a grinding sound, the riverboat *St. Honorine* grunted and pulled away from the waterfront, plodding slowly through the muddy ruts and out from the bank.

Aimée stopped and straightened herself with dignity. The main deck was crammed with army supplies and other cargo. She had no idea where she would sleep, but anything had to be better than where she'd been.

"This way, Lulu," she finally said, maneuvering herself and her companion through the crowded passageway towards the stairs.

After ascending towards the boiler deck, both discovered most of the passenger quarters located above, but by the time they reached the top step, all appeared occupied.

Aimée stopped again at the promenade deck to join the other passengers, whose eyes stayed glued on the shrinking countryside as the boat worked its way downriver along the Mississippi. As she glanced over the rail, she half-searched for the officer with the wide-brimmed hat.

She recognized two of the officers she had observed from before, but the captain was not standing with them.

It was not that she *wanted* to see the man she'd spoken to again…certainly not. 'Twas a fact, she wasn't sure exactly why she found herself searching for him at all.

Good riddance to the lot of them.

As far as she was concerned, there was no love lost for *any* adult male who dressed in the color of navy and wore the buttons of brass. She determined in her heart right then she would continue her loathing of all northerners until the day she died.

A disastrous thought crossed her mind. What if, at the last minute, old Smoke and the worn out carriage turned out not to be satisfactory payment for her trip? She did not want to be yanked from the boat or ordered back to the docks before they got too far out.

Well, I won't leave! They can try to order me off if they want to, but they would have to discover me first! I shall find a place to hide myself if I must!

Had she not recently learned how to conceal herself well in an underground cave? There, on the *St. Honorine*, she would do it again…if she truly had to.

* * * *

"Where you gonna sleep, Miss Aimée? Does you get your own floor spot?" Lulu asked anxiously.

Aimée grinned. "No, honey, I don't get my own designated footage on deck anywhere. I'm in the same boat as you…literally!"

She smiled. "There doesn't appear to be a vacant space anywhere, does there? It certainly is a tight squeeze around here. Let's check out the next deck. I know these boats like the back of my hand, honey. Been on them before with Papa. We'll find us a place."

"Yes, miss. I'm comin'."

The hurricane deck, up one more ramp of steps, housed a small group of rooms reserved for the boat's officers called *Texas* staterooms, not unlike the quarters below. But what caught Aimée's eye were not the quarters so much, but rather the rows and rows of makeshift beds filled with wounded soldiers. Some appeared to be sleeping, some whispering.

The only thing distinguishing the men in the beds from one another was the color of their hats or coats hanging on the posts at the end of the cots.

"Miss Aimée, what you doin' up here!" said her servant. "Won't them men folk come get you?"

She shook her head. "Hush. They cannot see us that well down here," she whispered. "Stay quiet."

The closer Aimée approached the makeshift infirmary, the more offensive the smells became, exuding odors of sickness, medicine, and in some cases, impending death.

"Miss Aimée! We's getting' too close."

Aimée pulled out her soiled handkerchief and held it to her nose. "Let's keep moving. Once I find the commander of this boat, we'll be okay. Papa might have known him and that would be good for me! He'll be able to help us."

"Wait!" said Lulu. She'd turned her head and fixed her eyes toward the cots again. She stopped and pulled on Aimée's arm.

"Miss Aimée," she whispered too loudly, "I think them boys is over there talkin' 'bout you."

Aimée shook her head again. "It's nothing important, honey."

"Mmm-hmm…I heerd one of them called you a *Sandhill Tacky*! That's what! And they's sayin' you prob'ly downright stink, Miss Aimée. That ain't right!"

Aimée put her arm around the servant. "Don't you fret. They stink plenty, too. And right now, whoever is saying that is pretty close to right! I'd give anything to have a bath. It's probably another Yankee carrying on anyway. Just keep walking, honey."

She searched on until she found the pilothouse snuggled in the middle section of the deck between two ascending smokestacks belching black smoke up to the sky.

"I shall simply have to go up to the pilot stand and find out if the commander of this thing is up there," she mumbled, wanting to get as far away as possible from the sick and infirm soldiers. He can tell me where I can rest."

"Oh, my!" said Lulu, who didn't budge. "You think it be okay to go up them stairs where all that smoke's be blowin' out?"

"You're with me, Lulu!" Aimée countered boldly. "I'll take good care of you—not like those heartless Yankees that left you for dead! Haven't I always?"

A moment later she noted the familiar boat commander, Captain H Moreau, standing from the top step of the pilot stand smiling down in recognition.

Aimee saw pleasure in his eyes as he descended the first couple of ladder rungs to greet her.

"Amethyst Rose Lebrún, little Aimée," he said, "is that you behind all that *saleté* grime and there in your soiled and bare feet?" He winked. "I almost did not recognize you, *ma chère*."

"It is me, Captain," she replied quietly. "I can't tell you how glad I am to see it's you!"

He laughed. "And who could miss that ball of fire what covers *zee* head so much like your *père*, and those eyes…the eyes of your *gentil mère* ? "

He cocked his head sideways. "What *eez* this smudge I see on your dainty leetle nose and this droopy frown I see on your sad leetle face? Have you no pleasant news to report from home for me? If you please, how *eez* Cecil and his little woman?"

Aimée softened her stance as he placed his hands on her shoulders and gave her a gentle twist. She turned back and allowed him to guide her back down the steps. When he turned her around again, the captain gave her one of his familiar bear hugs.

Aimée hoped by crossing her arms she might disguise her noticeably thin appearance.

He gazed at her downcast look. "What brings you to *St Honorine*, child?"

She tried to brighten her smile. "Captain Moreau! I…"

Horatio Moreau, the man with the hard to forget flat pancake cheeks and beady eyes staring directly into her eyes. Captain Moreau. One of Papa's dearest friends for years. How wonderful to be entrusted into his care for a few days. Her return hug was strong and genuine.

"I wish Papa were here with me."

He stopped to look her over again. "Is your *tristesse*, your sadness, because of this war?"

"My sadness — the war, yes...and because of my family — they are gone, Captain — Papa, Mama, and Christopher, too."

"I am so sorry. But you are here. And how did you take care of passage my *ma chère?* I would to help you should I have known."

She shook her head. "It is of no matter now."

"I know of your sister. But where is your older brother, David?"

"David? Had he been home from France, surely I would have lost him, too. *Shadow Grove*...also destroyed. There's almost nothing left of anything."

Aimèe reached up and touched his cheek gently. "I feel now as if I am no longer with purpose, Captain Moreau." She turned away to hide her face. "Why should I bother to go on?"

"Ah, *Ma chère.*," he turned her face back toward him, "I am so sorry for you."

"Lately, I have simply wanted to die," she cried.

"Do not talk such ways! Tell me, child, when did this happen? Was it summer last when the soldiers took your city? I remember zee *problème* when it came to your town."

Aimée nodded. "Indeed it was."

"And when did you last have good food to eat?" He squeezed her arms and looked her over carefully. "You are much too frail."

She sniffed and shrugged her shoulders before turning toward Lulu. "I cannot say — a while. We have managed though, the two of us."

"Yes, we's managin', like all them other folks," said Lulu.

"*La seule pensée!*" he lamented again. "Come with me, little one. You need a quiet place to rest your weary body and food for your belly. I have just zee place! You shall take my room! Yes, it shall be yours for *zee* duration of *zee* trip."

Moreau chewed on the stem of his old black pipe. "Let's see," he said as he went on rubbing his chin. "I can have water brought in with a small tub for you to *prendre un bain,* ha, ha, I should say, have a hot, steamy bath of bubbles...and a cozy bed with which to rest your pretty little head. It is a wonderful plan. No?"

"But, Captain, I couldn't take your room!" Aimée replied. Where then would you sleep?"

"Ha, ha!" He winked and continued laughing. "Do you not know, dear one, *zee* captain of *St. Honorine,* he never sleeps? Besides, what does it matter? It is already done!"

He lifted two fingers and pinched Aimèe's cheek. "Dry your eyes, *ma chère,* and smile. After you are all rested and prettied up...then, my child, we shall talk of new things...yes?"

Aimée glanced at him sadly. "I suppose we could then talk about my sister."

* * * *

Aimée's heartbeat quickened at the knock she heard at the door. It had to be the captain. She rolled over on her small bed. "Lulu, see if that is Captain Moreau, will you, honey?"

"Yes, Miss Aimée, but he shouldn't be botherin' you none. You ain't got 'nuff rest yet."

"Just check, Lulu."

At the next hesitant knock, the maidservant turned the latch. "If it be Miss Aimée you wantin', her's sleeping in here still," she mumbled.

"I only came to see how she was faring and if she was still able to sleep. She did not look—shall I say, *en bonne santé,* uh, healthy, when we first shared

31

conversation zee other time we spoke. I will come at another time."

"Wait, Captain," Aimée called out. "I'm quite awake. Don't listen to Lulu. She has a mind of her own. She sat up eagerly. "Give me a few moments to freshen up. I'll be out directly."

"*Magnifient !*" he called back through the door. "I'll be here waiting," he replied.

Lulu shut the door in his face.

Aimée stretched. "Don't be rude, Lulu. He has given us a place to stay. We need to be thankful. Get me some water, will you?"

"Yas'm. I worry about you is all. You was dreaming about Mr. Jonathan again!"

"Jonathan Dewey... again?"

"Yes, Miss Aimée. I heered you say his name three times in the night."

"Oh, mercy me," said Aimée. "I suppose I did, Lulu."

"I knows."

Hot tears escaped and rolled down Aimée's cheeks. "I've tried not to think about him much lately, but my memories of him are still before me."

Lulu nodded and passed her a hanky. "Wipe your eyes, Miss Aimée. I gots a happier surprise for you. You don't wants to think about the Dewey boy no more. Your trunks is back!"

"What's this?" she asked, blowing her nose. "You have my clothes?"

"Mr. Elijah, him brought your trunks up."

Aimée smiled. "He brought them after I went to sleep? You should have awakened me! You are my ever-faithful one, you know that. Thank you, honey; I didn't even have to tell you to tell old Elijah where we were, did I!"

"No, miss, I be knowin' what to do before you's ever has to ask me stuff. I always knows what you wants, Miss Aimée," giggled Lulu.

Following Aimée behind a folded screen, Lulu brought her back a gown. She hurried her into her black crimped dress of delicate gossamer. "And I can get your cape for the cold air, too."

It had been months since Aimée had been able to dress properly.

"You did want the black one, didn't you, Miss Aimée?"

"Oh, yes, honey. Thank you for remembering. One must be able to grieve," she reasoned.

"Folks don't get much time for grievin' no more, does they?"

"Not as they should, and heaven knows, I'm still in my state of mourning. For the sake of my family, 'tis crucial to show it. Many, during war times, cannot bewail the ones they love in proper fashion. 'Tis a terrible, terrible thing. I am bound and determined to do so for as long as necessary."

"And for the Mr. Dewey boy, too, Miss Aimée?" asked Lulu. "I never did like him."

"Yes, Lulu. I must also wear my mourning dress in memory of Jonathan, too, and I know you never liked him much," she mumbled.

* * * *

Was she not after all almost a widow herself? It was true the charming and handsome Jonathan Dewey had never quite taken her to wife for there had not actually been a writ of marriage between them.

The banns *had* been ready to publish; it would have only been a matter of time. They had made plans to take their vows at the chapel on the precise weekend he had disappeared. Was it not as good as complete?

Not that it was Aimée's idea. Not from the start.

The fact was, Jonathan Langston Dewey was the grandson to an English Baron, and her father had been interested in the family bloodlines when he had heard the family had moved to the area and had taken over the neighboring tobacco plantation.

The marriage was all her father's and the Baron's idea. Her father had the Dowry. The Deweys had the bloodline. Aimée had little to say in the matter.

"You will be connected to a prominent family, and because of me, you will be well taken care of," her father had told her. "Besides, they need our help financially."

"Yes, Papa," Aimée remembered replying. "But must I live around all that malodorous tobacco?"

She had never liked the smell of those strange burning tobacco leaves that had gained popularity around the area. In truth, she never cared much for Jonathan Dewey, either. However, when her mother interjected her own thoughts about the marriage, Aimée came to understood better the principle purpose for the arrangement.

"Think of it this way," her mother had reasoned. "The lucrative proceeds you'll collect from tobacco growing will keep you in finery for years to come—and you know you like nice things. Always remember, Papa knows best, dear." And didn't all girls of her status feel that way?

Aimée tried hard to remember her mother's comments up until the night before their wedding, when everything changed—when Jonathan had been ordered to report for service. It was interesting how he suddenly disappeared.

"Watch for me, Aimée Rose," he had said.

But he'd been called out the day before they were to exchange vows. His commanding officer had promised to give him a few hours the next day for his marriage ceremony. Jonathan never made it to the chapel, leaving Aimée waiting for hours in the narthex with the reverend and his wife.

Various reports came in that the dandy of Vicksburg was missing-in-action. Some said he had fled the area. Later it was reported he had run off to avoid his commitment to serve. That he did not want to care for a new wife.

Finally, after six months with no further word, the Dewey family decided to hold their son's funeral and return home to England about the same time the Yankees had come and seized what was left of their property.

Was the charmingly handsome, the debonair Jonathan, truly missing-in-action, or had he abandoned his troops? Was he dead? Did he in reality run off to avoid responsibility?

If he were to return home alive, would he still be interested in taking Aimée to wife with her family now gone and her father's property destroyed—her holdings now no longer of any value? Had her father truly known what was best?

Alive or dead, debonair or not, in truth, Jonathan meant nothing to Aimée. He was certainly nothing at all like her father. Not once had he showed the slightest interest in physical labor. In fact, the man was downright lazy. Unfortunately, she never once had told that to her father. Perhaps it was better that way.

Although she felt great sorrow for the Dewey family's loss, at the same time, she was relieved she hadn't been trapped into a marriage she knew she would later regret. After all, wasn't she the one left standing in the chapel?

* * * *

Lulu tucked Aimée's curls up in a net pouffe and tied them back with black silk ribbon away from her face. "Don't you worry none. I won't never tell no one I knowed what you's thinking, Miss Aimée."

"You never cease to amaze, me, Lulu Jean," Aimée said, shaking her head.

"Mmm Hmm."

"I suppose I really mustn't keep the captain waiting any longer," Aimée finally said, turning to give her servant a hug. "Perhaps there is something I can do to help the captain out around this old boat—you think?"

She stepped outside and walked behind the waiting captain. "Captain Moreau?" she whispered, giving him a start. When he bent his head toward her, she smiled. "I apologize for my delay. You wished to speak with me?"

He gazed down at her and sighed. "Oh, *oui, Mmlle Lebrún*. I now can see your familiar and lovely face in the light! How I wish I were young again!"

He took her hand and brought it to his lips for a whisper of a kiss. "Are you happy with your *pied-a-terre*, my child?"

Aimée blushed. "My room suits me fine. I don't know how I shall ever repay you."

He glanced down at his boots and then rolled his eyes her way. He spoke slowly, almost inaudibly. "There is one way."

"Whatever you want...tell me," she answered, her own bright eyes sparkling.

"Let us walk that we might discuss the matter further."

Heavy snickers floated out from the infirmary into the quiet of the night as several of the infirm soldiers Aimée noticed a moment earlier eyed the couple as they disappeared along the deck.

Captain Moreau took hold of Aimée's hand and placed it in the crook of his arm, quickening his pace to get her out of earshot of the heckling men.

Chapter Three

Not far from Moreau and the young woman, Palmer stood in the shadows, leaning against the railing, watching them. He, too, was having a difficult time taking his sight off the young woman whose creamy skin glowed in the moonlight. Were he to dare, he would have liked to reach out and touch her face from where he stood. It looked as soft as fine silk.

Her golden red hair was pulled back in some sort of netting. A stray curl fell softly along the side of her cheek.

From where he stood, he wanted to mend it. He'd as soon see the rest of the lady's bound up tresses somehow fall from their bondage and flow free down her back... until he shook that idea from his mind.

As he watched her in the evening moonlight, he was drawn to her immediately, not merely because of her ravishing beauty, but because of something else—a sadness or melancholy, perhaps, some heavy burden she seemed to portray. The woman looked quite lost.

He did not enjoy making habits of staring at lovely ladies...most of the time. Over the last several years, he'd made maintained his dignity in matters such as that, being a Christian gentleman and all.

Yet, left with the impression of *this* woman—with both her loveliness and as someone apparently in great duress—he had not been able to help himself.

What *was* it about this young woman that kept drawing him to her?

Heat burned his cheeks. *Indeed, what is my problem?*

With a shake of his head, he turned away quickly. This was not the time to be thinking about anyone of the opposite sex, regardless of the reason.

* * * *

"What are you thinking about, Captain Moreau?" Aimée touched his arm.

A lull had pinched the air, allowing for a peaceful repose as the captain listened. The sidewinder continued creating its own sounds—the hissing of the rising steam and the clacking of paddlewheels.

"Not much," he quibbled, "just *zee* river and its strangeness, and you *ma chère?*"

Aimée took note of the blanket of heavily illuminated stars, resembling ornaments of silver lace that covered the phosphorous sky and pointed.

"I am watching the fireflies leaving their calling cards here and there, and I hear hundreds of crickets rubbing their forewings together, chirping their customary sounds; the same sounds I hear frequently along these banks of the bayou, Captain." Aimée continued gazing out into the night. "I love the sounds that remind me of home."

The Mississippi River may have been under Union control, but no one could take away the haunting beauty surrounding her, the sounds of life or the evening glow of the Deep South no matter what the circumstances.

"The night, it lightens your eyes, *ma chère*," said the captain, glancing over from the side. "You wish to stop and think some more?"

"I want to memorize it all," she replied softly, "I must, you see. Mississippi is over for me now."

"Do not worry, child. I shall do what I can to help you. You will now go see *zee sœur*, sister?"

She nodded. "My life will never be the same as it was back with Papa," she murmured, especially if the rumors about her sister were as true as her heart hinted.

No one in Vicksburg cared much about Florette due to her arrogant attitude. Aimée had heard all the stories. She remembered enough herself. Things she'd never told anyone…and never would..

Florette gained her self-seeking, unkind reputation early in life. Even the suitors Papa brought home never got anywhere with her after she claimed she would choose her *own* husband when she had a mind to. Her animosity towards men took greater priority than the need to wed.

When she left Vicksburg, word soon spread the woman had become a well-known Madam, amidst gamblers and liberated octoroons, going as far as collecting women slaves to resell on the block.

Naturally, Aimée was not sure if any of it was all that true...early on. If it was, she had chosen not to care. It had made life easier...up until the fire.

The friction between her and her sister developed rapidly when her older brother, David, left Shadow Grove and sailed off to France. Shortly after that, Florette departed for the city. She did not have to look for long for a husband. That was how it was with Florette. When she wanted something, she simply went out and fetched it. In her case, it turned out to be a short,-squat, babbling Belgium man, old enough to be her grandfather.

In no time, she convinced Mr. Brusque to take her to wife. Then she'd had the daring to ask him to purchase for her as a wedding gift a large townhouse once utilized as a bordello, which he gladly did.

Within days of the ceremony, however, Florette falsely accused the man of bringing her physical harm and had the marriage annulled. With little care for her personal reputation, Florette then made full use of her new name, and within six months, her townhouse, already known as The Paramount, became one of the most notorious sporting houses in the red light district of New Orleans.

Some folks back in Vicksburg sadly rumored Mr. Brusque had returned to his home country and died a broken old man.

It sickened Aimée's heart to think about it.

"Does so much trouble your mind, my child?" asked the captain, interrupting her thoughts.

"Yes, Captain, many things and nothing. I often don't know anymore."

"Ah, sweet one, if I was only thirty and five years younger, I might *conseeder* taking you to wife myself, since my dear Marcella is twenty years now gone, rest her sweet departed soul," he said with a sigh. "Such is not possible, of course, with all the years which lie between us, ha, ha!   Come, let us continue walking."

The two of them walked on.

"*Jeunesse dorre*, the right young man will come one day for you to take your mind off sorrow! Perhaps, *zat eez* what you find yourself dreaming of more than your *seester*."

Aimée smiled. The nice captain did not know about Jonathan, and she saw no need in bringing up his name now.

"Was there any other particular reason you wished to speak with me?" she asked, changing the subject.

Moreau gnawed on his lower lip. The two of them were far enough out of ear distance to the patients, so he turned to face her but kept his eyes fixed on the cluttered deck. After shaking his head slowly, he glanced back at the darkened area of the crowded infirmary.

Aimée joined him, taking in the lined up rows of occupied beds several yards away, which she had purposefully ignored when she stepped outside her room. Now, even in the dim light of night, she found it impossible not to notice.

The smell of dried, caked blood and sweat mixed with grime made her nose wrinkle. Stark shadows of the soldiers took residence in her mind, branding her brain. Even from where she stood, she heard the moans and groans of some of the sleepless writhing in pain.

I don't want to think about it anymore! It's over.

Determined to hang on to her composure, she slowly closed her eyes then opened then again and gazed over at the captain.

"You, Mademoiselle," pleaded Moreau, "are my only hope." He paused then went on. "I have stayed busy round the clock, taking little time for rest."

"Yes, Captain?"

"There is no one who will help with the injured men. Many of them mere boys!"

40

He cast a sidelong glance at her and then slowly stared fixedly on the soldiers. "The colonel doctor, he comes to me. He say we need volunteers, but I look to everyone, and they say 'no,' so now I ask you, my young friend."

Aimée would have done anything…almost but what he asked. Yet how might she possibly assist with the selfsame men who destroyed her home and family?

"You expect me to play nursemaid to those, those, soldiers?" she argued suddenly, pulling herself away from his side to lean back against a heavy post. "Have you so quickly forgotten what they did to my family?"

The stiffness in her voice caused no small stir amongst the men in the bunks, as well as the other passengers below whose gazes shot up to see her own eyes flashing in the moon's shadows.

"I thought you were Papa's friend!"

"*Ma chère*, I was and am, and I shall always be," he replied.

But the captain had wounded an already broken spirit. His request had come too soon. He'd opened up a tender sore not yet healed. Aimée wondered if he knew it.

"Please believe me. I do not ask you to be unkind to your treasured memories. *Ma chère*? Mademoiselle Aimée? This boat, *St. Honorine*, it is as if she is no longer mine. The Union, they have taken control of her, and if I do not follow the orders given me, I may never have hope of making her mine again someday. I wish it was possible for me to make *zee* understand my *détresse*."

Nevertheless, Aimée had ceased listening. She'd already begun walking back towards her quarters. Slumping her shoulders, she wrapped her shawl more tightly about her.

She made a firm decision in her mind. It didn't matter how nice the captain was—or who he was. It didn't matter he'd been her father's friend.

She was not going to leave her room again until the boat reached port in New Orleans.

Once again, she could hear the whispers of the men further down the deck. She also felt other eyes upon her, as if she was being watched from the shadows when she moved toward her door.

Glancing over her shoulder, she noted the soldier standing a few feet away. He seemed harmless enough simply taking his ease, but whoever it was, she wished he would go away.

Aimée quickened her pace then stopped in midstride before turning the latch. With a deep sigh, she opened her door, stepped inside, and slammed it shut behind her. She glanced out the window into darkness.

Papa would never have had me act in such a way toward the captain.

He so loved his boat. And he, indeed, was her father's friend.

Naturally, he wanted no trouble, not with whoever the colonel doctor was, nor for her…but especially not for *St. Honorine* – his pride and joy.

But at the moment, she didn't choose to care.

* * * *

Inside the stateroom, Lulu gaped at her wide-eyed.

"Miss Aimée?" she asked, hurrying over as Aimée's tears fell in full force, spilling onto the ebony gown. After searching for a clean handkerchief, Lulu handed it to her. "Miss Aimée?"

"If you only knew what I was asked to do!"

Her servant nodded as Aimée rambled on. Without a word, she helped her off with her dress and crinoline. Nevertheless, after several long moments of sheer silence, she could keep still no longer. "Was you able to offer help to the boat man, Miss Aimée? It was a mighty nice thing you was gonna do."

Aimée looked at Lulu in dismay. Of course, Father and Mother would've considered the circumstances and jumped in to assist without a second thought. Father and Mother without a doubt would have never been rude to a dear friend.

But that was them.

"We'll talk about it tomorrow," finished Aimée, climbing into bed, beneath the covers and turning her head against the wall.

* * * *

Aimée came awake instantly...wide-awake. Turning her head slightly on her pillow, she saw Lulu laying out a clean set of garments for her. "What time is it?"

"I seen the sky say 'bout six when I were outside," said Lulu, looking up to send her a smile.

With little effort, Aimée rolled out of her bed, feeling a touch of coolness in the dawn air as it penetrated the small window of the cubicle-sized room.

Dipping her linen cloth into the basin of fresh water, she soaped herself down and breathed deeply of the fragrance of lavender oil Lulu had only moments ago added. The words that passed between her and Captain Moreau the night before were still fresh in her mind. She knew what she had to do.

"I bet that old captain, he knowed how to get his way, hmm?" Lulu said a few minutes later as she helped Aimée dress.

"Hush now; I must hasten," Aimée scolded. "Yes, I'm going to assist the captain. He doesn't know it yet, but 'tis only for Papa I'm doing this...only for Papa, mind you, not for those dreadful mean Yankee soldiers. Finish helping me get ready now."

Lulu nodded and giggled as she cinched up Aimée's corset tightly behind her until she laughed so much she couldn't hold still. "I knows. Hee hee; I knows. You got a mighty big heart just lakky your pappy."

With a brief nod, Aimée studied her profile in the captain's looking glass. Her creamy magnolia-rich complexion gave her a look of fresh innocence. The dark circles around her eyes were now long gone. She was pleased with what she saw.

"You is as pretty as a pitcher now, Miss Aimée. No different than before. Don't see how them warrior boys gonna get much help with you out there, hee, hee!

They's gonna have heart flutters when they sees you in the light of day."

"Posh!" Aimée glanced once more at her reflection. For the last several months, how she looked hadn't mattered. This morning for some reason, it did...even if only a little.

"I'd best go see if I can find that captain now. He must be somewhere nearby making his rounds." She walked over toward the door. With a wink at Lulu, she turned the latch to hurry out.

Aimée took a deep breath of the warm air. She saw the captain walking away from the doctor, pulling his pipe out of his pocket as he walked. He refilled his bowl and stopped, leaning against the mainstay to search for a sulphur match. When he glanced up, she grinned, her cheeks burning.

"I'm here, Captain," she said softly. I'm sure you aren't surprised."

"No, I knew you'd come, *ma chère*! You are Cecil's *fille*, as I thought." Moreau stuck his pipe between his teeth, walked over, and took Aimée's extended hand then led the way down the corridor to the infirmary.

* * * *

The surgeon greeted Aimée and directed her to a chair where she waited as he spoke with the captain.

"Your assistance is greatly appreciated, ma'am," he stated a few minutes later, "I'm Colonel J.J. Bonn. I will make myself available as you need me. You can see by looking around we are significantly short staffed."

Aimée listened intently to the doctor. She glanced over at a lone soldier lying still on the cot beside her. "This soldier has not stirred since I sat down beside him over ten minutes ago. Is there something special I can do for him?"

The colonel bent down to listen to the young man's chest then brushed his hand across his mouth to check for the movement of air. "We weren't able to give him the appropriate attention when he needed it most." He shook his head. "It looks as if he is about ready to take a final turn."

Aimée tossed her head back and rose to walk to a different cot. *He is just another Yankee, after all. What should it matter to me if he loses his life? Weren't three precious lives taken from me?*

Yet it did matter, and she knew it.

"Unless you need me further, Colonel, I...I'll simply move along, if you don't mind." Already, she felt numb, and she hadn't yet begun.

* * * *

Looking up as she approached the cot near his, the Army Lieutenant openly studied the graceful form of the young woman with great admiration. He drew his lips in thoughtfully.

It was impossible for her to see him as he watched her move about from cot to cot, her petticoats swishing gracefully beneath her dark day dress. The animation of her character as she passed by enchanted him.

Some of the beds were unoccupied, giving her the occasion to change and freshen up the bedding, while at other bedsides, she gave fresh shaves or offered a hand of comfort. Sometimes, she would simply sit and read a letter for a patient.

He only saw her dimly with his one good eye — the rest of his face and head still buried beneath worn bandages. He stirred uneasily on his cot. It was difficult still being a patient.

She appeared withdrawn to him...like someone lost or distant. The war did that. Anxious for the moment she would come closer to his cot, Philip sent up a quick prayer to hurry her his way.

A few moments later, he watched her move two cots over to where Southern Boy slept. Philip pulled back and listened.

* * * *

"Soldier?" Aimée whispered softly to the patient on the cot.

As she spoke, she witnessed the sandy-haired young Confederate as he turned his head and opened his eyes. "Am I dreaming?" he asked groggily, looking up. "You can't be real."

She smiled. "Quite real, Soldier."

"You smell like a handful of blooming purple flowers, ma'am."

"Thank you, Soldier. I'm here to be of service."

"I ain't seen me a girl in a while."

He grabbed her hand and placed it on his chest. "Maybe you better give me a closer examination...ma'am."

With gentle-like firmness, Aimée pried his fingers off her wrist. "No hands on the help...Colonel's orders." She touched a finger to her lips to hush up her patient then took a clean cloth and began wiping the damp rag across his forehead and cheeks.

"I only came to refresh you. Here, let me wash you up a bit."

His peach fuzz made her smile. "You're not in much need of a shave, soldier boy... not yet, anyway. How old are you, if I may be so bold as to inquire? What's your name?"

He reached up again to touch her arm. "They call me Southern Boy, missy, and I'm ten and four today, but I can be whatever age you're wantin'... pick a number."

"And they still let you in the war?" Aimée pursed her lips.

"Wait a minute!" he shouted. His gaze came up to study her face closer, and Aimée knew the exact moment it dawned on the rebel patient exactly who...and what...she was. His eyes came up to study her face closer until it dawned on the rebel patient exactly who she was.

"Why, you ain't no purple flower, Southern lilac, ner Georgia peach. You's that stinky Sandhill Tacky, poor, white-trash wench we seen steal yer way onto the boat!" He poked an unsteady finger at her face.

"I know you, lady! We all seen you with the boat Cap! Musta' pleased the old fella' right good, huh? How else would ye be comin' up with all that fine garb you're wearin' on your back?"

He guffawed. "How's about me and the boys next? Come on. Jump in here to bed next to me—I gots plenty of room." He slid over and patted the sheet next to him.

Aimée, being the person of genteel upbringing she was, felt her face immediately redden. She'd been caught off guard and now found herself speechless, feeling ill prepared for the young soldier's vulgarity towards her in such a way.

How could this Confederate talk to her like that, him not even being a Yankee? What had happened to good, old fashioned Southern honor? Was it all being destroyed with the heartless war?

* * * *

A moment later Aimée thought she heard something from behind the partition then felt two large hands reaching around for her.

"Wha!" She felt herself slip out from beneath her as she fell backwards into the cradle of someone, obviously a huge hunk of a man. It could not have been Lulu.

It was the way he engulfed her and pulled her away from the soldier's cot so gently that amazed her, that shocked her.

"Excuse me…excuse me? Do you mind?" She tried to pull away and to get a look at her rescuer but found she was in almost a daze.

What is wrong with me?

"Don't worry, ma'am," he whispered. "I'm not going to hurt you. I came to take you to your room."

The stranger's presence somehow had made her feel greatly at ease. With his arm around her waist holding her steady, she had indeed felt completely engulfed by his presence. Instead of continuing to pull away, she allowed herself to lean against her rescuer's husky body, resting her head against his warm chest.

It wasn't like her at all.

"Will you let me take you to your quarters, ma'am?"

"I—I suppose so."

47

Aimée noted right away a gentleness as the stranger began to weave her in and out between the rows of cots. As they passed by the men, the others kept calling her rescuer *Angel Wings*. He only smiled at their foolish jesting.

They didn't speak as they continued back to her stateroom. When Lulu opened the door, she gasped.

"Miss Aimée!" she exclaimed rolling her eyes anxiously. "What is you doin' wrapped up in that big man's chest? Who is that man, anyways?"

Coming to her senses, Aimée blushed then instantly pulled away from the soldier's comfortable embrace. She stumbled through the door.

"The lady is emotionally distraught," he answered for her. "She needed my assistance."

"It's okay, Lulu." said Aimée.

Leaving Lulu standing in the doorway, her rescuer eased her inside the stateroom and directed her to the nearby window seat. He stood over her, looking down into her upturned face.

"You done it good, sodure man. What you waitin' for now?" challenged Lulu, following behind him. "You can get on out of here. Looks like you got my mistress' insides all queasy-like."

"Not him," whispered Aimée glancing up. "He did not hurt me."

"You are okay, ma'am?" One gentle gray eye continued to gaze down at her. Bandages concealed the rest of the soldier's face.

"But you are one of the patients!" she exclaimed, taken aback. "Should you not be in your bed?"

"I'm fine, ma'am. You are the one about which to be concerned." He reached into his pocket, took out an embroidered handkerchief with the initials *PJ* on it, and handed it to her.

"I could not let Southern Boy talk that way to you." Although she could not see him well, his flushed face made Aimée curious.

"I don't know what to say." She wiped her eyes. "Southern Boy. Does he have another name?"

"That's what they call him out there. My given name is Philip—Not *Angel Wings*. That is what they call me to make fun of me. You may call me Philip if you wish."

"Okay...Philip. Listen, I appreciate what you did, but you had better leave now. I'm all right, truly."

Aimée started to rise but tripped on the soldier's boot, falling dead center into his arms. When she pulled herself away, her face burned with embarrassment.

Philip backed towards the door, a sheepish grin on his face. "I'll see myself out, ma'am."

"Well, good bye," she mumbled behind him, raising an arched brow. Sitting back in her seat, she quietly observed the soldier-patient as he left the room. It was difficult to tell whether he was from the North or South without him wearing his complete uniform.

Aimée glanced down in her lap at her rescuer's handkerchief. *PJ*. Such a nice man. Would that more men might be like him. Running her index finger across the embroidered initials down in the corner, she made a mental note to have Lulu wash the cloth and return it to the man before they departed the boat.

"Is you goin' back out there?" Lulu glanced towards the door.

"I must. I need to ignore the offensive things some of those boys out there might say to me. I declare I'm acting like a frightened school girl and worse yet, the one who spoke so rudely was a southern neighbor no more than the age of ten and four! I declare! Imagine what Papa would say if he knew. I am simply going to have to take what comes."

Chapter Four

As planned, *St Honorine* made her scheduled stops at the various ports, slowing the trip extensively. No matter where the boat docked, more wounded soldiers and additional supplies found their way onboard.

Finally, Aimée's task of nursing the wounded soldiers became more of a pleasure than a chore. If she kept her eyes off the color of uniforms and hats, it helped. When she shut her ears to the unpleasant comments and went about her job with a smile on her face, the derogatory remarks eventually ceased. Many of the men even began expressing their appreciation for her presence.

* * * *

After stopping for a brief meal a couple of days later, Aimée glanced up to see Captain Moreau walking towards her with a heavy frown on his face.

"Captain?" she lifted her brow, "All is not well?"

"Not as well as could be, *ma chère.*"

"It is not the same as before, is it?"

"Since docking at the last Port, I have learned from the colonel doctor that our Confederate leader, General Gardner recently surrendered to General Banks." Moreau shrugged. "Bonn should have been pleased, but somehow, it only adds to his sour face."

"Is that bad for you and your boat?" Aimée asked.

The captain's eyes darkened as he held her gaze. "Ah, *ma chère*. It does not look good at all, but you don't want to leesten to my *mélancolique*. All I now hear from the doctor is to clean here, do more there, fix this, fix that. More beds, more supplies. It makes my eyes want to weep!"

"Truly I am sorry for you, Captain"

"The doctor told me more passengers are to come. There is no space for which to fit additional beds. I cannot grow my boat to be bigger. That *eez* the problem."

Looking out at the serrated stumps of once-decorative trees and the ruined buildings and other scars from the recent battle-tide, the captain continued.

"The Colonel made up his mind. It will be necessary for me to ask you and many others to disembark at the next port. I am so sorry, *ma chère*."

Aimée took the captain's hand and smiled. "Don't be so bleak, Captain. It's all right. We can catch a ride on one of the next southbound ferries."

"You do not worry, Mademoiselle?"

"I heard some of the patients say there were four or five other boats still to come. There is sure to be one for me."

Captain Moreau had been more than gracious, Aiméé knew, but priorities were priorities, and this was a time of war. She'd also heard about the sniper attack threats rumored amongst the men as a response to the shipment of guns on board...just like everyone else. No one truly knew if *St. Honorine* would even safely arrive in New Orleans. It was best she get off now while the she could.

"Captain Moreau. You have been more than kind. I will miss you."

He fixed his eyes out at the river. "*Il n'y a que le premier pas qui coute!*" he exclaimed vehemently, reverting back to his native French.

"It is not a fair *décision*, and I intend to tell the *Docteur* so! *Selon toute probabilité!* Who knows ! He could be leaving all of you in *probable* despair! Why, you and many others, *ma chère*, won't even have a place to spit at the wind!"

Aimée wanted so to ease his discomfort. "I don't need a place to spit, Captain," she said smiling, "and we all know many are *already* in despair. Do not worry about us. We all know many will probably die of infection before they ever arrive at their final destination...*if* they even get *there*."

The captain grew quiet. Clenching the stem of his pipe between his teeth, Moreau studied the yellow eddies whirling beneath his beloved boat. "The colonel may have his *hotel-Dieu*, this hospital he wishes, or whatever it is he has here with my boat, but I no longer wish to help him, *ma chère*. That is how angry I am! Now I must notify the others. Please, please forgive me."

Aimée touched his shoulder. "I understand. You go."

He gave her a brief nod, made an about face then walked off sadly to inform the rest of his passengers of the unfortunate news.

* * * *

Nothing was ever certain anymore. Nothing good ever lasted it seemed—not for Aimée. Like the confusion of the last several months in her life, once again, she was losing control over the choices she had to make for her future.

The more Aimée had busied herself the last few days, the further the thoughts of her lost family moved to the recesses of her mind. It had been good. She'd thought she'd even found purpose for a while.

All that was gone now.

A sense of inadequacy swept through her. *I don't even know who I am anymore.*

While Lulu organized and repacked her trunk, Aimée sat on the window seat and stared down at her hands. She thought more about the patients.

It would be difficult she knew. Most had grown to be kind, thanks to the daily help of her new friend, Philip. She'd begun looking forward to being with him every morning. Now that she was being ordered off the boat, she would never again see him.

She glanced out her window at the tall slender Union officer standing down by the smokestack. Once again, he was looking her way.

She was almost certain it was that same officer she had seen the first night she had gone out walking with Captain Moreau. *Why is this man forever eyeing me?* She bit her lip. Perhaps it meant nothing.

I must speak to the captain about him.

"You thinkin' 'bout them soldier boys again, Miss Aimée, or that tall warrior what's been watching at you? I seen him around the boat."

Aimée twisted around quickly. "Mind yourself, Lulu. You don't need to know what I'm thinking." She wrinkled her forehead. "You've seen him, too?"

"Mmm Hmm. I seen him. Always around, him is. Anyways, how does them boys 'speck you to get supper when you ain't gonna be here no more, and there ain't gonna be no food no more? Besides, Miss Aimée, I *always* knows what you're thinkin'."

Aimée blinked. "First off, I was not thinking about any *particular* warrior man. I had my mind elsewhere. Also, they say we can get the next steamboat which should take us on to Florette's. And, Lulu Jean, what is this fuss about food? We need not worry about food for the patients here; someone else will take care of that. To tell you the truth of it, I am plain weary of the whole matter."

She rose and busied herself around the room. "I can't help but think about that poor man, you know, Philip, the officer with the bandaged face out there who was helping me. He must have practically lost his face from someone's rifle or something! You've seen his head. I wish — "

"Miss Aimée," said Lulu, shaking her head, "you best be careful about them wishes you get when it comes to them boys. I seen him look at you, too."

Aimée gazed over at Lulu in complete innocence. "Never you mind about that. You wouldn't understand. Besides, I'm a changed woman about boys, Lulu, and have been for years. You'd best remember that."

* * * *

53

The landsman called out his orders, and the passengers readied themselves to depart.

Aimée walked beside Captain Moreau, keeping a firm hold on his arm.

"Do not worry *ma chère*," he assured her, "*Que je dis*, that is to say, things will work out. I'm sure *zee* next boat will arrive *queekly* to take you on to see your sister. And when this war finishes its course, I promise I will come to visit."

"I regret to say I didn't get to say farewell to Philip," said Aimée. "I don't believe I even told him my name. He just kept calling me nurse."

"I can bid him *adieu* if you wish it. I saw the colonel taking the young man off with him to greet *zee* new patients. It looks as if he has become *zee* doctor's new assistant. Was there someone else you wish me to speak to, child? I saw you had been searching for someone else a moment ago — another friend, perhaps?"

Aimée's eyes widened. She had not had a chance to speak to the captain about the Union Officer who'd been watching her. Had her quiet search for the man been that obvious?

"No, no, that was all, Captain."

"I will say *bon voyage* to you then and remember the same to your *bon ami*," Moreau said. "If the stars tell us right, who knows; maybe *zee* two of you will meet again when times are different, you think?"

She laughed while Lulu frowned. "It's ok, Lulu," she reassured her. "Captain Moreau doesn't mean one should actually read the stars. 'Twas only a figure-of-speech."

"Humph!" nodded Lulu, "Them stars, they can look mighty pretty, but they don't do nothin' good for you."

The captain smiled at them both and placed his hand on Aimée's shoulder. "Extend my greetings to your sister, Master David as well, should you receive a post from the wayward boy."

"I will, and thank you again for your kindness."

He bowed his head as they turned to walk off.

Aimée turned back once more and waved then ran back and kissed Captain Moreau on the cheek. A tug of sadness pulled at her heart.

* * * *

Finally reaching a safe distance from the boat, her trunks sitting on the dock at her side, Aimée watched the bridge as it lifted and the gangplank rise again. Her gaze lingered there and then around the dock. She found herself still searching for the familiar face of the Yankee Captain, though she'd never admit it aloud.

Behind her, the steam whistle blew, and the black smoke ascended as the engines continued building up steam. Slowly, the side wheels began turning, sloshing the muddy water up against the levee. Their familiar clacking sound gradually became more distant as she and Lulu watched the *St. Honorine* disappear from sight.

The last hours of her journey were yet to come.

While she sat down on one of her trunks and watched the water splash up against the dock, the warm wet spray of the late August shower hit Aimée's face.

Lulu had already doffed her shoes and was soaking her feet in the mucky river. "We gonna just sit here all afta'noon drippin'?" she asked irritably.

"I don't know." Aimée leaned forward and rested her elbows on her knees, cupping both hands beneath her chin. Sheltered from everything outside of plantation life but for the occasional balls, she was not well experienced with travel or for what to do from one moment to the next...not without someone around to tell her. She was endlessly aware of Lulu who always seemed as carefree as the afternoon sky while Aimée herself felt like a fish out of water.

Should she remain waiting for the next boat without any idea of how long that wait would be? Could she leave the trunks unattended and head towards town with the others?

She turned and listened as Lulu sat on the edge of the dock humming that same familiar hymn she'd heard for years. Aimée frowned.

At least she has her religion.

* * * *

It was apparent the Lebrún woman was not without some kind of means. Dressed in her subdued black, she exhibited a stately look, her gown looking anything but drab...even on the drizzly overcast day. Her long and flowing skirt of silk lawn emphasized her tiny waist and small bone structure. Fiery red hair, though pulled back into a net of pouffed ribbon and white cap, still drew immediate attention to the glowing satin of her cheeks, giving her an almost wreath-like appearance.

Nothing about her went unnoticed to the Frenchman who stood off to the side. He lifted an eyebrow as he scrutinized her. The time was right. She was completely alone.

He drew in closer, missing nothing. He had begun his perusal hours earlier when she got off the boat, examining every curve even to the sway of her walk. When his gaze followed her departure from the captain, he smiled, noting the tears periodically trickling down her face.

Now as far as he could see, she appeared as if she needed help. What better time than the present to make oneself available, to offer assistance at the shedding of tears? The Frenchman stepped forward with a ready smile. He would find a way to relate. He'd certainly done it before.

He had remembered that morning to don his most costly sport suit, taking care to button it in the latest manner. Always fascinated by the fashions of men, he had picked up this particular style from the Prince of Wales when he had last visited the States around the same time of his own arrival from France.

Since English sporting clothes had caused a considerable stir to the women in Europe, surely they would do the same in America. He wasted no time in adding a few to his own wardrobe.

Resting his left hand in his middle pocket with his free hand just so, he removed his felt hat with his other hand and slowly worked his way in closer to the damsel in distress.

* * * *

Aimée did not hear him coming. With her chin still cupped in her hands and her elbows on her knees, she stared ahead.

"Hmmm, if you look this good when you are cheerless, I cannot imagine how you must look when your life is filled with joy!"

Snapping her head back, Aimée gazed up at the man, noticing how a couple of strands of his greasy hair had slipped out of place. "Pardon me?"

When his eyes followed hers, he reached up to rearrange the straggles then spoke again, his voice carrying a lazy French accent. "*Bon jour, Mam'selle*. You appeared in distress. How can I be of assistance?"

At the sound of the man's voice, Lulu jumped up, her wet feet dripping, and hurried over. "Her's gonna be just fine!" she interrupted. "That is, if you don't mind leavin' her be, man!" Boldly stepping around, she tried to move her body in front of Aimee.

"It's all right, Lulu," said Aimée. "You can step aside, honey." She explored the vicinity around her then back at the man before explaining. "I'm fine, sir. Truly, I am. I'm in no more distress than anyone else here at this harbor."

A bone protruded awkwardly from the man's tight-fitting britches, making a popping sound as he bent his left knee.

Aimée blushed. "I'm just waiting for the next boat to New Orleans. Isn't everyone?"

"A coincidence, indeed," he answered gleefully. "I, too, am bound for the great Crescent City! I have conversed with some of the other individuals on the dock. Many have stated they are going only as far as the port that will take them on to Baton Rouge. Now, at least, I shall have a traveling companion."

Aimée shook her head. "As you can see, I already have someone with me."

"Unquestionably," he chided himself. "Please do not misunderstand me, miss…? Perhaps you might inform me as to your given name, so if we come across one another while on the craft, I can offer you a pleasant greeting." He lifted his razor thin shoulders and raised his palms heavenward.

"Lebrún, Amethyst Rosette Lebrún."

"Ah," he sighed, "Your name is as arresting as are you, Miss Lebrún … as a jeweled flower, they say."

She thought he appeared congenial enough. His comments came as nothing new. Familiar with the constant flattery of males, Aimée wanted to giggle at his attempt to sound like that of an Englishman when he obviously was not.

"How thoughtless of me," he continued, "I should have responded with my name in kind. I am the Honorable Beauregard T. Proctor. You must have heard of me. My family's name travels only in the proper most places."

"No, I'm afraid…no," said Aimée.

"Captain Moreau, are you acquainted with him, then? The two of us are esteemed friends. Perhaps he has spoken of me."

"Why, no," Aimee exclaimed. "I know the captain well, but he did not mention you."

"…a pity."

"I was busy helping out in at the infirmary most of the time and—"

"I know, I…" he replied too quickly then caught himself. "Rather, I say people spoke tenderly of your charitable work throughout the vessel. My *friend* Moreau often talked of your kindheartedness the many times we chatted. Surely he must have said *something* about me."

He had often seen the woman around the captain. He had also been told dropping the name of the riverboat captain was certain to be an excellent ploy, though, in reality, he knew nothing whatsoever about the proprietor of the *St. Honorine*.

"I'm sorry…he did not."

"A shame, Mam'selle, but at least, you can easily see, because of the good captain, we are not strangers at all. You might as well consider me an old friend. You are well acquainted with the city, yes?" He winked.

Aimée's expression changed. In truth, she had no idea where she was going or even how to locate her sister even if it was only to tell her of the family then to find out the whereabouts of her aunt. Her level of anxiety had risen several times because of it. "Unfortunately, I'm not at all familiar with the state of Louisiana, nor its fine city, New Orleans."

"You must not fret then because I personally know the city like the back of my hand. Any place you wish to journey, I will gladly steer you in the right direction. In fact, if you will permit it, I will be most happy to give you a tour of the entire town, that is, if your *minion* here," he pointed to Lulu, "has no problems with leaving your side, only temporarily of course." He subtly lifted his chin towards the slave.

"How kind of you to offer, sir," said Aimée, "but Lulu is not—"

His mouth twisted oddly. He turned back towards her. "And then there is the situation here with your trunks, Mam'selle." He slanted his gaze at her side again. "We would not want to leave them untended with your slave either now, would we?"

"I'm afraid you misunderstand, Mr. Proctor," said Aimée.

"Miss Aimée?" Lulu asked, eyeing the man with skepticism. "Don't you wants to get to the house of your sistuh soon? I means, stead of dilly-dallyin' all over tarnation? Maybe you should be thinkin' about the next boat, what's comin'."

The Frenchman slowly licked his lips and turned back Aimée's way, ready to speak again.

Aimée glanced first at him then at Lulu and wondered at the look in her eyes.

"His eyes is too close to the bridge of his nose, Miss Aimée," she leaned in closer and whispered so only she could hear, "and his mustache way too skinny. It ain't right."

"Lulu, hush."

Lulu's eyes appeared to grew larger. "But look at him sweat! That ain't right, neither. I knows what I sees."

"Lulu," scolded Aimée again just beneath her breath. "Stop that."

Though she thought she watched over her maid, the tables were often turned with the young servant was convinced her mistress *depended* on her for everything, especially when it came to the perils of men folk.

"Lulu *is* right, I'm afraid, about time constraints, Mr. Proctor," Aimée finally agreed, looking from her to him. "There won't be time for tours of any town."

"I see. And where did you say your sister lived?"

"Her didn't!" Lulu argued with a frown.

"I will gladly accompany you there at any rate…for your protection, of course. One cannot be too careful, can one?"

Before Aimée could respond, she heard the sound of the oncoming paddlewheel and stood up to peer along the waterway. She was weary from sitting and feeling soggy from the air's dampness, and the familiar clacking sound of the approaching boat came to her ears as a welcome relief.

"I will appreciate your assistance Mr. Proctor," she decided, looking up at him.

"Consider it done then. 'Twill be my honor. I shall leave the two of you and meet you as the boat nears the harbor. Until then," he said with a nod, "I shall bid you adieu."

* * * *

The vessel, a steam-powered ferry, was much smaller than the greater sized *St. Honorine*. Since there wasn't much room, the girls looked for a small area on deck where they could sit and rest. It wasn't long before they both dozed in and out of sleep.

Darkness descended as slowly the boat steamed southward, the climate noticeably changing to a warm gentle breeze.

"How long it gonna be, Miss Aimée?" asked Lulu groggily.

"I don't rightly know, honey."

"I can tell you," interjected Mr. Proctor as he walked up, swaying with the boat's movement. He glanced at his watch then replaced it in his pocket just as Aimée and Lulu looked his way.

"I say we should arrive at the harbor by dawn. Tell me, where did you say your sister lived, and what was her name? I recall your mentioning you didn't know how you might locate her."

Lulu grimaced. "Anyways, her didn't said, Mister! I thought you wasn't comin' 'round till we docked!"

"Don't mind her," said Aimée, stretching and smiling. "Lulu is somewhat protective of me. Florette...that's my sister's name, oh, I should say, Florette Lebrún, Mr. Proctor."

"Do call me Beauregard," he replied, flashing his teeth and moving in closer.

"She lives in a four-story townhouse in *The French Quarter*."

Beauregard's slow smile increased. "*The French Quarter* you say?"

"Yes, her home is called The Paramount. Do you know of it?"

"What was her name again?" he queried, his brow lifting.

"Florette, Florette Simone Lebrún. You can't tell me you are acquainted with my sister. *Do* you then know of the whereabouts of her home?"

He grinned and nodded. "Indeed I am...only vaguely, mind you."

"But that's extraordinary!" exclaimed Aimée. "Lulu, did you hear that? How terribly fortunate it is that we have met."

"Exceptionally!" he tittered. "'Tis my good fortune, indeed." As he mumbled on, he licked his lips. "I render there's a slight resemblance betwixt the two of you."

He reached up and began twisting his pencil thin black mustache. "I can deliver you right to your sister's door, in fact! I know the square where her place is located and the district where it can be found; I have passed there often enough!"

"You have!" Aimée announced excitedly, clasping her hands together.

"Indeed. Now if you will excuse me, I will leave the two of you to rest. I shall return to collect you at the end of the trip."

Aimée took Lulu's hand, grasping it tightly. "See, Lulu, 'tis a wonderful thing how providence happens. Isn't that what you always say? Something like that? Look at our good fortune all because of Mr. Proctor. Thanks to that man, I will soon be able to see Florette. Oh, I do hope she will be pleased to talk with me, after all."

Lulu pulled her hand away and frowned.

"What is it, honey?"

"'Scuse me, Miss Aimée. You knows I don't take much likin' to that fortune stuff. And what that man doin' not bein' a warrior man like all the other boys? And…and why him's got that awful skinny hair on his lip. I don't trust that neither!"

Tossing her head back, Aimée laughed and then closed her eyes. "Lulu, go to sleep. You worry too much."

Chapter Five

New Orleans, Louisiana

The Matilda's official whistle blower took his position up by the large instrument. He proceeded to press down on the treadle, announcing the pending arrival of the ferry to the Port of New Orleans. The riverside levee was coming into full view just as dawn rose softly over the Southern Louisiana horizon.

Sticky dew covered the ground in the town, which had not yet awakened. At the sound of the triple-chime, the full-throated chord shook the pilot stand, causing the ears of the nearby officers to ring with havoc.

Aimée and Lulu stood up and gazed out at the oncoming city, watching it increase in size the closer the boat neared the landing dock.

"My reverent knows 'bout this place," Lulu mumbled quietly. "He told the folks of some of his relations, what got sold on the block in the center of town for no more than fifteen hundred dollar to them terrible masters, what took the folks to task bad!"

"I'm sure his confession resulted in numerous negative responses from the congregation," said Aimée.

"Yas'm!"

She saw Lulu shudder. "It coulda' been me!"

"I've heard people say several of the slaves around this area have been able to purchase back their freedom lately," Aimée soothed, hoping to ease Lulu's troubled face.

"Just lakky your pappy done?"

"Yes, just like my father did. You know, honey," reassured Aimée, "You still understand you're free to go at any time. That hasn't changed."

"Not unless you be wantin' to send me. I ain't got no cause for leavin'. I'm thinking the good Lord, He wants me here to protect you anyways."

Reaching over, Aimée gave Lulu a hug before the two turned and watched the shore together. She stared down the side of the ferryboat, where the lapping of the tepid shoreline waters splashed against the bow as it eased in between the two docks.

"Looks like we've arrived." She glanced over at the man dropping the ferry's anchor with a heavy splash.

"What do we do now we's here?"

"Don't you worry about a thing. Let's go let them know where to take my things."

"You scared, Miss Aimée?"

She gave Lulu a kind smile. "More numb than anything. That nice Mr. Proctor will help us." Aimée inspected the area to see if she could see him anywhere near,

A scowl crossed Lulu's face the moment her eyes caught sight of Beauregard's raised arm.

The two women hurriedly moved along to get close so they could get in the rear of the line where Aimée could find her trunks.

"You can have them delivered to this address," declared Proctor, stepping out to hand the trip pilot some numbers on a piece of paper. "We shall arrive ahead of them forthwith."

"I truly thank you, Mr. Proctor," said Aimée when he returned.

"How could any proper man resist when being around you?" He followed his vocal gesture with a bow then reached over to place her hand on his arm. "Do let me assist you in stepping off the dastardly gangplank. We would not want you to lose your footing!"

* * * *

Over at the edge of the dock near an empty carriage, Aimée noticed the comely officer who stood watching her as she came off the boat. As she got closer, she recognized him immediately. It was the same officer she'd seen back in Vicksburg.

What is he doing here? Is he going to intercede again? There's no way he can know who I am. Not now. The last time he saw me, I looked like such an urchin.

Admittedly, the officer had not been at all rude that first morning back in Vicksburg. In fact, he'd acted to the contrary. It was just in knowing he was a Union soldier, who, apparently with great pride, served the North. He'd also had the audacity to waste her time there at the harbor long enough to make her almost miss the boat.

How then did he arrive here in New Orleans before I did?

Aimée glanced around the area. There was no way to avoid him. The carriage behind him happened to be the only one available to take her on to Florette's. He was certain to see her when she passed by for he was already looking right at her.

While she waited for Mr. Proctor's return, she continued studying the officer's face, which was heavily tanned by the sun. He had a dimpled, square chin, and he filled out his uniform so beautifully it was difficult to take her eyes off him. Unfortunately, he was clad in the dreaded garb of the North she detested.

His thick, black-lashed eyes seemed to bore a hole into her heart. What was it that gave the man such a resolute look of self-confidence? Aimée didn't want to notice his attractiveness, but it was difficult not to.

She reminded herself a third time; he was a Yankee, typical of all the soldiers of the North—self-possessed, overbearing pride. Yet, this man, with his kind smile, appeared somehow more gracious than any Southern gentleman with whom she had an acquaintance, including Jonathan, rest his poor unloved soul.

With relief, Aimée turned her head back toward the boat and saw Mr. Proctor walking up to her. Behind him, the ferry's gangplank lifted.. The *Matilda* was disappearing from view much like the *St Honorine* had done earlier, with just a few turns of its paddlewheel, removing yet another link to home.

Goodbye Mississippi…once again.

"Miss me?" asked Proctor with a slight grin.

Aimée glanced over at Mr. Proctor, confused. "I'm sorry?"

"Never mind; let us be on our way," he said, guiding her towards the end of the harbor by the unoccupied carriage. Proctor soon raised his arm to hail the driver.

* * * *

"Welcome, ma'am," greeted the Union officer, stepping up close. "Captain Palmer Jordan here at your service. You are needing a ride into town, I presume?" He tipped his hat at both and then gazed into the beautiful young woman's face with a broad smile.

"You have come from the *Matilda*, but it seems we have met before, have we not? I'm sure we have… somewhere. Perhaps you can refresh my memory. Those crystal blue eyes of yours do appear familiar to me."

"We seen you before, warrior man," charged the servant stepping out from behind the beautiful woman.

"What you doin' up here? You chasin' after my mistress lady?"

Palmer laughed and shook his head in disbelief. He had not recognized the redheaded beauty at first. This would be the first time he had seen her close up…like this. How was he to know she was the same lost ragamuffin girl who stood on the docks at Vicksburg…the same discourteous female who had barked at him so tersely. His eyes flickered at the amazing change.

"Of course not, but I should have known the moment I saw you exactly what I was up against when I walked over here! Where's the other one?" he asked, glancing around for her other companion.

"Mister Elijah? Him's gone," replied the servant girl.

Just as the young woman started to open her own mouth to speak, Mr. Proctor pulled in front of her, blocking her view. "This woman is with me, officer. If you wish to speak, you can do so directly to me!"

With a nod, Palmer clicked the heels of his boots together and stepped back. Leaning to the side of Proctor, he set his face again towards Miss Lebrún.

"Let me simply say it is indeed a pleasure to see you again...all cleaned up, I mean. I might add 'tis a remarkable improvement! Wait...a minute! Of course." He looked a little closer. "*You* were also the volunteer nurse on the *St Honorine,* weren't you? You don't remember me, do you?"

"Sir?" She stepped to the side of Mr. Proctor and lifted her chin.

"I was also on the boat, ma'am. I should have recognized you then." The gleam in his eyes danced.

"You cannot be serious! That was *you* who stalked me?" She backed up a step.

Her belligerent tone shocked him. "I was not *stalking* you, ma'am, only greatly admiring you...from a distance."

Her eyes flashed. "You should not have—I was..."

He backed up a step and stared at them both. "My apologies, ma'am, if I caused you concern. You'd best be on your way. If you need any help, I shall be around. I'm sure you probably will eventually. "

* * * *

"Excuse me," Aimée declared, her eyes narrowed, as she pushed her escort further aside. "If we need anything, *Billy Yank,*" she said, puckering her brows and wrinkling her forehead, "you can be sure you will be the last person we shall call upon! Now, if you please!"

"My pardon, ma'am," he replied, tipping his hat and backing up further. He grinned. "I was just stating a fact."

"It doesn't matter to me if the two of us just met, are meeting again, or that this is the twentieth time we have made acquaintance! All of you warriors look the same to me, and I want nothing to do with any one of you! Can we please go now, *Mr. Proctor*?"

Turning her attention to her escort, Aimée placed her hand back in the curve of his arm. "The color of that man's uniform is greatly clashing with my dress!"

"Indubitably," Proctor replied, sneering at the Union officer. "Let us be on our way, Miss Lebrún."

She watched as the captain saluted, turned, and walked off, going in the opposite direction.

* * * *

Aimée, Lulu, and Mr. Proctor sat in silence as the conveyance disappeared around the bend and led them down the dusty road over a slight dip and away from the harbor.

From what Mr. Proctor had suggested earlier, New Orleans had taken a downturn from its prosperous past. What once thrived had only slightly begun to build up once again. The area all around now showed the aftereffects of the war, the town and road more rundown than the busy port. It saddened Aimée's heart to have to see it.

She glanced back just in time to see the Yankee disappear completely from her view. She was appalled he'd ridden in the same boat almost all the way to New Orleans without her having realized it.

Had it truly been so necessary for her to be *so* rude to the man? She sighed and settled back in her seat then looked down at her hands.

Indeed, Mama and Papa raised me better than this. She was disgusted with herself.

I wonder if I shall ever see the man again…It would be no wonder if he didn't want to see me again.

The pearly reflection from the river made it easy to observe the entire area clearly. The four-story stucco manse, badly maintained, sat flanked by extended cast-iron balconies around each window, hardly serviceable, nothing much to look at. No morning gaslights hissed along the roadside, nor was there much sign of life around the townhouse itself.

Just as the driver halted the horses next to the structure, the front door at the portico opened, and a portly man well past his prime and slight of neck, stumbled out the door, trying to make his way down the stone steps without falling.

Aimée watched as the man placed a worn hat atop his dappled bald head then glanced in both directions with his bloodshot eyes. He appeared to focus on nothing, missing the snorting horses directly in front of him. Within seconds, he wandered off down a small alleyway. Eventually, he disappeared from view.

Mr. Proctor snickered. "That incoherent gentleman looked rather inebriated. Did you observe the continual swaying?"

Aimée, believing it was no business of hers, felt sorry for the poor man.

Mr. Proctor cleared his throat. "This is the place. The Paramount, located in what the town folk here call *The French Quarter*. I told you I would accompany you within, did I not? 'Twould be captivating…er, gripping to present you to your, uh, sister."

"No, no. You are too kind…but no," Aimée answered. Having no idea how Florette would receive her, she preferred to present herself without the help of any outsider.

"I am appreciative of your assistance, especially with that loathsome Yankee soldier. The man appears to be popping up repeatedly."

"Well, one can not be too careful, can one?" Proctor lifted a pencil thin eyebrow and leaned against her. He reached across her to open the small door and hesitated far too long than what was proper.

After stepping out of the carriage and onto the stone walkway, he turned around and reached for Aimée's waist. Ignoring her outstretched hand, he took hold of her and lifted her up.

He pulled her in close until she attempted to wiggle free from his spider-like grip. Finally, after a long pause, he released her and allowed her to regain her bearings — the entire ordeal bringing a great blush to her cheeks.

"My greatest pardon, *Mam'selle*! You would not want me to let you fall and soil your pretty feet and dress! 'Twould be dastardly!"

Lulu, who helped herself out, turned and made a face at the man.

Aimée folded both her arms together to stay out of arms reach of her escort. "I do think I can handle myself. I will just say thank you for bringing me here, Mr. Proctor."

"My pleasure," he flared his nostrils, ignoring the servant's glower. "I'm sure we can find a way." He licked his lips and reached up to replace his hat. "We will meet again soon, you can be sure."

Still flushed, Aimée took Lulu's hand and drew her up beside her. "Shall we go, honey?"

* * * *

Proctor nodded and then turned to climb back up into the rear section of the carriage. He leaned back and smiled. Tapping on the wall, he alerted the driver to move on. "Yes, Miss Lebrún, you can be certain I will be back...perhaps as your customer," he whispered across the aisle to the empty seat.

* * * *

When no one answered Aimée's consistent knock, a troubled look creased her brow. The last thing she wanted was to be stuck in the middle of a strange city. And it was difficult not knowing much about her own future. Besides, her trunks were to arrive later that day at the same location.

"What shall I do now, Lulu?"Just as she lifted her hand to pull the bell, hoping to arouse someone's attention a different way, the door came slightly ajar.

"What you all be wantin'?" asked the frail sounding voice from within. The servant behind the portal was a youthful girl no more than the mere age of ten plus three, with large and expressive eyes that peered through the darkness. She stood quietly, holding the door ajar little more than a crack.

"I'm here to see Florette Lebrún," stated Aimée. "Is this her home?"

After an uncomfortable stillness, the shy young servant girl stepped back and made way for her entrance.

Inside the poorly lit hallway, long and narrow and tightly enclosed, Aimée got an eerie feeling...especially after standing outside where the warm rays of the early morning sun had pushed their way into the bright luminous morning of Southern Louisiana. Outside, it promised to be a bright day. Where she stood inside, it felt as dark and cold as a night in the dead of winter.

She turned to observe the girl, standing timidly in the darkened shadows as she shut the door behind Lulu.

Looking up at Aimée and Lulu with her hollow-like brown eyes, the girl pointed in the direction they should follow.

The room next to the entry hall looked cluttered, gloomier than the front hall. One hissing gas light sat lit on a small table over in a corner. Wallpapered walls, heavily patterned and ripped in several places, hung busily around the room.

Rug remnants lay scattered about on the badly disfigured wood floor covered by layers of thickened dust. On each window, faded blood red velvet drapes hung from large bold brass rings, which sat tightly closed, apparently to block out all light and unwelcome outside intruders.

It all seemed bizarre to Aimée who, with her sister, learned early brightness meant happiness and cleanliness was next to godliness back at *Shadow Grove*. Ruby Lebrún had instructed her daughters on the mannerisms necessary for any respectable woman, even if one looked to a servant to accomplish the task.

Aimée continued gazing around the room. Three garish settees sat tattered next to small but ornate, rickety tables in the large salon all rather haphazardly. The over-used room was apparently arranged to accommodate individual conversational groupings rather than as a comfortable parlor suitable for family entertaining.

The musty odor of stale smoke lingered as it stung and burned her nostrils. There was also the smell of sour liquor rising from half-empty decanters missing their protective tops. She found it impossible to miss the dirty crystal glasses strewn about the room on several of the tables — almost too many to count. To her right a tattered tapestry cloth dragging on the floor draped a large hexagonal-shaped table sat over in another corner.

Aimée's eyes darted from one place to another while her servant quietly watched her, unable to hide her own horrified look.

"Lulu, look there," she whispered, pointing down to the floor, "someone has burned the rug in several places." She found herself incredibly saddened by the evident marks on the once beautiful wool rug blanketing part of the floor, probably caused by dropped ashes or a dropped pipe.

"She don't take no pride in nothing, Miss Aimée," whispered Lulu.

"Hush," she corrected. Nevertheless, inside, Aimée felt sick. She missed *Shadow Grove*. She didn't want to try to remain in this new environment — this formidable place for long. Hopefully she could let her sister know about the family and get a hold of Tante Fran's address and be on her way soon.

The quiet young house servant followed Aimée's gaze as she continued perusal of the room. Walking over, she tapped her on the shoulder and pointed to another empty settee not far back from the entrance. It, too, was covered with tapestry. There the rich red, black, and darkened green stitching on the covered seat was attached nicely to an ornately carved frame of dark mahogany, intricately etched along the back and arms and legs. It was the only well-kept furniture piece in the room. And it was clean.

"This *is* truly the home of Florette Simone Lebrún?" Aimée asked, sitting down. "If not, I shall gladly take leave and beg your pardon for the interruption."

The girl nodded and turned to walk out of the room through some dangling baubles. Before she disappeared from view, she turned around. "Her name be Misses Simone Brusque, ma'am. I'm guessing her be the same one you's wanting." After a quick bob of her head, she turned again and walked away.

Lulu ground her teeth. "This place don't look like no nice place."

"Perhaps Florette needs me and...and I can help her," Aimée reasoned.

"That ain't what I sees." Lulu firmly shook her head. "Not that she don't need help! Don't you know what this place be?"

"Well, I know for certain it belongs to my sister! Perhaps she has recently had guests, or..." Aimée reasoned again. "...well, I guess I don't rightly know. But that could explain all the...the furniture all over the place." She looked around and flashed her arm about the room, then went on. "...perhaps."

Lulu hesitated. "No...Miss Aimée...this place...is...well, you sees, my reverent, he tol' us 'bout these places here in the *quarter* place. They's..." She bent down and leaned in close, as if praying the walls would not hear her speak. "My' reverent, he say this is well—oh my, it's for one of them ill-puter folk!"

Aimée leaned back and stared pointedly at her. "Ill-puter? You mean a house of ill-repute? Why, Lulu Jean! I wouldn't have thought that of you! Have *you* been listening to those rumors back home?"

Yet as she spoke, her heart sank. All she had to do was look around. In her heart, she knew something was amiss, but she didn't want to believe the horrible things she knew her servant was considering. "Let what you say not be true."

"No, ma'am," said Lulu sorrowfully.

Yet it was impossible not to see the obvious. Even the earthen sculptures sitting atop the larger pieces of furniture in the room were of questionable nature.

Startled, Aimée jumped at the tingling sounds of hanging baubles at the hallway entry. Looking across the room, she saw Florette push the beads aside and walk in, her hair extended down her back in a dull brown braid.

Although Florette's lips were not freshly painted, still they hinted of a forgotten deep brownish red. The rouge on her cheeks was smeared, and her eyes still wore an abundance of stale makeup plainly left over from the night prior, which now appeared beneath her lower lashes. Her shimmering red silk robe sat tightened at the waist with the upper portion of her wrapper displaying an embarrassing amount of cleavage.

Aimée veered her head away quickly, embarrassed by her sister's immodesty but not before noticing her bare feet and heavily painted toenails.

Florette glanced up with a frown. "Young Amethyst Rose. You are the last person in the world I expected to see this morning."

"Hello Florette," said Aimée, standing to avoid further embarrassment. She watched as her sister scrutinized her from head to toe with disapproval. "You must be surprised to see me. I...uh...."

Of course, Florette would have no way of knowing about Father, Mother, and Christopher, unless David had written. Did he even know? Aimée readied to speak again.

Florette's expression did not change nor did she come closer. "What is it you want here, Amethyst?" she asked stiffly, extending no arm of welcome.

Aimée wavered. "I...I needed to stay here for perhaps a couple of days is all until I figure out what I shall do next. I came to tell you.... I hope go to Tante Fran's I think. You see, I...."

Pulling back in case her little sister might want to reach out and hug her, Florette looked baffled. "What's the matter with *Shadow Grove*?"

"Florette, please, can we talk?" Aimée reached her arms out in despair.

She chuckled. "Obviously, you have something to tell me else you wouldn't be here, nor would you be getting me up at this ghastly hour! What time is it, anyway?"

"I'm no longer certain of the time—perhaps around seven. I haven't been certain of time or anything for weeks, even months, Florette."

"So what is it? Truly, I cannot fathom why you would come down here. When have you or I ever been endeared one to another...I mean in the way you want to be endeared? Tell me that."

"There is something I must tell you."

Florette smiled contemptuously. "If you are in a quandary at the house, that doesn't surprise me. If you need money, you need to see Papa not me. You have always his been his favorite, you know. Mama and Papa didn't kick you out, did they? Ha! Never you, sweet and perfect *Aimée*; oh, how I've always loathed that empty-air-headed name...not the darling of *Shadow Grove*... and all of Vicksburg...not you, Papa's little princess."

She laughed harder, but her sarcasm bode rich. "And weren't you betrothed to that rich brat down the road? What's his name? Dear Jonathan? What did he do, Amethyst—dump you? It cannot be such as that. Pray tell, I must hear your news."

Tears rolled down Aimée's cheeks as she blurted out her memories once again. Looking over at Lulu, she lifted her hand. "Please, I...I need my handkerchief."

Lulu rushed over to her and found her linen kerchief in her sleeve, wiping the tears from Aimee's eyes and her own smoldering ones.

Keeping her back to Florette, she whispered, "Don't you worry none, Miss Aimée. The good Lord, Him gonna take care of you—Him and me, both."

Florette let down her guard only slightly and walked over. Yanking Lulu away from Aimée, she gave her a rigid embrace. "I didn't know. And David? What about him?" she cracked, a strange look briefly shadowing her eyes as she pulled back as quickly. "The house...is the house gone, too?"

"There is nothing substantial left as far as I know." Aimée paused. "'Tis why I came."

"David, I asked...is he dead?" Florette pressed again. "What do you know about him?"

"I haven't heard from David. I guess he's still in France. I was hoping maybe you had. I doubt he has any knowledge of what happened yet."

Florette waved her hand as if to push him out of the room and away from her thoughts. "Never mind him. I suppose for now I can find you a room upstairs...somewhere. I shall figure something," she went on. "How old are you now? I doubt you would have much care for my type of business, but there are things...."

Aimée felt obliged for her sister's kindness. "I shall turn ten and nine soon. But I don't plan to stay long, Florette."

She was not listening. "You're more than old enough. I'd forgotten that. Whatever happened with you and that ghastly boy?"

"Jonathan?"

"The one. Wasn't he the boy Papa pressured you to wed?" She stopped and looked her over from head to toe. "I'm sure the two of you must have, you know..."

Aimée looked confused. "You mean the wedding? Do you speak of the wedding? It never occurred, Florette. Jonathan was killed in the war...it is assumed, anyhow."

Florette shook her head. "Then the two of you never did...oh forget it." She motioned Aimée towards the dark hallway. "Come with me. I shall take you upstairs where you can settle in. We'll chat later. Right now, I'm too tired. I don't often rise until after the noon hour, and I'm not about to change my habits for you now. It's different here, you'll see."

Chapter Six

Aimée followed Florette up to the top of the stairs.

"I usually let this chamber out to my top girl, Nina. She's visiting a sick cousin for a few days, so it'll have to suffice." Florette shrugged her shoulders and walked over to the window to pull back the purple silk brocade draperies.

The textured walls were painted a fervid blue, the wide crown molding of brilliant purple separating them from their high ceiling of mottled gray. The huge hand-carved four-poster bed was covered with a plum-hued spread.

"It's bright, I agree," she asserted, when she saw the look on Aimée's face, "but, don't worry. Nothing's going to reach out and bite you. You'll be fine in here until Nina returns. Don't act so shocked, Amethyst."

Florette walked over to corner of the room. "Behind the closet here and this folding screen," she said, "I have a small cot. When Nina returns, if you're still around, you can sleep in there, as long as you don't interrupt her while she's working."

"W…working?" asked Aimée.

"Yes, working."

"And Lulu?"

"What about Lulu? Your slave can sleep on the floor in the other room with the others…with Etta May and Daisy." She watched her sister. "Listen, if you need her or one of the others, just call through the paper-thin walls. There's sure to be someone in that room most of the time. They like to listen in."

Florette tapped on the wall. "Etta May? When I'm finished in here, come and show the slave where she's to stay."

"Yas'm, Misses Simone," Etta May called back through the wall.

"See what I mean? I added the partition. It's not as sturdy as it could be, and you can hear everything, but it serves its purpose. None of my girls are modest. Oh, and there's something else that has been on my mind."

"Yes?"

"Since you arrived, in fact. Wear something decent tomorrow, Amethyst. That black is dreadful on you."

Eyes wide, Aimée stared back in shock. "But I'm wearing this in honor and respect of our parents and Christopher! 'Tis only right!"

Florette shook her head. "Not here it isn't! You are in my home now. As long as you're here, you'll do as I say. Discard that horrid thing and put on something bold and bright. Now, get some rest so I can."

Without another word, Florette left the room, making sure Lulu was out first. She then shut the door behind her.

Aimée heard the click in the knob and knew her sister had not only provided her a place to stay; she'd also decided to lock her in. It wasn't her intention! She hadn't yet had a chance to mention Tante Fran at all.

Plopping down on the large bed, she stared at the dark walls then fell back against her pillow and sobbed herself to sleep.

* * * *

When she awoke, the room felt darkly oppressive with both windows shut tight. The sour smell of second hand smoke seeped in beneath the floorboards.

Aimée's head throbbed from having sobbed herself to sleep. She hadn't removed her dress and shoes before she'd collapsed. Not only did her feet throb and ankles feel swollen from the pull of her kid boots, she could see that her black crape skirt was now deficiently wrinkled and no longer of any use.

Briefly sitting up on the bed, she peeked across in the mirror at her messed up tresses and the darkened circles back beneath her eyes. After a few moments of sitting in the dark and silence, she rose to remove her clothing.

Why did I come here at all?

78

Perhaps it had been the giggling laughter and the mordant smells of liquor seeping into the room through walls that had stirred her into consciousness.

Why did I come here?

"Lulu?" whispered Aimée a few minutes later through the wallboard. "Are you still over there with the others?

"I hears you, Miss Aimée" she answered back. "I's here."

"Do you hear the music playing downstairs?"

"Yas'm and the laughin' from them men."

High-pitched sounds came up through the floors from a couple of girls, surely not old enough to be away from their homes at that time of night.

"What am I going to do?" Aimée cried. "Why did I not listen to you earlier?"

"I's been talkin' at the good Lord. He knows the sitchashun, Miss Aimée."

She tried to smile. "It's what you do, I know, honey. Don't know what good it'll do me."

"Well, I'm figurin' if the good Lord will show me what He's wantin' to do, I can let you know, too. And He'd talk at you, too, if you take the time to listen."

"You go ahead, Lulu. If your good Lord is there for you, He'll listen to you better, I suspect."

"I'm just gonna keep on praying like I been praying every other day then, Miss Aimée. You just gotta hurry up and open your ears and heart and them lips and start talkin' and listening, too!"

"Perhaps one day." Still standing in the dark, Aimée finished removing her garments down to her pantaloons and turned back towards her bed. "Right now, I'm going back to sleep." Climbing back on the bed, she pulled up the coverlet and buried her head beneath her pillow in an attempt to force out the sounds below.

* * * *

It was mid afternoon by the time someone, other than Lulu had entered the room and opened Aimée's drapes, apparently to allow the beams of the midday sun to filter in through the dirty windows, which were now cracked open.

As she opened her eyes and sat up, Aimée breathed in the fresh air and then took advantage of the large ivory pitcher full of hot water that had been placed at her bedside on top of its porcelain basin. She reached for the cloth and washed herself down then grabbed the folded linen towel at the base of the stand. With a sigh, she glanced down at the old rug on the floor in the center of the room.

"My trunks!" she exclaimed happily. "They found me!" She glanced up to see Lulu sitting in the corner. "Lulu." Aimée handed her the pitcher. "When did you come in?"

"Wanted you to see your trunk."

"And I do! Why don't you go downstairs and get some more water when I'm through? Then you can wash up when I have finished with my toilette."

"Thank you, kindly," she answered, lowering her head slightly and rising. Before she got out the door, she saw Aimée bend, struggling with one of her cases. "I can get that," she said hurrying back over to her. "Move aside." Squatting down, she slid in beside her and worked the lock.

Aimée reached inside to find a garment suitable enough to please Florette without bringing shame to her deceased family. "'Tis only right I continue mourning father and the rest for the proper amount of time."

"Yas'm, Miss Aimée, and the Dewey man, too."

"Yes…him, too." Aimée pulled out her lavender gown accented with its tiny black dots. Ebony tassels hung from long fitted sleeves military style. It was one of her favorite day dresses. "Florette cannot disapprove of this one," she declared, holding it up.

"No Miss Aimée, it's one of your best." Within the hour, she finished tying Aimée's stays together with its dangling black silk ribbons. Carefully she fastened her white cuffs and the loops closing the front center of her crisp white collar.

Once she straightened out the braided loops, she tucked Aimée's hair neatly back into the net of black ribbon away from her face.

"You's ready now, miss."

There was a clicking of the knob and a knock at the door. "Is you ready? It's me, Daisy."

"She's ready." Lulu looked over at Aimée, "Don't you worry none about the key, neither, Miss Aimée," she whispered. Lulu quietly gave her a wink and pointed to where she left the key in the door.

As she slowly descended the stairs, Aimée made up her mind what she was going to do. When she could find a way, she would leave. Florette did not care a whit about the family.

If anyone would welcome her with open arms Tante Fran, Francis Alba Simpson, her deceased mother's sister-in-law, would. She would need to hear about the family, anyway. Aimée knew she lived somewhere in the area. She only needed to find out where.

Tante Fran was said to have only one fault. People claimed she had the habit of talking religion too much and actually boasted about having conversations with God.

That was what her father always said. Someone even once mentioned God spoke back to her a couple of times! *Anyway*, thought Aimée, *I suppose a little religion couldn't hurt...as long as Tante doesn't force me into believing something different from what my father and my mother taught me.*

As she reached the base of the stairs, Aimée saw Florette stride into the hall to meet her.

"I see you decided to rise. It's well past the 2:00 hour, Amethyst." Florette turned away curtly, as if to look at a smudge spot on the nearby drape.

"I would have descended sooner, but I was waiting for you to open my door. When did my trunks arrive?"

"Yesterday, as you slept. Why did you bring so many?"

"So many?"

81

"What are you planning to do with all that stuff and nonsense? There's a millinery shop and dressmaker right here in the *Quarter* where you can pick up some gowns and hats if that's your desire. One of the proprietors is a good friend of mine."

"The trunks contain all that is left of home," reasoned Aimée. "Perhaps you would like to come up and see if there is anything you might wish to keep for yourself...at least for memory sake?"

"I'm interested in nothing to remind me of *Shadow Grove*," said Florette.

"I don't understand you at all," said Aimée. She no longer knew her, in fact. Just observing Florette made her feel as if she was around a complete stranger.

"I don't need memories of *family*!" Florette went on. "What did any Lebrún ever do for me? It's always been you, Amethyst, the ubiquitous Amethyst Rose. Always you!"

"But that's not true."

"Oh, but it is. What you see here," Florette waved her arms about her, "Except for that fancy settee in the corner of the parlor, I have obtained myself, mind you, myself! I didn't need the family to help me make my way or to dress me in fancy finery! I've pulled my own. You'd never understand. You were always such a submissive child, and in doing so, you always got your way."

Florette glared at Aimée's beautiful dress then spoke again before turning to walk off. "At least you did not wear that ugly black number today. Oh!" she added before turning to walk off, "You might as well learn this now. As long as you are in my house, *sister dearest*, you shall address me as *Simone* not Florette. I despise the name *Florette*."

"I see."

"As with Aimée or Rosie... they're all pure silliness. *Florette* makes me feel like a side dish at a meal. Here at The Paramount, I go by the name of Simone, because for once, I am the main course!"

"Florette," Aimée spoke out her name defiantly anyway.

Her sister stopped and spun around the two women staring fixedly at each other.

"I won't be staying here. I shall even leave today if you 'd rather."

"You shan't be going anywhere. Not now."

Aimée watched her in question with a mingling of fear. "What do you mean?"

"Don't stare at me like that. I've done some rethinking. Since I was looking for someone to help me out for a few days, I've decided to let you fill in where Nina left off." Florette cast her eyes up more thoroughly and down her younger sister. "You might be good for business after all—due to your experience with the Dewey boy."

"I don't understand."

"If you don't now…you will. Think back little sister. Quit pretending to be so dull of mind. You must know what we do here. I have guests…visitors…clients—of the male species. Some are lonely; some come looking for an ear. Others… come to make use of The Paramount…for other purposes. You're mature enough to handle it, and I'm well aware you enjoy the likes of men. I certainly know they like you. They flocked at our door long before you came of age, and our good father tied you up with Jonathan Dewey."

She watched Aimée's eyes widen. "If I'm remembering correctly, you have your flirting down pretty well! Don't deny it," she added with amusement.

"I do not flirt!" argued Aimée.

Florette laughed sardonically. "I know of no woman who does not flirt with a man, especially you. Oh, you shall fit right in…once you get used to it."

Walking over and taking Aimée by the arm, she led her into the drawing room, a much smaller, tidier area. "I shall give you a brief respite; then after a week or so, if you tire of your new occupation, I will consider sending you off to Tante Fran's. How's that?"

She chuckled again. "As long as you are using Nina's room, you can make me some money! And don't plan on running off either. You won't get far. There is no place to go remember? Oh, and do remember my name, Amethyst...it's Simone now."

Aimée watched in dismay as her sister turned to leave. At one time, she thought she knew her. Those days were long gone. How she wanted to go home. But she had no home...anymore. What she really wanted was her father.

Aimée closed her eyes. *Why, God, whoever you are, didn't you just let me die with the family?*

Florette walked back, just as Aimée rose to stare out the window. "Listen, we must all gain knowledge of what it means to earn our way. Now you have interrupted my life without invitation, why should I not treat you any differently from any of the others who stay here under my direction?"

She stared at the younger sister bitterly. "Remember, Father and Mother are gone. They *aren't* coming back. I'll call on you when I need you."

Aimée slowly ascended the stairs to her room. Was this the reason God kept her alive when all the others died? She groaned at the absurdity of it all. If it was God's doing, even with Lulu's suggestions she pray, perhaps for her He wasn't worth the effort.

* * * *

During her three-day reprieve, Aimée let her mind wander back to the handsome Captain Jordan, the Union officer who'd observed her on the boat then again in the harbor. It was amazing how the two had run into each other a thrice of times. She also remembered him saying he would make himself available if she ever needed his assistance.

Had he truly meant what he said? Was it actually possible to call upon him now? How could she reach him if she wanted to?

What about the kind and gentle Philip—from the boat who didn't even know her name? There was no way she could call upon him if she needed him. Who knew where *he* was.

Besides, after her sister was through with her what man would there be willing to assist a soiled woman? *But I will not be soiled! I won't!* Aimée lay back against her pillow as both the lieutenant and the hazel-eyed warrior in deep blue lingered strangely on her mind.

"Godspeed to you, ma'am." It had been that captain who had said those words to her right before she boarded the riverboat back in Vicksburg. She knew that now.

"Godspeed to you." He hadn't known she was listening back then.

Both him and the gentle man, *Angel Wings*, had to be somewhat religious…perhaps they were something like Tante Fran. Perhaps they talked to God, just like she did!

Sitting up quickly on her bed, she continued to stare back out the window, feeling the blood drain from her face with fear for the unknown, her throat feeling parched and dry.

She glanced below her. It was a long way to nowhere. Could she jump? But where would she go then?

Discouraged, she leaned back on the bed and tried to contemplate the coming evening as she reached over to pour herself a tumbler of water from the pitcher.

Aimée had been informed earlier she would no longer be known as Amethyst Rose Lebrún. "Simply Rosette Badeau," Florette had said. How convenient.

Rosette…Rosette, she repeated in her mind. Now she would become as a pretty decoration or prize for the client who chose her. But she would *not* allow herself to be tarnished by any man, not if she had anything to say about it.

I will not become a pawn for my sister! Not like in my earlier years. She shivered and fell back against her pillow. She would get around Florette somehow.

There had to be a way to find Tante Fran.

* * * *

"Your guest has arrived, Rosette," Florette sang out from the bottom of the stairs three hours later. "I hope you're ready."

"I been prayin' for you, Miss Aimée." Lulu eyed her as she straightened her skirt. She turned to shut the door and walked out the door.

"Thanks, honey," Aimée called back softly, hearing her head down the stairs. She stood quietly, studying her face in the mirror, knowing there was no longer any place to hide.

As a young woman who had faithfully saved herself for Jonathan Langston Dewey, the chaste Lebrún virgin she could almost laugh at herself now. Who would care anymore?

The fact was she was now about to *look* as if she would lose the flower of her youth forever in one night in less than a few moments.

Certainly, if Florette had *her* way, no one would even look at Aimée respectfully again, after this night, not once Florette (and her clients) were finished. Well, Florette didn't know her as well as she *thought* she did. She headed out the room and started down the stairs.

Her sister met her from the bottom of the stairwell. "Your guest has explicitly requested you!" She continued teasing, speaking loud enough for the other patrons to hear while Aimée cringed.

"I'm coming, Flo...Simone."

"It looks as if you've already gotten the male population well in hand even here even in New Orleans, Rosette! I should've figured as much! Just make sure you don't try hustling my other girls' clients, and I insist you stay away from mine!"

Aimée wanted to curse her sister, but their mother had taught never to do such things. It wasn't proper for a respectable Southern girl. Biting her tongue, she pressed her lips tightly together and pretended not to hear.

As she walked past Florette and on through the beads and into the parlor, Aimée recognized the gangly man instantly, giving her a moment to collect her wits.

Perhaps the night would not be a disaster, after all. She did have a way out.

When she walked in, Beauregard T. Proctor looked up and smiled.

* * * *

His eyes smiled enjoyment at the rustling sound of her petticoats, his ears at hearing the soft whisper in her voice when she greeted those around her pleasantly, as if she had known them for years. The animation of her character enchanted him.

If she was frightened, she did not let him know it, for all he saw was a woman completely at ease in the room, more dazzling than ever. She gave him the impression a few nights at The Paramount had been no worse for wear at all on her.

After bowing, he gave her an exaggerated wink. "'Tis grand to see you again, Miss, ah, am I to say *Badeau* now?" he asked. He began twisting his curled mustache, his familiar habit, and with his free hand reached out to take hers, kissing her fingertips. "You do remember me."

"I do. You guided me here. Yes, 'tis lovely to see you, Mr. Proctor."

"I knew I'd be in the area this evening, so I made arrangements to drop by. I recalled our earlier encounter on the *Matilda*. I hope you don't mind, Miss Lebrún, excuse me, *Badeau*. Interesting how you have changed your name," he said with a gleam in his eyes. "Call me Beauregard, please."

She shook her head. "Indeed, my name is no different. My sister suggested it. Feel free to call me whatever you like. Shall we sit down?" She nodded towards a couple of free chairs. "What can I do for you this evening?"

His eyes were hungry as he gazed at her from head to toe. "You ask so soon?"

She turned her head back and smiled, keeping her guard up slightly. "Actually, I believe I am to say, 'What's your pleasure?' but it all means the same, I suppose."

87

Beauregard responded with a hearty guffaw and another wink. The settee off by itself was unoccupied, and with his hand, he steered her away from the singular chairs and towards the far corner instead.

Before answering, Aimée glanced behind her catching sight of Florette working her way past the other guests.

"I see the two of you are getting blissfully acquainted!" A knavish smile curved across her mouth. "Has Rosette invited you to her room yet perhaps for a — more intimate visit?"

Beauregard saw Aimée's face turn pale and lifted a brow as she spoke. "He's only dropped by to say hello, Simone."

"I see," said Simone," gritting her teeth. "I suppose I can work it out this evening so the two of you can *chat* in the drawing room if you both would prefer rather than go upstairs. I shall leave you to get further acquainted then."

She glanced at the two of them. "Oh, that's right. By the way, Beau," she added turning towards Proctor. "We've missed you the last few days since Nina's been away. Have you, perchance, been out of town?"

Beauregard frowned as she continued, a smile lingering on her lips. "Now that Miss Badeau is with us you must no longer make yourself so scarce!" She turned and quickly disappeared behind a servant who stood nearby.

* * * *

Although he tarried late into the night, Beauregard's meddling questions began to make Aimée feel ill at ease.

Why did he want to know so many essentials about the family, namely her father? He'd hardly mentioned himself, only that his name was well known in Louisiana and further north. What nagged at the back of her mind was the remark her sister had made before she left the two of them unaccompanied there in the parlor.

What had she meant when she said, *"It is good to see you again, Beau. We have missed you the last few days."* Had

88

she been implying that Beauregard Proctor—*Beau*— was a regular customer at The Paramount?

Aimée moved reflectively up the stairs towards Nina's Boudoir, bone tired. A shiver ran up and down her spine. It was well past 2 A.M. by the time her guest left for the evening but not without a promise she would see him again.

It looked as if her steady customer *would* be Mr. Proctor. Better him than someone else. As reasonable acquaintances, at least they could enjoy each other's company without becoming involved physically. Aimée was determined to keep her arrangements with the man at a respectable level.

She opened the door to her darkened room and walked inside. With a loud plop, she fell down onto her covers and buried her head beneath her pillow—lately, the only place where she felt she could hide.

Her grief came sudden as the tears began falling. She knew Lulu could hear her muffled weeping through the paper-thin walls, but Aimée was beyond caring. Lulu knew her heart anyhow.

Sure enough, more of Lulu's soft prayers began pouring forth through the walls, loud enough for her to hear and hear well. "Lord, please help Miss Aimée find You. Her just plain don't know how."

Chapter Seven

Beads of warm rain splattered against the upstairs windowpane, dripping lingering puddles on the sill and down onto the muddied road. It was a refreshing shower amidst the break of the day, leaving no necessity for starting a fire in Aimée's room. The hypnotic sounds of each droplet floated through the back of her mind as she slept on.

At just before noon, she stirred. As she turned her head, she glanced across the room to see Lulu sitting over in a corner watching her. Always Lulu with her—always as familiar as before.

"I have a tremendous headache. What time is it?"

"Noon...I brought warm milk up."

Aimée sat up, angling her pillows behind her.

"I prayed for you 'gin last night. What did the good Lord do?" Lulu looked up.

"You pray for me every night. He helped I suppose. Maybe you can help me learn how to get your good Lord's attention for myself. I try talking to Him, but I suppose He doesn't know I exist."

Lulu smiled. "He knows, Miss Aimée. If you been praying, Him's been hearin'!"

"Okay, so He's hearing."

"I seen that man here last night, that Proccer fellow. What you gonna do 'bout him?" asked Lulu.

"About him?"

"Mmm Hmm. And you still gonna go see that auntie of yours? You said you was. I'm sayin' when you going to get yourself outa this horrible place?"

"I don't know, Lulu. I don't even know how to find my way there."

Lulu smiled again. "Think a minute, Miss Aimée, 'bout what you teached me when we was chillens."

"What did I teach you?"

Then it dawned on her. Aimée knew Lulu couldn't read well, but she had taught her some of the rudiments early on, at the same time her governess taught her. How to read. How to add. She watched Lulu bend down to open the third trunk.

"I seen something in this here trunk what might give you what you is lookin' for, Miss Aimée."

Aimée pushed off her coverlet and jumped out of bed. Slipping into the nearby dressing gown, she tiptoed over and crouched down beside her. "You mean in here?"

Lulu nodded.

"Let's look inside."

"Is it this folder you're talking about?"

"Mmm Hmm."

Aimée lifted up a large leather bound folder and got up to carry it over to her bed.

"Well, Miss Aimée, what you think?"

"Papers my father would've wanted me, Florette, and David to have," she said.

"'Specially you, Miss Aimée. Maybe there be a map or sumpin' to your auntie's place."

"This is the deed to *Shadow Grove* and much more..." Yet after a thorough searching, there was nothing to provide her with the whereabouts of Tante Fran.

She glanced over and saw the disappointed look in Lulu's eyes. Discouraged, Aimée stood up and walked over to stare out the window. It suddenly came to her.

"I know what I shall do. I shall sneak into Florette's library and see if I can find it there. I know my father gave it to her when she left *Shadow Grove*. He would never have sent her away without doing so. She must have it written down somewhere."

"Oh, Miss Aimée! You sure about that?"

"I simply must do something, Lulu. On the morrow I am invited not only to a luncheon to meet Florette's other girls, but she also has a new customer coming in to meet me in the evening." She swallowed. "Florette expects him to come to my chamber, and I know he is looking for more than idle time."

Aimée wrinkled her brow and chewed on a nail. "It is the perfect time to do this. Tomorrow night could be too late. I've got to get out of here. Like you said, Lulu. I must."

* * * *

"You has to eat with all them others at the food table?" asked Lulu, when she walked into Aimée's room the next morning.

"I told you I would. Florette wants me to meet the other girls to understand more of what is done around this place. In the meantime, this afternoon, I shall do my best to locate Tante's address. Wish me luck and hand me my dress on the bed, will you?" asked Aimée stepping into her soft leather boots.

"I wishes you God's blessings; there ain't no such thing as luck, Miss Aimée! Besides, none of this don't seem right to me…this sneakin' stuff," huffed Lulu.

"Hush now." She walked to the mirror.

Lulu grumbled on as she tied the stays to Aimée's wine-velvet, bretelle corselet then placed the richly textured jacquard skirt over her head. "Miss Florette, her can be right mean. That's what I'm thinkin'."

"Florette? She is as she is. Maybe one day she will explain it all to me."

* * * *

It was a small gathering for teaching Aimée the meaning of turning fast tricks for she had a big night ahead of her. Florette even stayed civil during her introductions, while Aimée did her best to remain tolerant of her sister's profoundly different ways. She observed each girl closely as they introduced themselves.

Two called themselves traveling girls, octoroons, while three or four had been long time residents of The Paramount, including Ginger Jean, who was plumper than the rest and looked like a child of little more than twelve.

The shorter one with the raven black hair, thick and long, wore her tresses in a single braid wrapped around her head. She acted sure of herself. Not so, the timid one sitting next to her with a blank look on her face, her eyes as big as watery pools.

Did any of the girls have homes of their own? Aimée wondered how they could have gotten into a profession at such a youthful age. They certainly looked young.

As she quietly observed them, she realized they were probably asking themselves the same question about her, the now infamous *Rosette Badeau*, who had only days earlier turned the age of ten and nine without fanfare.

When she glanced up again, she noticed how the timid one was watching her with almost frightened eyes. Perhaps she wanted to speak.

* * * *

"Did you hear what I just said, Rosette?" asked Simone, with a frown.

"I'm sorry, no, I did not," said Aimée, clearing her throat.

Florette stood up and repeated her announcement of the changes coming to The Paramount. Instead of its customary $5 nights, the girls were now to raise their prices a quarter for each fast trick. Simone stared pointedly at her.

"You, too, Rosette. Your guest shall come directly to your room this evening—a Yankee soldier." Then she narrowed her brows. "I want you to invite him in and be prepared to meet *whatever* pleasure he seeks. He's paying good coin for you. As is the case with all our clients, he'll leave his fee on the dresser near your bed."

How *could* she respond? It was difficult to believe Florette would have the gall to link her up with a Yankee...especially on the first night she was to lose her virtue!

I simply cannot do it. I will not do it.

* * * *

93

After the others left the room, Aimée spoke guardedly. "Perhaps I should drop in on Tante Francis in a few days, Simone, to share the news of the family. I told you when I arrived I wanted to go by her place. She should be told about the family. Mama was her sister-in-law, after all."

Aimée tried to hold back her feelings of resentment. "I know you want me here a few days, but I shall need to be able to locate her…when the time comes."

"I suppose," said Florette shrugging her shoulders, "there's no problem in letting you know where she lives. I shall have to inform you later in any case. I have her address written down somewhere.

She rubbed her chin. "Abel, the stable man, drove me there ages ago. He knows. You can ask him the directions too, but be prepared. The stupid man is mute and cannot communicate. You may find him a lost cause." She laughed.

"Why do you say that, Simone?"

"I keep him around to humor myself, I guess. Heaven knows why. I often ask myself the reasons I bother to do decent things for people."

Aimée looked at her sister in amazement. "How shall he tell me anything if he cannot utter words?"

Florette shrugged again. "Perhaps your ingenious slave can understand his garble. In the meantime, I have a few errands to run this afternoon. I'll leave the key unlocked at your door if you wish to go out back and tackle the cause." She laughed again. "Like I said, everything he communicates is pure garble."

Aimée breathed a sigh of relief. Florette was making it easy! Fortune was indeed with her…or was it perhaps an answer to one of Lulu's prayers?

* * * *

In Aimée's opinion, the stable hand was an amiable young man with freckled nose, looking much older than probably his tender years. Right off, she could understand his responses to her questioning.

She smiled often to show her appreciation.

Although she did not ask, he gave her the impression he wanted to drive her and Lulu to the Simpson house that afternoon if that was her preference. She watched as he disappeared into the tack room then return with a harness and hold it up with a smile on his face. As far as she was concerned, the trip was a standing order.

With a nod and a smile, Aimée acknowledged then turned and ran back to the house and up the stairs. "Lulu, pack my things!" she hollered, reaching the top. "We're leaving right now!"

Once on the road, the travelers journeyed upriver towards the east bank surrounded by magnificent manses.

Aimée felt the driver pull back slowly on the reins to slow the old chestnut down then heard the mare's whinny. She turned to Lulu. "I'll bet that beautiful horse up front isn't happy with all the weight in here with my trunks!"

"Yas'm."

Aimée viewed the countryside outside the carriage window. "We are coming to a much nicer district now. We're to look for a place called *Primrose Ivy*, Lulu. I guess this is it," she said. "There's the sign above the porch."

Abel pulled the horse to a stop, jumped down, tipped his cap, and stood at the door with his toothless smile.

"Wait upon my trunks until I see the lady of the house is at home, Abel." Aimée motioned before taking the steps.

Reaching up to give her a hand, he nodded and helped her down.

Aimée turned around and waited while he reached in for Lulu, causing her to blush. He stepped back out of the way while the two walked up to the opened door of the large manor.

A slender servant girl stood waiting and smiled broadly at the two visitors. "I'm Millie," she said. "Come in."

Aimée gazed at the softly painted walls and the fresh bouquet of flowers on the corner table, making it particularly cheery inside. The intense darkness of the place she recently left now appeared in her mind as even more shadowy, disquieting.

Her heart leapt when she heard the rustling sound of a woman's flowing skirts and she saw Fran Simpson waltz up with a merry smile on her face.

"Why, I declare! If it isn't Ruby and Cecil's youngest daughter!" With her silver hair pulled back, it was hard not to notice the crinkling edges of her cornflower blue eyes. She held her arms out for a full-sized embrace. "But my, how you've grown my up, dear, and into such a princess!"

Aimée almost lost her breath. "Hello, Tante."

She cocked her head sideways. "What is this? I had no idea you were coming. Ruby did not write...or at least I have not yet received her letter. And who must this be?" She bent around to look at Aimée's house servant. "You know, I met you ages ago, Lulu Jean; I believe it was when the family first took you in."

She shook her head. "Why, you were merely a child back then. How you have grown into a young lady yourself!"

"Yes, she is still with me, Tante."

Lulu lowered her head.

"Tante, I hope you will forgive my intrusion. I have just come from Florette's, and..."

Her aunt held up her hand to stop her. "Say no more, darlin'. Listen, I was about to take tea. I do hope you will join me."

"It sounds wonderful," said Aimée.

"Perhaps after that tedious ride from the city you would first like to freshen up, Amethyst Rose."

"I would appreciate that very much."

"I hope you plan to stay a while. Do you have your things?"

Aimée's wide-eyed gaze followed her aunt's who looked behind her and noted, with a chuckle, Abel heading up the walk with a large trunk on his back.

"I see that you do. Good, good!" Clasping her hands together and pulling them towards her heart, she continued. "It is glorious to see you my child. You favor your uncle, my dear husband Cyrus, God rest his soul. You know he had the same golden rust hair as you! Like fire it was. Yes, yes, my dear Cy, such a love…"

Aimée tried to smile.

"How long might I have you, darlin'? I do tend to talk a mile a minute when I am eager! Oh dear, I must slow down. Do stop me if I get carried away."

Flapping her hands into the air, she shook her head. "'Tis my age; it must be, or perhaps, or…or am I using that for an excuse? Remember, now, you must stop me if I…"

Even in her aimless rambling, Aimée recalled her Tante Fran always did have a way of making one feel completely at ease, simply by the way she babbled on and bubbled over with joy and goodness.

Aimée had heard all her life from both her parents about Tante Fran's love of life and how she wasn't afraid to show it. Right now, she needed that loveable vitality desperately.

"I'm so anxious to hear all about Ruby and Cecil and the boy…oh, yes, that sweet boy…how old is Master Christopher now, seven or eight?"

"That's what—"

"Oh, yes, and David…did the young man ever return from his lengthy trip? Come give me another hug, Amethyst Rose. How I have always loved your name!" She stopped again and looked Aimée up and down, joyful tears falling from the corner of her smiling eyes. "Here I go, all blubbery."

"'Tis good to be here," said Aimée'. "I'm glad I came."

"But of course," announced Fran, wiping her eyes with her lace handkerchief and then stepping back. "You know, I think I'm the one who picked that name out for you. Yes, it *was* me! Of course, I had to do a little bit of convincing. Your mother — she wanted to name you after Cy's great-great grandmamma, Pearl Violet...or was it Pearl Iris...or Pearl Hyacinth — oh my, where is my memory? Did your mother ever tell you that?"

"No, I'd not heard that."

"Oh," Fran stepped in once again, "you look so like her...but also like my Cy."

"I'd heard that too," Aimée faded out.

As Tante Fran chattered away, she began walking in circles. Finally slowing down, she touched her hand to her warm forehead, as if the touch would summons her to stop, scurrying back over to her, with her skirts rustling behind her.

The two tightly embraced for the third time, when Tante gave her a gentle peck on both cheeks.

Aimée could no longer withhold her own tears.

"Whatever it is, dearest heart," she whispered, "it will be all right now, but let's not talk just yet. Go now and freshen up and then we shall have a serious chat over tea in, say, forty-five minutes. Would that do?"

Aimée nodded, wiping her eyes. Taking Tante Fran's extended hand, she walked with her through a large hall and the two ascended the nearby staircase.

Though Aimée listened to her continue with her prattle, most of the time, she could not be certain about just what she was talking.

"Will this do? It is one of my favorites and gives the best view of my garden." She led Aimée into the chamber at the top of the steps. "I used to come in this room and sit and look out when your Uncle Cyrus was off serving his country."

"'Tis fine."

"Settle in then, and after tea, I insist you take some time to rest."

"Yes, I shall look forward to it. I shall look forward to it more than you can imagine!"

* * * *

While upstairs, Aimée refreshed herself and searched in her trunk for something comfortable to change into.

"Help me with my dress, will you, Lulu?"

She handed her the fragile gown of pleated ivory gauze with its tiny periwinkles dancing throughout. As she stood quietly, Lulu fastened her up, tying the silk blue ribbons at her throat and along her long trimmed sleeves.

After brushing out Aimée's hair, Lulu held it back with froths of tulle, while Aimée gazed around the room at her aunt's fineries.

"'Tis so like home here. Did you see Tante Fran's lovely silver tea service downstairs? I wonder how she is able to still keep her good china what with the war and all."

"She didn't let no war mess her stuff up, Miss Aimée. You is in the right place, now." Lulu pulled back and turned her towards the looking glass.

"That's fine. I'll go now."

Turning a few minutes later to run out the door, Aimée hurried down the stairs with purpose.

When she heard more than one voice in the parlor, she stopped abruptly at the entrance. She was instantly annoyed at the transparency of her feelings.

She glanced up.

Tante Fran and her guest both turned their heads as Aimée walked through the archway.

"Am I interrupting something?" asked Aimée.

"See, Beryl, honey? Isn't she something?"

"Oh, Francis, she is utterly charming," Beryl chirped back. "How do you do, dear."

Aimée's eyes veered the woman's way.

"She won't mind my being here, will she?" Beryl asked.

"Come in, darlin'," said Tante Fran. "I want to introduce you to my friend. The two of us have just been having a little tête-à-tête. I forgot to tell you we share tea most afternoons.

"Beryl, Amethyst Rose—Cyrus's niece...Aimée is Ruby's youngest daughter. I have mentioned Ruby and also Florette, the older sister."

Aimée nodded and managed a small smile, trying to hide her war of emotions. "How do you do? I'm sorry, I didn't get the name," she said, sitting down beside her aunt.

"You can simply call me Aunt Beryl, dear. All the young people do here."

"Aunt Beryl it is then." Aimée turned to concentrate more fully on her aunt.

"Tante Fran, I must be the bearer of bad news. Is now a good time?"

"We aren't going to bring up your recent visit with your sister...are we? Let's not talk of those things here at tea—not..."

"'Tis not regarding my sister," explained Aimée. "Is this then not a good time then?" she asked, glancing over at Beryl.

"Tell me first, darlin'. How are Ruby and Cecil, David, and of course the boy?"

Aimée struggled with her words. "That's the news that's difficult to share. The family is...dead...since a year ago July."

"Dead? What are you saying?" said her aunt. "Gracious me, you poor child!" Fran instantly rose and scooted in closer to her, tears rolling down her face. "I am so sorry. I knew there was something, with you traveling down this way. I had no idea 'twas that! The war, I'm sure."

"Yes, and there is little left even of family memories now."

A hot tear rolled down Aimée's cheek.

"Oh, my!"

"Let me pour you some ladies some tea," said Beryl, so you can talk, then perhaps I should go and see if I can be of use in the back."

"Wait," said Aimée. "Don't go. As long as you don't mind listening to my story, that is."

"Not at all," said the tall older woman, pouring the tea then turning to sit back down.

Aimée had wanted to talk to someone, and was grateful her aunt would listen and care.

To someone else, everything that had been building in her heart for so long would finally matter to someone besides her. One more time she poured out her heart revealing memories from the past she wished more and more would just go away.

* * * *

"…then after the fire," she said when she was almost finished, "I housed with neighbors, but no one had much to share."

Tante nodded and covered her hands with her own as she continued.

"I did not want to eat their food, Tante. Most had no spare room. They were trying to house others also. I slept little. After I left them, I returned to the place Elijah had dug out for the family. Oh, Tante! It was dreadful!"

"Go on," said Fran, choking back further tears. "Tell us all of it."

"Day in and day out, hunkered down, waiting — waiting, and hiding in that underground cave along the banks. Not only me, mind you; others too, yet, we all felt completely alone…and abandoned."

Aimée felt the touch of her aunt's arm ever so lightly.

"It was bearable, yes, but still dingy, horrible, and miserable. I felt as if my own existence was a struggle between life and death. We must have waited for months, Tante, for those hateful men to open that muddy river up again to us."

"Yes, darlin'," she nodded, "I knew the river was closed…for oh, so long."

"We merely wanted to get out of Vicksburg…that's all."

"Yes, yes."

"But at least the wretched Yankees could not find me!" Aimée's mood veered sharply toward anger, "and—and if they had, well, if they had—perhaps, I would have done something that would have brought much shame to the Lebrún name! Oh, Tante..."

As Aimée's voice rose with her story telling, the wretchedness she had felt in her heart and mind for so long peaked, enough to shatter the last threads of all control she'd held on to for over a year.

Aimée stood and gazed at her aunt and the speechless woman beside her, swallowing hard and biting back her tears.

"Elijah and Lulu stayed with me the entire time. To be honest, I think the blue coats knew where we were all the time." She soured. "They were too busy destroying anything and everything of value to bother with us there."

She suddenly felt weak and vulnerable. "Truly, I don't know why they didn't simply come and take me away. They might as well have." Sitting back down, her voice broke off.

"Bless Elijah and Lulu." Francis shook her head. "Bless you all! What happened in Vicksburg was no secret. Everyone at my church discussed it, but we didn't realize..." Fran's eyes met Aimée's as she looked back up. "I don't know how you managed, but it is certain the good Lord watched over you."

Aimée nodded and gave her aunt an attempt at a smile.

"My nephews were fighting in..." Beryl stopped short of finishing when Aimée briefly glanced her way.

"You will stay here, of course," said Tante Fran.

"I am truly much obliged," Aimée replied.

"And, Aimée...you would have never done anything to those Yankee soldiers that would've brought you shame...remember that. You mustn't think such things. "

Aimée could only stare back at her aunt wordlessly.

* * * *

The three women drank the last of their tea in silence. As the hour ended, Aimée listened attentively as her aunt's friend, Beryl, finally mentioned again that her own nephews were out fighting the same war. She hadn't heard from either of them since '61 and said she had been praying she would receive word soon.

"Maybe you will soon," said Aimée.

"Did David ever go to war, darlin'? He is still of age, isn't he?" asked Fran, interrupting.

"He's getting on towards thirty," said Aimée, "but was out of country when the war began. If he returned to the states, I wasn't told. It's been years since I've seen or heard from him."

Beryl reached over and touched Aimée's arm. "Your aunt and I pray daily this war will come to an end. You should join us in our endeavor, Miss Lebrún."

"Perhaps one day I shall," she replied, looking down at her skirt. "Right now taking time for prayer is not a priority." She still had no way of knowing whether anyone was truly up there listening. She still did not know if she cared.

When she lifted her head, Beryl smiled.

"Listen, darlin'," said Fran, as the three stood to say goodbyes a few moments later. "You need to know Beryl and I help out in the hospital annex the doctors set up in the South Wing here in my home. I did not mention it to you earlier."

"You service soldiers here? Yankees?"

"I've more than enough room to spare in my home. It causes no harm here. It is for all who have a need whether men from the North or South, dear. The doctor in charge said our assistance is making a difference."

"Tante Fran?"

"You mustn't fret, darlin'. We try to remember many of those boys and young women, too. They are doing what they can and what they believe is right, no matter what side. Do you understand that?"

Aimée scowled. "Those bluecoats are nothing more than invaders! They've destroyed so many homes and broken apart numerous families." Her face reddened.

"I guess I should at least mention the riverboat captain had me assist in the infirmary on his boat. I tried hard to turn a blind eye there to the color of uniforms, when I could."

"Now, that's the way," said Tante nodding.

"I suppose I *could* do the same here with you. I actually learned a lot," said Aimée. "In fact, it felt good to be able to be doing something worthwhile such as…"

"That's right," said Tante.

"Just don't ask me to like the men."

Chapter Eight

Aimée received a complete night of slumber, feeling comfortably rested — the first time in weeks.

"Miss Aimée," Lulu whispered from out in the hall, "Can you hears me? I knows you're stirrin' in there."

"I hear you, Lulu. I decided to get an early start. I figured you were up. Will you bring me some water and prepare a bath?"

She opened the door and peeked in. "You ain't sick or nothing? You ain't usual been getting up this time of the morning, not no more."

"I'm in good health. Draw that bath, will you, please?"

"Yas'm, I do that now."

Aimée donned her dressing gown, stretched her tired limbs then walked over to her window to gaze down at the courtyard. Her eyes fell upon a soldier sitting below on a stone bench with his head bowed.

Why, that man is praying. Her heart stirred as she watched, until she abruptly recognized the color of his uniform.

'Tis a Yankee soldier praying and out in public of all places!

Stunned, Aimée spun around and hurried back to her bedside. The soldier certainly did not have a right to flaunt himself in such a way, praying before the world and everything…where the whole world could *see* him!

Wasn't religion supposed to be a private issue?

No one did that. Not even Lulu.

Aimée glanced around the room. What if she was to take the time to try? Privately. What if she tried to talk to God herself, at least in the privacy of her room? No one would know. Who was to say she could not?

Looking around again to make certain she was indeed alone, Aimée knelt down beside her bed. She laid her head down on her tousled covers and waited.

Nothing happened.

All she could feel was the coolness of the polished wood floor on her bare knees through the sheer cloth of her dressing gown.

Repositioning herself, Aimée tried scooting over a few inches to the bedside rug. This time, before she closed her eyes, she clasped her hands together in a steeple like fashion. She waited a minute longer.

Nothing.

What was she doing wrong?

Did I ever talk to God as a child? Of a truth, I cannot recall. As the budding flower of Vicksburg, I was either too busy chasing after the boys or later as the flame in the hearts of all the males, they were chasing after me! Ha! Look at me now!

Here, I am on my knees bending, trying to talk to a God about whom I know nothing. Perhaps He has no interest in me at all...if He is even out there.

Even if she did reach Him, she didn't know what to *say* to Him. The entire exercise seemed completely futile.

Feeling suddenly silly, Aimée rose quickly and walked back over to the window to gaze back down at the garden. A sense of great disappointment filled her heart when she saw the soldier was gone. She glanced at her reflection in the windowpane.

What is wrong with me? Why is something always missing from my life?

Was it not only the night before she had visited her aunt's library and come across those interesting scriptures?

It had seemed the perfect place to go, where she could sit down with her note pad to write her poetry or read a good book. Yet, when she arrived there, instead of thinking of anything to write or finding a simple book to read, she had come across her aunt's leatherbound Bible, which sat open on a drop-leaf table over in a corner.

Her curiosity had pulled her to it, down the opened page, where she read the scripture verse that seemed to call her to it.

"He was in the world…the world was made by him…the world knew him not. He came unto his own…his own received him not…."

It was true. Aimée knew nothing about him…this God, just as it said, even though Lulu had tried for years to tell her. Yet, right there in her aunt's library, there was the strongest sense in her heart she *needed* to believe in something — in someone.

She recalled reading the passage one more time.

"He came unto his own…his own received him not…"

Now, in the quiet of her chamber, her whole body cried out to receive or know him…to know something.

What am I supposed to receive? You, God? I don't understand? Am I lost too? I don't know, Lord…If it is as the book said, until I do, I presume I shall be lost forever as well.

Tante's library had been much like *Shadow Grove*, like Aimée's Mother's day room, where the two of them had sewn together, read together, and written in their diaries. Yet at *Shadow Grove,* Aimée had no memories of either parent ever telling her about God or scripture verses.

"The world knew him not."

Aimée sighed deeply. Had her mother or father ever spoken to her about God? Would she ever become acquainted with Him? She looked up then closed her eyes again.

Is that why others can so easily talk to you, God, and I cannot?

The room remained silent.

Gazing down at the empty stone bench yet again, Aimée visualized the soldier there praying.

Perhaps it will never be possible for me.

She lost track of how long she stood in her room gazing down, thinking about nothing anymore.

* * * *

"Good morning, darlin'," said her tante, looking her way. "Join me for some weak coffee? There's plenty and an extra cup here."

Aimée entered the dining room and sat down. "It smells good."

"It's drinkable. You rose early this morning." Fran poured and smiled.

Aimée's heart beat faster. "I was hoping I might find you up. I'd like to go with you today to the annex. I guess I am a bit nervous."

"Wonderful. I was just getting ready to head that way. We are receiving transfers from the hospital this morning — boys, who will furlough soon but need a place to rest while they convalesce. Some arrived in port not that long ago. I've heard tell there will be about a dozen arriving. I can use your help registering them. How does that sound? Grab you coffee, and I'll show you the South Wing now." She got up to walk out the door.

The South Wing was only steps away from the kitchen and passed the garden in an area with its own private entrance.

Aimée saw a table with a registration sign above it. "Is this the desk where I shall sit?" she asked.

"This is it," declared Fran setting her own cup down. "The docket here will give you a list of names sent over from the hospital. The doctor has sent over an assistant, who will work with you in assigning men to their appropriate beds. Beryl won't be by until later."

"Thanks. I will appreciate the help."

Fran helped her Aimée into her crisp cotton apron, then lifted her cup and turned. "I'm just going to mosey on to the back for a moment to where we have the beds just to say good morning to a few patients. I'll be back."

"I'll call you if I need you." Aimée settled into her chair and readied herself to greet the first group of arrivals.

* * * *

"Good Morning, Ma'am," said the decorated soldier dressed in the blue of a Union officer to Tante Fran, tipping his hat, as she started to disappear behind the curtain toward the back behind the younger nurse beside her. She walked past and gave him a smile and a nod.

"Good morning officer."

He continued through the hall behind the nurse's desk glancing casually her way. When he became even with the desk he stopped, turned, and stared.

"And good morning to you! But I know you!" he exclaimed, his mouth increasing to a wide smile. His gray eyes sparkled beneath the thickness of his long curly black lashes.

She turned her head and gazed first at his doubled-breasted coat, at each button lined up vertically in groups of three, his collar of dark velvet then directly at him.

They both could not stop staring.

"Yes, I do know you!" He said, grinning from ear to ear.

She took a closer look. "Ph-Philip?" she asked, her face turning crimson.

Lieutenant Philip Jordan answered back warmly, "It's me all right. I thought I would never see you again. And yet, believe it or not, here you are right in front of me. And wouldn't you know it I still don't even know your name."

He neared the desk.

"'Tis Amethyst Rose Lebrún." She shook her head. "B-but what are you doing wearing *that* uniform?"

He laughed. "Ah! Such a question you ask. How long has it been now? I cannot believe this is happening!" He lifted his hands and touched his face. "But of course!" He laughed again. "You would have had no idea at first seeing me before as a patient! Indeed it is I, Lieutenant Philip Jordan, at your service."

"Sir?"

He grinned wide.

An infinity of a moment passed by.

"I have never forgotten you, the wonderful nurse from *St. Honorine*. You didn't recognize me at first without so many bandages, did you!"

She continued staring. "But why did you have to be a—"

* * * *

Aimée found speaking suddenly difficult. She tried to look nonchalant by lifting her chin and giving the lieutenant a cool stare. It wasn't working.

She studied him from head to toe before she spoke, her voice rising in surprise. "I-I honestly didn't realize you were a—a Yankee, Philip...Lieutenant!"

The shock of her words had caught in her throat. Lifting a hand in front of her mouth, she hoped she could hide the turmoil she was feeling inside with her struggling emotions.

She'd wanted so to see the man again, nevertheless, she'd not intended for him to be a Yankee soldier...not Philip.

Restless patients hooted and hollered from the door, waiting to enter. She could see them from the corner of her eye.

Aimée took a deep breath, put her hand down, and turned to recognize some of their faces as well, men from the boat. Why would it not be so? Had she not been there as well?

"Apparently it makes a difference to you...my being a Union officer," he said to her.

"Apparently it does...officer."

Aimée realized quickly her feelings would have to go on hold, at least until she was able to get the men waiting at the door registered. "I must get back to my work, *Lieutenant*. Truly, I—I cannot talk just now. I must tend to the men, you see." She blushed.

Looking away then down at her roster, she bit a lip and tried to concentrate, blinking nervously.

Land sakes! What shall I do? 'Tis Philip! He was my friend. But now he's a Yankee!

"I get the picture. If you will excuse me then." He turned and walked over to the door to bring order to the rowdy group, glancing back briefly before disappearing from the room.

A tear fell from Aimée's eye as kept her eyes on her list of names. Once again her life felt lost and alone, without a friend in the world.

Why did he have to be a Yankee?

"Looks like you already know ole' *Angel Wings*, huh, ma'am?" said the noisiest patient after he stepped up to the table. "Everyday that boy gets a few more of them wrappings off his head, and we find out what's 'neath 'em. He's like a reg'lar Christmas present! No one can call him *Mask Face* no longer."

"I'd like to get your name, please," she said wiping her eye quickly with her sleeve.

He gaped at her. "We didn't know he was full on rank before! Don't matter him bein' a…" The boy's eyes followed Aimée's as she lifted her eyes towards his to get his name.

"Hey! I know you!" he said. "You're that *Sand Tacky* from the boat! Look at you now! Remember me?" Southern Boy viewed Aimée more closely.

Aimée blushed. "May I please have your name?"

"Name's Corporal Benjamin Joseph Craft," he said, "and I ain't no *Billy Yank*, as you can see. My home's down Georgia way…out nears Habersham County! I'm *me* from the boat. Remember?"

Aimée nodded. "I remember." She searched the roster down to the *Cs* and crossed off the name *Craft* then wrote down all the pertinent information to in-process the corporal. It would have been impossible to forget him.

"Nobody *fergets* me. What you all doin' over here, girl?"

"Let's get a move on, Corporal," admonished the lieutenant, walking up beside her. "There are others behind you."

"I'm goin', I'm goin'. You be sure to tell the little lady out front she can come on back to my cot anytime."

As Southern Boy followed the lieutenant to the back, he continued carrying on loud enough for Aimée to hear until the officer returned to the front for the next patient.

Masking her inner turmoil, Aimée tried not to listen and watch as she went on with her duties.

It was almost impossible to forget she had not seen Philip since he passed by her every few minutes, but they didn't spoke again that morning.

* * * *

By thirteen hundred hours on the military clock, Aimée watched him lead the last soldier into the back. Closing her roster quickly, she set her quill down and put the cork back onto the inkbottle.

Removing her cap and apron then returning them to the peg, she ran out the door and back towards the garden walkway as fast as her legs would carry her. As she headed for the north wing, she vowed in her heart not to look back.

Her stomach churned. She wanted to get away, but where would she go? Could she speak to Philip again? It was probably too late now. She had been rather rude after all. Inside the house she could hear her aunt and Beryl chatting in the parlor.

"Is that you dear?" Tante asked, glancing toward the door. "Come join us. We were just discussing the scheduling."

"Yes, all right," she replied, dragging her feet.

"What is it?" asked Fran. "Was this morning too upsetting for you?"

She touched her fingers to her lips. "Beryl mentioned earlier it might be too soon to expose you to the turmoil of the sick and wounded men. Was she right, dear?" asked Tante.

Aimée shrugged.

"Do you want to tell us about it?" Hurrying over, she took hold of her arm and led her to a nearby footstool.

Aimée swallowed her tears. She had no true justification for releasing them—not just because of a single man who happened to be a Yankee soldier. The problem was the man was Philip, her dear friend Philip.

He was there.

112

Why did it have to be him?

"Why don't you go have a rest in the library, and the two of us will talk later, shall we?" said Tante.

Aimée nodded and rose to leave. Reaching over, she gave her aunt a tight squeeze.

* * * *

She had not moved a muscle except for the needlework project in her hand.

Tiptoeing up to the door of the library, Tante Fran peeked in.

Aimée stared down at her small sampler.

"Are you ready for that visit?"

She glanced up with a smile. Her lashes still glistened with dampness from weeping. Reaching into the cuff of her long sleeve for her handkerchief, she wiped a stray tear off the bridge of her nose. "I think so."

"Good. Then let's talk, shall we?"

Fran walked over to sit across from her as Aimée set the needlework down. "Tell me now what happened this morning."

"On the *St Honorine* I helped Captain Moreau with the floating hospital. There was another gentleman there who worked with me...one of the patients."

"Go on."

"He stayed by my side and even protected me from some ill-mannered boys from the South."

"And?"

"Philip and I worked side by side for days, and when I had to leave..."

Frances smiled gently. "I know. You're missing your young man, is that it? Then when you saw the young men in the back, did it make you pine for him in a greater way, perhaps?" Her eyes sparkled.

Aimée frowned. "He wasn't my young man, so much," she answered awkwardly. "Tante, that man, Philip, he's here...in your house!"

Fran stood up and clapped her hands together, her hooped skirt rising with a whoosh. "Why, darlin'! How simply delightful! I must meet your boy! We could have him join us for supper — if he's able to get away, that is!"

She started to turn. "I'll have the cook scrape up a little extra. Yes, yes, that would be just the ticket! Oh, I cannot wait to tell Beryl! We shall have her join us — that is, if you wouldn't mind."

Hardly stopping to take a breath, Fran hurried to head out of the room then spun around to continue. "Were the two of you able to chat much? My, my, he was not one of the severely wounded, was he? Oh, dear heart! I wonder what he likes to eat."

In her rapid ramblings, she twirled her body around again then sat back down, her forehead wrinkling.

She pursed her lips. "Was there more…dear?"

Aimée watched her aunt's face redden as she began to fan herself and lean in closer.

"You don't understand. Philip, you see, Philip, oh, Tante…the man is a *Yankee*, a Union officer! Well, he is *the enemy*!" Her tears tumbled down as she buried her face into both hands.

"Oh my!" declared Fran. "This indeed puts us in somewhat of a quandary doesn't it."

"I'm not trying to cause problems, Tante," Aimée apologized.

"Yes. But this could prove a dilemma," she said, "for what I see here is either a friendship gone sour or perhaps more."

"It was merely a friendship, Tante, but what can I do?" Tears trickled down as Aimée whispered. "I want to work with you and help you. The work in back will give me purpose, but I don't know if I can face him again. I was even rude to him this morning when I saw him."

"You are certain?"

She shook her head and bit her lip. "What if he was with those other Yankee invaders who killed my family?" She looked up. "What if he was, Tante? Don't you see? Who knows? How am I to know he was not?"

"Oh, darlin'. You cannot know that." Tante stared at her.

"Well, he could have been! Those...those people almost destroyed my home, and...and well, I think I might come to hate them all. Yes, that's it. I do. I've decided. I hate them, and I simply want to die!"

Jumping up, Aimée turned to run out of the room, but Fran was quick, catching her sleeve to stop her before she got to the door. Taking her niece's hands into her own, she smiled gently and spoke even softer.

"Sweet one, we mustn't be repulsed by those boys, for it turns us into such ugly creatures. That is not like you, Amethyst Rose. And you must *never* want to die...not like that. I realize how terrible this war is, what with all the changes going on all around us. The good Lord knows, too. Don't you see? We must keep our hope and faith in him."

Aimée fixed a stare out the window.

"Amethyst Rose, look at me."

Fran drew her niece into her arms and rocked her back and forth. "God *will* fix things. I promise you, He will...in His designated time." She let go long enough to look her in the eyes.

"Maybe you can point out the young man, this friend to me," she declared. "Then we'll work things out so you do not have to work in the same area he is in at the same time. Would that help?"

"I—I guess so."

"That's the girl. And darlin'," she finished, "...we must pray this horrible war ends soon so the color of uniforms and who we are will not continue to be a factor in making enemies anymore, shall we? That is the way God would have it. Can you see that?" she continued to stare gravely at her. "Don't turn away from me, child. Can you see that?"

Aimée could not answer. She wanted desperately to turn away. Pulling back, she bent down and picked up the sampler from her lap setting it on the table, studying her fingers as if they might choose for her a better answer to return to her aunt. In any case, she decided, she would at least consider her words.

115

What else could she do? It was only right she knew that now.

"Will you at least join me tomorrow morning for church, Amethyst Rose?" Fran asked when she turned to leave the room.

A hesitant but affirmative nod brought a smile to the elder Simpson woman as Aimée made to follow her out of the room.

Church.

Perhaps she could do it. She had never gone before.

She would have to deal with it eventually anyway — that and prayer about the war with her aunt's friend Beryl.

Getting through the rest of the war without hatred, letting go of her bitterness about her sister, and looking to heaven for answers, all needed to be dealt with before long and she knew it.

Soon, Aimée thought, quietly, she would maybe consider all that was on her mind.

Soon, perhaps — but not just yet.

* * * *

"I'm looking for a Rosette Lebrún," said the man to the house servant from out on the porch.

"Rosette?"

"Amethyst Rose," he corrected himself.

"Her's here," she answered with a bob.

"Beauregard T. Proctor here, the honorable one," he announced, nudging his left foot forward into the opening of the door before it shut in his face. "Just be kind enough to give her my name. I'm sure she will choose to send for me."

"Move your feets, man. I's always told I must shut the door."

"I was just considering it is a might chilly out here. Mayhap I could position myself within...until you announce me?"

She nodded and cautiously admitted the man.

Beauregard stood in the foyer with his right thumb holding onto the closing of his lapel. With his other hand, he removed his hat and set it down on a nearby table while he watched the housemaid tiptoe into the parlor.

* * * *

Fran and Aimée sat in the parlor in silence with their needlework.

"There's a man here to see Miss Amthys'," said Millie. "He say his name is Borgard Proccer, something like that."

Aimée quickly went back to her work.

How did he find me?

Her aunt glanced over at her then at the clock. "Are you acquainted with this gentleman, darlin'?"

"Only slightly," answered Aimée glancing up. "But how would he know to find me here?"

"Perhaps by way of your sister. If you do not wish to see him, I can always have Millie send him away. It's up to you."

Aimée hesitated. "I suppose there would be no harm in seeing the man."

After all, he had been helpful in showing her how to locate Florette in the first place. With reluctance, she got up from her chair.

"I know the man. I'll see Mr. Proctor."

* * * *

Aimée took a deep breath and forced a smile when she saw him.

"I've missed seeing you, Rosette," said Beauregard, from the hall, a frown on his face. He bowed before her with an exaggerated gesture. "How long has it been—two and a half, three weeks?"

"Hello, Mr. Proctor," she said quietly.

"You were supposed to begin calling me Beauregard." His eyes glistened as he perused her from head to toe, lingering in areas where Aimée was beginning to think any respectable man would not venture. "You look charming this evening, my dear!"

Since there had been no word from Florette, she had hoped her sister had become resolved she had simply left with no intention of returning.

"Did my sister send you here?" she asked curiously, reaching out to shake his hand.

Taking hold of hers, Proctor pulled it up to his soggy full lips and nibbled at her fingers. "And if she did?"

Aimée yanked her hand hastily out of his grasp.

"This is the way to the parlor, sir."

"My dear Rosette," he said, stopping her. "Wait. I came to pass along some grave information."

Aimée spun around looking perplexed. "'Tis Amethyst Rose, Mr. Proctor. Anyway, what is it?"

"Your unfortunate sister has taken ill and is calling for you." He cleared his throat. "Mademoiselle Simone is down with a fever, she and a few of her—the others, as well. I just happened by the other week…on business. And in my passing I came to look in on you, ascertaining you were not there."

His tone was cool, reproving. "She invited me in, rather I should say, her slave did—you recall the one with the hollow eyes—that was before she ran off with the other one—what was her name… Etta Jean?"

"You say run off?"

"As I was saying, upon my entrance, the colored child informed me the mistress was unable to rise." He watched Aimée closely.

"I took the liberty, most naturally, of scurrying up the steps to her private chambers to see if there was something I could do…to help. Anyone of my good character would naturally."

He paused to clear his throat again then gazed deeper into her orbs.

Aimée bit her lip. "Is there yet more?"

"Tut! Tut! Oh, yes. There the poor woman lay, unmoving upon her bed, terribly heated and seeming rather frail. So sad it was. I say, it was difficult to look upon her," he continued in his practiced English.

Aimée wondered if there wasn't a slight accusing edge in his voice as he stopped, sighed, and shook his head.

Her brows arched in question. "So what happened to Florette?" she asked uneasily.

"She'd been weeping, unmistakably, for several days actually."

"My sister, *Florette,* weeping? That is difficult to believe, Mr. Proctor."

"Yes, Simone…weeping. I presume because you had departed without a word. Then she took poorly this last week. In fact, the entire household began ailing soon after."

She was glad he didn't feel the hammering of her heart.

"Since that first day, I've made an effort to go by and visit often…as any benevolent person would," he continued. "The poor woman has weakened terribly, calling out mostly for you. Thus, you see me here imploring you to return to the aid of your ailing kin."

Raising his eyebrow, he spread his nostrils and breathed in. "Take note," he added, "as the others remain quiet in their rooms, you've no need to fear contracting whatever it is plaguing the household. I do believe, however, you should be there and not here lounging in luxury while your helpless sister suffers."

"She needs me then?" questioned Aimée, staring down at the floor.

"Terribly so."

Aimée's heart suddenly ached, for it seemed her sister, for the first time was perhaps calling out for her. Florette had never needed her for anything before. Was this an opportunity where she could be of some assistance to her for a change?

Of course, she would return with Mr. Proctor.

It was also a way not to have to run into Philip again. Although Aimée ached for his friendship, she knew it was impossible…now.

"I shall come with you, Mr. Proctor. Wait here."

Chapter Nine

She glanced up. Heat burned in her cheeks.

He was watching her, grinning, exposing his slightly oversized teeth. His lip curled up on one side. "Let me get the door for you, love."

Aimée, now repelled by him calling her his love, could not respond before Beauregard reached across her and rubbed his arm against her bodice. Shocked and embarrassed, she pulled back stiffly and leaned against the seat, to try to break free from his nearness.

"My pardon," he mumbled awkwardly, climbing over her lap.

When he swung open the door and jumped out of the carriage, he turned and grabbed hold of the small of Aimée's waist, sidling her off her seat. Grasping her too tightly, so she could not pull away, he lifted her off the ground and drew her into his embrace, causing her to shutter at the nearness of his soggy face. The man dripped in sweat even in the cool of the night.

Aimée started to choke . She smelled his breath and body, both of which reeked of sour odors and stale spirits.

"Let me go!" She jerked out of his arms.

"Indeed!" he announced, setting her down on the stone road. He pushed her slightly forward then at the small of her back towards the front entrance. "I shan't harm you, *Rosette*. Now, come along. Don't be shy."

Mr. Proctor had taken complete authority, and Aimée could only stare after him. She watched him kick the door shut behind them once they stepped inside the house. He almost did not seem like the same man she had met back at the dock.

"Simone said we should walk right in, so *that* we will," he continued, dragging her by the arm.

Aimée nervously ran her fingers through her hair with her free hand. Why could she not pull back? Why did she no longer exert herself? What had happened to the courage she had had as a child? Before, she was known for her stubbornness, her strong will. She had not seen it in years.

Fighting back her tears, she stepped further inside.

The stuffy room was still musty. Odors from leftover drink and rancid smoke from cheroot ashes still filled the air. The hallway was now filthier than before.

"Etta May and Daisy are truly gone?"

"As I before stated." Proctor shrugged. "Were you not listening? Besides, am I their keeper?" He motioned for her to follow him up the stairs.

Feeling a combination of fear and dread, Aimée bit her lower lip. In her heart, the same phrase rang out continually. *What have I just done*?

When they reached the third floor, the door to Florette's room at the end of the hall was already ajar.

Aimée could barely recognize her sister's voice when she heard her call out.

"Is that you, Beau? Did you get Rosette to come?"

"I have her with me, Simone, my sweet," he answered back. "Are you ready for visitors?"

Aimée stared at the door ahead then at the man. *My sweet?*

"Come in," she called out again, slightly out of breath.

Aimée followed Beauregard into the chamber. Florette sat with her back leaned against a number of pillows, resting against the backboard of her bed. The worn velvet spread on her bed of intense blood red, with its gold silk threads laced throughout, looked much too hot for the warm fall evening.

The logs in the fireplace crackled fiercely. Florette's room was sweltering. The tapestries draping the wall behind her dresser were perhaps to draw attention away from the threadbare rug and torn wallpaper Aimée assumed.

On a small table beside her bed, Aimée noted several partially filled bottles of strange tonic and empty spoons, now dirty.

A half-full vial of stale water sitting on Florette's cluttered dresser with an empty glass beside it appeared as if it been there for days.

Aimée sat down beside Florette and touched her sister's hot, dry forehead with her cool hand.

"How long have you been this way?"

Her sister's hair, damp and disheveled, lay sprawled across her shoulders and down her flimsy gown, revealing more than it should, in the presence of a man. She didn't seem bothered by its transparency. Her dark shadowy eyes stared out, yet looked vacant.

"I took fever a few days ago and have no energy. I cannot seem to pull myself together. Then one of my girls came down with something then another. Those who escaped this vile disease abandoned me! All of them, even the darkies!"

She waved her weakened arms about her. "Even the stupid cook took off, but for some reason, Doris later decided to return. I guess she didn't know where else to go. I insisted Beau give her a whipping. Served her right."

"You whipped Doris? But what about their freedom?"

Florette tried to crease her brow. "As long as the coloreds remain beneath me, they'll know of no such word as *freedom* in *my* house. 'Tis a shame, Rosette, *I* receive no appreciation for all *I* do—dullard, ignorant fools...all of them! What do they know?"

Florette stopped to cough phlegm into a nearby canister. "No one cleans up after me, no one helps me bathe, no one does a thing—no one, except for dear Beau here."

She reached out to take his hand. "'Tis disgraceful! I fear I shall lose my business at this rate. I am close to ruin."

Aimée watched Florette with dismay. "What did the doctor say?"

"He refuses to stop by. And you! You are no more the gracious than any of the others, Rosette!" she stated. "That in itself is deplorable — but for now, I suppose I will let it pass. I have you here now...and here you will stay." She stopped again to catch her breath. She slowly twisted her head over toward the man with tired eyes.

"If it wasn't for this wonderful man, I probably wouldn't be here talking to you today. Beau carried me up to my chamber five days ago. He's been with me ever since."

When her coughing started up again, this time uncontrollably, Aimée observed her, not with the love a sister should have for her sister but instead with confusion.

"Listen, Florette... Simone, I shall stay and help out in whatever way I can, but understand — this isn't permanent." Aimée refused to apologize for leaving the first time. "We must get the doctor back here to find out just what is wrong with you and the others."

"Posh on the obtuse doctor! As long as I have my tonics and *you* around, I'll be fine. All that matters is that *I* am fit again. Your job is to keep me in medicine and to clean this place up — oh, and to check in on the others when you aren't busy helping me. When the others show improvement, I want them back and doing what they were trained to do. Right now, I want you to give me something to help me sleep." She pointed to one of the bottles. "I think it's that one right there. See that powder?"

Aimée nodded.

"In the meantime, you need to line up customers for next week. Do you understand, Rosette?"

"Me?" Aimée stared at her blankly.

Never in her life had she thought she would find herself a part of what was now being thrust upon her. She sat in her chair stunned.

"You don't know what you are demanding," she whispered softly.

"I most certainly do, *sister dearest*. I most certainly do."

* * * *

Far into the night, Aimée stayed up scrubbing walls, woodwork, and floors, ridding the parlor of soiled glasses, bowls overflowing with ashes, and leftover bottles of stale brandy and liquors.

She opened up the heavy velvet curtains on the first floor and unlatched many of the windows to allow September's morning sunshine and breezes to enter in. Her sister's well-used enterprise was beginning to look and smell almost presentable.

As she looked around exhausted, she sensed a note of satisfaction. With two floors yet to go, she was amazed at what she'd been able to accomplish in one night. Aimée's bones ached. She felt both hot and cold at the same time. Her now stained and sweaty muslin gown clung to her body. She could feel her skin beginning to crawl.

Sensing a gnawing in her stomach, Aimée wanted to maintain energy enough to continue. She knew she should eat. It would also be a welcome thing to be able to sit and shut her eyes if only briefly…just long enough to recharge.

She needed to look in on Florette again and the others who were hopefully sleeping peacefully. She also needed Lulu.

Every now and again throughout the night, Aimée had glanced over at Mr. Proctor, who had lingered too long into the night.

By the look on his face and his raised brows, his cat-like smirk, it appeared he was enjoying the fact he could watch her toil away as he sat there watching.

The stench of the stale smoke he left behind from his lit cheroot clashed with the clean fragrance of her wood wax. Aimée was glad to see him finally leave.

By the time she picked up her pail of dirtied water and carried it to the back of the house, it was close to daybreak. After dumping the foul liquid, she rushed back into the house and turned to the far corner of the large storage area where she came across the chamber pot and an old brass portable tub. She eyed the tub with envy.

As she stood there staring, Doris walked up and tapped her on the shoulder.

"I can bring you some hot water, miss, if you set yourself down at the table and eats a slice of warm bread. You been working mighty hard, girl. I already got water steaming in that there bucket over to the stove."

"That would be so kind. I heard you came back."

"Yes, miss, I come back. Where's your Lulu girl?"

Aimée frowned. "I just wish she were here with me right now is all I can say, Doris. She is over at my aunt's as we speak."

Yas'm, I was wonderin' 'bout that. I'll say a prayer for you tonight to get your Lulu girl back right quick. Miss Aimée, I think you're gonna need her with you, is all I can say," said Doris just above a whisper.

* * * *

Back at *Primrose Ivy*, it was his time again for morning prayers again and reading in his prayer book.

The lieutenant hoped the lady of the house did not mind him coming outside to sit a spell as long as he didn't bother anyone. There was something about her garden and that bench. It reminded him of Gram's garden up in Virginia.

The sound of voices caused him to open his eyes.

"I'm sorry to interrupt you, Captain," declared the woman stepping up. "Do you have a moment?"

He stood up and reached out to shake her hand. "Lieutenant Jordan here, Philip Jordan."

"I'm Francis Simpson. *Primrose Ivy* is my home."

He offered her and the young woman behind her a sudden, arresting smile. "What can I do for you folks?"

"It's you," said Lulu, peeking at him. "You be the one all right. You be the nice warrior man what helped my mistress at the ship boat! You be the one what saved my mistress from them nasty boys!"

"Can I help you, ma'am?" he replied again, trying to direct his attention only to the silver-haired woman.

She smiled.

"I hope I wasn't disturbing anything," he said setting down his prayer book. He glanced back at Lulu. Don't I know you?"

She eyed him. "Um Hmm. You knows me all right. You was more taped up on the head bafore."

He narrowed his brow as the other woman spoke to him.

"Sir, do you recall this servant? Lulu Jean, you're sure this man is the one that helped Amethyst Rose? I just want to make certain."

The servant nodded. "Right friendly-like." She peeked all the way around and showed her face. "Hello, Mr. Warrior man."

After staring briefly, Philip gave her a wide grin. "Of course! Well, hello there. You *are* the lady's maid from the boat aren't you? And an extremely protective and loyal servant at that! How interesting to discover you here!"

Lulu giggled.

"I heard you say your surname was Jordan. Is that right?" asked the woman.

"That's correct," Philip replied, picking up his prayer book and tucking it under his arm. "My father's roots are in Northern Virginia, but the family has been up in Ohio the last few years. I'm here waiting to be furloughed."

"I wondered," she asked. "And you are fighting with the North, I see." Her eyebrow lifted as she scanned his uniform.

Philip nodded. "There was a time, Madam, in Virginia, where many of the families struggled over which side they stood on. I am fortunate my primary function is to serve as a medic. It is because of where my family resides, up in Ohio, I must represent the Union. Many of our Jordan relatives not only reside in Northern Virginia but over in the Carolinas and down in Mississippi as well. The Jordans are Southerners at heart, I must admit."

She smiled. "Understandable. You are a doctor I'm told. I have heard something to that effect."

He gazed over at Lulu. "Not a doctor. But I've had medical training, yes. Right now, I'm convalescing. Back at the hospital, Colonel Swift finds ways to make use of me when he gets the chance. Once I get the rest of these bandages off my head, I'm gone from here."

"Home? "

"That is my hope, yes."

"You know, Lieutenant," said Mrs. Simpson, "I have a friend with the same surname as you. You would not perchance be acquainted with a Beryl Magnolia Jordan, would you?"

Another jovial laugh sounded from Philip's lopsided smile. "Beryl Jordan is my aunt, ma'am! You cannot tell me you know her."

She smiled in return. "She is my dearest friend, Lieutenant; may I call you Philip?"

"Please!" He beamed.

"Were you aware she is here in New Orleans?"

"No ma'am. I've not seen my Aunt Beryl for over five years. Perhaps I can look her up before I head back to my folks."

"You shan't have to look far, son. Beryl helps me here at the annex! I am surprised you've not run into one another."

"You don't say! How fortunate for me! I will indeed welcome seeing her. I hadn't been told where she was off to after she left my grandparents up in the valley. This becomes a wonderful turn of events!"

She smiled. "I will try to make arrangements for you to see her, shall I?"

"Please do."

"Right now I have another more pressing request," she added.

"Her needs you for something else right now, Mr. Warrior Man, to help out Miss Amthys'," Lulu blurted out.

"Amthys?" he asked. "I'm sorry; I don't follow."

"Amethyst Rose, my niece, sir," Fran interjected, "the young lady from the admissions desk the other day. Surely you recall."

He looked down again at the servant. "Oh yes! You see, she neglected to give me her full name."

His eyes lit up. "I would be glad to do whatever I can. I don't think there will be a problem. But," he added, "I cannot guarantee the lady will accept any assistance from me. You see, Mrs. Simpson, the color of my uniform has become anathema to her."

"Leave that to me, son," assured Fran. "Leave it to me."

* * * *

Morning arrived early. As the hired hand finished attaching Mrs. Simpson's horses to the landau and led the horses out onto the drive, he handed each a lump of cane then gave them a loving swat on their rumps and waited in silence.

Philip walked up and nodded before climbing up and into his seat where he placed his medical bag down on the floor beside him.

Fran, with her parasol and satchel and Lulu behind her, walked out the front door and off the veranda. "Good morning, son. Are you ready?" she said with a bright smile, handing Joseph her bag and sliding onto the seat, Lulu climbing in after her.

"I am indeed. Madam, you look mighty fetching. This being Sunday, do you have a nearby church you attend?"

"The chapel is not far from where we're headed. I will have plenty of time to look in on Amethyst Rose and her sister before going over. I would love to invite you to join me."

"I would like to do that sometime. Did I tell you my father is a minister?"

"Is that so?" She smiled. "And have you considered filling in his shoes at a later date?"

"'Tis in prayer, if God should call me to it. Either that or use my talents for medicine—maybe both. I'm interested in making use of both the fields of medicine and missions once I finish the service. Much depends on this war. I have a great curiosity for the uncultivated lands out west—places untouched. It is either into the vast wilderness or up to my grandfather's."

Philip chuckled. "The ranch is up in the Shenandoah Valley where my cousin and I used to work during our summers. My cousin loves ranching and farming. I must decide soon what I'm going to do as I am not the keenest sort in farming. "

"And you still want to venture out west? You may find yourself in the middle of much farming out that way, son."

"That's what I understand." He smiled. "Did my aunt ever speak to you of the family, Mrs. Simpson?"

"Feel free to call me Fran, son. I've joined her in prayer for her nephews for quite a while now." Fran wiggled in her seat and patted the lieutenant on his knee. "At least you are now here."

"Yes, and I would like to see my cousin soon, myself, ma'am."

"For now, Captain, I am grateful to have you with us and that you are able to help out. I'm sure in the long run, Aimée shall be pleased as well I'm bringing you along."

"Please remember I am a Yankee Lieutenant not a captain yet. Do call me Philip." He grinned wide. "You know you are promoting me well before my time!"

She grinned.

He turned his face towards the window, his mind suddenly clouded with uneasiness. "As far as the girl is concerned and how she will feel about my coming…"

He slowly turned back. "I cannot guarantee anything, ma'am."

* * * *

Feeling refreshed in the clean day dress she brought with her in her satchel, Aimée found her way up to the third floor. Her sister was still asleep.

She tiptoed over to touch her flushed cheeks and forehead, noticing Florette felt hotter than the night before. Florette had kicked off her heavy spread in the night, and her gown lay twisted around her thighs.

At the sound of Aimée's soft breathing, she woke up and lifted her weak arm to wipe the sleep from the edges. "Is that you, Rosette? It is so cold in here. Cover me back up."

Aimée took the covers and once again laid them over her.

"No, no, now it is too hot," said Florette again. "Go open the window."

"The window *is* open."

Aimée rose and walked over and drew back the curtain to allow the morning sunlight to filter in through the pane towards the bed.

"Noooo! Shut those!" Florette shrieked hoarsely. "I hate the light!" She kicked off her covers again and leaned over to try to sit up, but in her faintness fell back against her pillow. "What in the world is the matter with me? This is ludicrous!"

"I don't know what's the matter, Florette."

"It's Simone! Call me Simone." The elder sister glared at the younger. "There you are, walking around looking grand, as usual. What about me; I couldn't feel more repugnant than I do now. I wish *you* would get whatever it is I have."

Aimée stared at her.

Turning over on the bed, Florette began coughing again, where she could not see her younger sister's face anymore.

"How can you say such things to me?" said Aimée. "Why have you always detested me, Florette?"

"Shut your mouth. Where's my pillow?" Florette bawled.

"I'm going to try to get the doctor today," insisted the younger, fluffing up the pillow behind her sister's head. "You are getting worse. We must know what it is you have before it spreads throughout the house, if it hasn't already or gets to the point where there is nothing we can do! Your pillow is right here where it was, and it is soaked."

Reaching behind her with all the strength she could muster, Florette snatched the pillow away and placed it over her head. "Get out of my room!" she whimpered from under the cushion, trying to hold back her ragged and persistent cough. "And shut the vile door! When Beau comes, tell him I want to see him right away."

When Aimée turned to walk out of the room, she swallowed hard feeling sick at her stomach. She wanted to die a thousand deaths right then. If only it was possible.

What am I going to do?

Why had God taken those that loved her away from her and left her with only her sister who despised her so?

She could not stop her trembling. Once she stepped out into the hall, she shut the door gently behind her. She slid down the wall and onto the floor, where she sat staring dully down the hallway. Blurring tears drowned her eyes.

It was not long before her head tilted down then back against the closed door. With her parched mouth falling open, Aimée soon fell asleep, not yet having looked in on the others.

* * * *

Philip, Tante Fran, and Lulu waited in the downstairs hall for Doris to turn off the fire she had going on the stove in the back of the kitchen. She had said she would only be a minute.

He glanced over to see her wiping her hands on her apron as she headed towards the entrance again.

"Okay, sir, what you folks be needin'? We ain't taken nobody today up them steps for nobody," she said.

"This woman here is your mistress's aunt. We have come to see how she is doing and Miss Lebrún."

Lulu nodded. "That be right."

"I am Lieutenant Philip Jordan. I am no client. Let us go up."

"Miss Simone? I don't know nothin'," apologized the cook, stepping back and making way for the trio to go into the large room beside the hall.

"They's all upstairs and most is sick with coughs and hot heads. I don't know where Miss Amthys' got herself off at."

"We knows they's sick," Lulu belched out boldly, as she followed behind Philip and Tante Fran.

"And Miss Lebrún?" he asked.

"Her must be up them steps, too. I's cookin' up some soup. If you folks want any come eat later, if you don't mind onions. It ain't much," said Doris. "Lulu, your Miss Aimée, she was missin' you the other morning when we visited."

Moving past Doris, the entourage walked over towards the hanging baubles. Lulu and Tante Fran gazed twice around the clean room as if seeing it for the first time.

By the time the trio climbed the stairs and reached the third floor, Philip recognized who was lying slouched against the door down at the end of the hallway. A muscle quivered in his jaw.

"Ma'am?" He nudged to Fran.

All three ran over and bent down to call out Aimée's name.

"I think you'd better be the one to talk to her first," he said. "She might not remember me at first. Or she might!"

"Yes. You are right."

"Amethyst Rose?" he watched and listened as Fran called out. "Can you hear me, darlin'?"

There was no response.

Philip stood stiffly. He bowed his head, removed his hat, and closed his eyes. He felt Lulu's touch on his shoulder. She had joined him he knew.

"Amethyst Rose, darlin'?" He heard Tante call out again.

"Don't worry, Mr. Warrior Man," whispered Lulu in his ear. "Hers gonna wake up this time. God told me so in my heart. You'll see."

Chapter Ten

Aimée gradually woke up, spotting Lulu first. She smiled.

"Oh, Lulu, Mr. Proctor brought you at last." Then she saw the shiny boots and blue striped trousers of the individual standing beside her, and her eyes moved up towards the man's face.

"Philip! 'Tis you?" she said, looking suddenly alert. Smoothing out any hidden wrinkles in the skirt of her dress, she reached up and tried to soothe the tangles in her hair, now hanging loose.

"What do *you* want here?" she continued, "I-I mean…" She tried to pull herself up."

"Philip, Lieutenant Jordan, as you know, has medical training, Amethyst Rose. He's going to assist you until the doctor arrives. Hush now and quit worrying, and instead, tell us how we can help. Have you had any sleep at all since last night?"

Aimée stared at them all in silence then shook her head. She saw all of them gazing above her at the portrait hanging on the wall behind her. It was impossible to miss the disgusted look on Tante's face as she took note of the founder of The Paramount, a harsh-looking woman dressed colorfully in a crimson gown cinched tightly about her bodice more-than-efficiently emphasizing her bountiful décolletage. Tante Fran turned from the portrait back to her.

"I…I was up most of the night getting the house presentable for customers, Tante. It was a debacle when I arrived."

"I can imagine. You poor dear. And where is Mr. Proctor?" she asked, glancing around.

"He left early this morning and is due back sometime before noon. I thought *he* was to bring Lulu in."

Fran shook her head in dismay. "He never showed up. The lieutenant and I brought her over instead. 'Tis just as well. Presentable for customers you say…my, my! Listen, I think it would be better to have you back with me at *Primrose Ivy*. I do not want you taking ill with all the rest…and let's not talk about Florette's *customers*."

"How long have you all been here?" said Aimée.

"Never mind that," said Tante turning to the servant. "Lulu," she went on, "is going to help you downstairs, Amethyst Rose. The lieutenant and I are going to have a look in on everyone and determine what needs to be done."

"Come on Miss Aimée," Lulu nodded walking over to take Aimée's arm. "Ever'thing's gonna be okay. You'll see."

* * * *

Once the girls left, Philip and Fran worked their way from chamber to chamber.

Philip determined most of the women suffered from consumption, while one was well into pneumonia. All had picked up a horrible rash probably passed on by local customers then spread to one another. Two he noted had been afflicted with the bloody flux.

The frailest of them all, Florette, whose cough was the most severe, appeared to be the only one with medicine. Her tonics apparently had come from the doctor the week before—prescriptions he could tell were left for all the other patients.

Lieutenant Jordan shook his head as they returned toward the stairs together.

"Some of the concoctions in your niece's room are highly questionable, ma'am, not meant for her at all," said Philip after looking at the bottles. "I'm not sure she should be taking what's in them."

"Is there anything we can do?"

He shrugged. "I realize medicines are scarce these days, and doctors must make do with what they have available. I'm just not certain how she managed to get what was assigned to the others."

"Oh dear," said Fran.

"I hope the doctor will be returning soon, Mrs. Simpson, Francis," he said. "Maybe he can fix things. Because if there is no improvement to these women soon, the survival rate here looks dismal. "I'm going to place a yellow flag outside the door to keep others from coming near the place."

"I'm so pleased you have come, Philip. Now, perhaps we'll get somewhere," Fran said.

They reached the bottom of the stairs.

"I don't know about that, but I will do what I can."

She patted him on the shoulder. "You'll do fine. I must be going soon."

"Ma'am?"

"Church services commence soon. If you need me for anything, Lulu knows how to reach me. There's an extra horse and carriage in the carriage house I understand from the cook, and Florette still has her stable man, Abel."

He looked up and saw Lulu walking over. "Lulu will take care of things won't you, Lulu?"

"That's right," she said. "Don't fret none, Misses Frannie. "I take good care of the mistress."

"I'll contact the doctor," Fran continued. She walked through the front hall. "Let me know if you need me for anything," she stated, turning around once more to say good-bye, one eye peeking in the other room at her sleeping niece. "Anything. I'll be back before you know it."

* * * *

Aimée could not stand it. The Yankee lieutenant had been there hovering over her almost a week. Merely watching him walk into the room upset her. Certainly the man was no different from any of the rest she'd encountered, and yet—

She also knew she needed to get upstairs to see her sister. She still had to finish her chores.

She still felt weak from her fitful rest, and it was simply too much to bring herself to go into the spare rooms.

What am I to do?

Unattended walls throughout the house remained moldy from the Louisiana humidity and recent rains. The odor in some of the upstairs rooms still smelled rancid when she walked by. As a whole, many rooms in the house had received little attention for months.

The top two floors hadn't yet been touched and likely carried contamination from the presence of disease. Whether Aimée liked it or not she would have to finish the job sooner or later.

* * * *

The morning Dr. Boswell finally walked in the door with his nurse, Aimée did not miss the shocked expression on his face.

"This cannot be the handiwork of Simone Brusque," he said as the two stepped inside the house noting the clean floors, walls, and furniture. "Add this to my notes, Nurse."

Aimée quietly followed them from room to room as they observed each one scrubbed clean. After visiting the other patients, they headed for Florette's room to make their observations

"Is she any better at all?" she asked as they stepped outside her chamber.

"Your sister is in dire straights, ma'am," Dr. Boswell acknowledged grimly in the hall. "Consumption is a dangerous thing, and what with Mrs. Brusque's varied complications, I could bleed her. But I cannot guarantee it would bring about improvement."

"Bleed her?"

"She's taken a turn for the worse since my last visit." He patted Aimée's shoulder.

"I don't know what to do," she cried, blinking back a headache, at the same time licking the salty residue of a single tear escaping her eye and rolling down her cheek onto her dried and cracked upper lip. "Whatever you think is best. Is there truly no hope for her?"

"Her hard lifestyle speaks for itself—her less-than-careful watching of certain, should I say, bad habits. All has brought me to believe she has developed a dangerous immune disorder for which we have no cure at this time."

"No cure," She repeated.

The doctor watched her with steady eyes.

Aimée lowered her head. "What does that mean then, doctor?"

"Your lieutenant filled me in on his findings upon my arrival. Although I think I have gotten a handle on the illnesses of the others, Mrs. Brusque, I believe, has been suffering from hers longer than she realizes."

"*My lieutenant?*" Aimée looked up and whispered.

"Yes ma'am," he replied. "My suggestion is to stay out of her chamber as much as possible and remain only in the rooms you've cleaned. Avoid touching your sister's soiled bedding or eating utensils—anything you know she's handled. If you can get away from the house now and then for some fresh air, please do so."

Aimée shook her head. "I cannot leave here. Florette needs to know I am here for her. I cannot abandon her now."

"Those are my orders, all the same. Your decision will determine the future of your own health, Miss Lebrún."

Looking away from the doctor and down the hall, Aimée grew quiet. What would her father have done?

* * * *

Outside, Philip grabbed his medical bag and found his way to the stable, where he waited for Abel to bridle the old horse for him. There was little more he could do since talking with Boswell. Now, the major expected him back at the hospital.

"Well, Abel, I know you can't talk, but while you're busy saddling my horse, would you like to hear about my experience with the interesting Florette Brusque?"

Abel looked over and smiled and nodded then returned to his task.

"I was determined to share my faith with the woman who was ill, you understand. Might be the last opportunity I'll have. That's what it's all about. You would, if you could hear or talk."

Abel glanced over and grinned.

"At least it appeared as if she listened. First time she's ever been quiet." He smiled in return. "Aimée, that's Miss Lebrún, on the other hand. She avoids me. Hard as I try, I might as well forget any chance of a friendship with *that* woman. What do you think?"

Abel mumbled something and looked up, giving Philip a wink.

"You think I should pray more about it, huh? Well, perhaps Providence can find another way for me to talk with her. Who knows? There must be a way to reach that girl. I doubt it will ever be through me."

He looked over at Abel and laughed. "I sure appreciated this talk, Abel, my boy. Are we about ready, then, my friend?"

Abel nodded, picked up the reins, and handed them over.

As Philip donned his hat and attached his medical bag to the back of the saddle, he climbed up, tipped his hat to the stable hand, and turned to ride off towards the hospital, looking over towards The Paramount as he passed by. "I doubt very seriously, I will ever be the one to reach that girl," he whispered softly to no one in particular.

* * * *

In his office at the hospital, Philip was almost finished going through the rest of the paperwork at his desk when he received his long-awaited orders of release from the Army. He looked through them again to assure all was in order. Then he heard a tapping on the door.

"Enter," he called out.

His Aunt Beryl peeked through the opened door and smiled. "Hello there," she clucked, grinning from ear to ear. "Surprised to see me?"

"Aunt Beryl," he exclaimed, rising and hurrying to meet her and giving her a hug, "Come in! Come in! And where did you come from!"

"I was over at Fran Simpson's working. Instead of returning home, I had Joseph drop me off here. By the way, I'm not alone!" she said with a laugh. "I found a stray out front. Shall I bring him with me?"

Philip threw his head back and laughed. "Certainly. I like surprises."

As she moved behind her, Philip caught sight of his elder cousin wearing a uniform of brass and blue, staring back at him.

A thick lump formed in his throat. He instantly stood at attention at the higher-ranking officer. "How long has it been now, Captain?"

* * * *

"Stand at ease, Lieutenant," ordered Palmer with a broad smile. "How long has it been, PJ? At least four maybe five long ones?"

Palmer walked all the way in and looked Philip over. "I heard about the bandages. I still see a couple. Want to tell me about them?"

Stepping back, Palmer extended a generous handshake to the younger officer. "You don't look too much worse for the wear. Fill me in on the details on a young man's life."

"And me, too!" Aunt Beryl said. "I'm anxious to hear, Philip."

"Oh, these?" Philip pointed to what was left on his face. "My face used to be covered. The last of the old binding come off today," he explained. "There were a lot more earlier. Just a few reminders of wartime I shall have to live with for a while, I suspect."

"I've shared in a few scrapes myself over the last several months, PJ, especially during our skirmish up in Vicksburg years back. That ordeal greatly affected folks who at one time were great friends with my mother's family—wasn't too pretty. You know the history. We'll all be glad when this thing is over," said Palmer.

"Any news to report?"

"Lincoln sees the necessity for this to come to an end, I hear. Perhaps that will take you back to the homestead. Where you going...Ohio or Virginia?"

Palmer waited for Philip to walk around the desk where he sat down, taking a moment to stack the papers he'd been reading. He handed him his orders.

"It's all here. It looks like the folks up in Ohio will be blessed by my presence in less than a month, war or no war. I'm ready, except for the fact I was in the middle of a project to which, unfortunately, I will not be able to continue."

"Your father will be comforted by your return, Philip," said Aunt Beryl. "Too bad you have to abandon your mission."

"What mission is that?" Palmer asked.

Philip looked at Beryl and nodded. "What's done is done. As for me now, it's time I head back and look up my old girl, Mary Ann. I doubt I'll get through to Virginia."

"Mission, PJ? Mary Ann...has that girl been writing to you, too, Cousin?" Palmer furrowed his brows. "What's she doing, playing us against each other? I've been receiving communiqués from the O'Hare girl for over two years."

Palmer hesitated to add, as time progressed, so had the intimacy of her letters. "I've often wondered at her seriousness. She was sometimes a bit frivolous in her thinking, if I recall."

"I knew she might correspond with others," said Philip. "I reckon I've no claims on her...yet. That's why I want to look her up. It's time I get serious about my own decisions for the future, and if need be, perhaps place those claims...if she will have me. Unless of course— well, you see, Palm, there's been an interest elsewhere, but I try not to think about that one too much."

141

"Oh, pray tell? Clue me in." Palmer winked. "Has it something to do with this so called mission to which you gave reference earlier? Whatever you decide, I've no doubt God will lead you," he finished with a grin.

"I'll let you know about the other interest, perhaps at another time," said Philip. "Right now, I'm doing my best *not* to think about that one."

"Does it have to do with this project or affair you mentioned?"

"Does it, Aunt Beryl?"

"Let me tell it," interrupted Beryl.

"Philip has been practicing his medical skills elsewhere. Just recently, he began to help out over in *The French Quarter* with several young women who have taken ill."

"*The French Quarter* you say? I'm all ears!" Palmer sat down.

* * * *

"It all sounds extremely interesting," remarked Palmer at the end of the meeting. "I'm due for a short furlough myself soon. Perhaps I can help you out, Cousin PJ. I was going to be taking a visit up at *Pencil Ridge*. Been missing Pop and Gram and hoping it will be safe enough to travel that way soon. If there's anything I can do to give you a hand before I go, I'll try. I don't have much medical expertise, obviously. But I have to admit I've wanted to check out that part of the city in more detail — as a part of my duty, of course. Tell me," he said, lifting his brow, "your personal interest doesn't rest with one of the individuals at this place you call The Paramount, does it?"

Beryl's gaze moved from Palmer to her other nephew.

"There is one there who needs greater assistance perhaps than others," Philip responded carefully.

"Consider me your man then, PJ!" Palmer stood up and reached across the desk to shake his cousin's hand again. "Aunt Beryl can fill me in with the details, and I'll work on the particulars with my colonel."

When two men saluted and the three finished their good byes, Philip followed them out of the office and into the corridor.

Palmer turned back. "This does sound interesting."

"You're sure you want to do this?" Philip called out just before the two turned the corner.

Captain Jordan glanced back and smiled. "You needn't concern yourself about me. I wouldn't miss going to *The French Quarter* for the world."

* * * *

Aimée sat on the settee and faced the wall. What would happen next? She could only wonder. The house was no longer peaceful nor in the least bit quiet.

Nina Burdett, Florette's *Queen Bee* had come home.

Nina Burdett—nothing like Aimée expected. She was only a slight woman. She wore her jet-black hair pulled back in a tight bun, and her eyes were nearly as dark, almost piercing. Yet somehow Aimée thought she made her presence known the moment she walked through any door.

Aimée also noticed even Mr. Proctor, once he discovered Florette's top girl had finally returned, wasted no time in finding his way back to The Paramount.

Before, with all the sickness abounding, he had begun to avoid the premises. She hadn't seen him in days, and she wasn't looking forward to his company now.

With Florette out of the picture, Nina acted as if it was *she* who ran The Paramount and Beauregard was right there with her.

Right away she had pulled Aimée aside and begun to order her around. "Since Beau is coming to see me tonight," Nina had said earlier, "I'd like you to stay out of the way. We have business to discuss."

"Don't worry. I'll not be around," Aimée remembered promising.

"Good. Then that's settled. You can let him in when he arrives if your slave isn't about."

Then Nina had turned and walked off, having established her position in the household quickly and without Florette around.

By the end of dinner hour, Aimée did overhear Beauregard coming in through the front door and working his way up the stairs. From the entry of the library, she followed him with her eyes.

"They is up to no good, Miss Aimée," grumbled Lulu behind her back.

"Nina doesn't much talk to me—why should he?" said Aimée, turning around. "Besides, why should I care? He has shown an interest in running the business here from what he hinted around with a while back. Who knows," she reassured Lulu, "perhaps he'll once again come to my rescue."

Lulu grimaced. "Oh, Miss Aimée, I don't know about that. When you gonna talk to the Lord about all this?"

Aimee stared back blankly. "Right now, I think I shall depend on you to do the conversing with your God. He doesn't know I exist, and I doubt He is in the least bit interested in things going on at The Paramount."

"Even if them two destroys the place, Miss Aimée?"

Gazing over towards the chair by the front hall, she turned and walked away. "Go away, Lulu, I'm tired. I cannot imagine what worse shape this place can be in than it is."

* * * *

Just as the downstairs hall clock struck twelve, Aimée awakened with a start. Rising in the silence and stretching her wearied limbs, she grabbed her dressing gown from off a nearby chair and found her way to the dresser to light her lamp.

When she opened the door, she noticed only one or two lights still burning in the hall and down the corridor to Florette's chamber. Only a dim light shadowed the floor space beneath her closed door.

Turning the knob, Aimée opened the door. The room smelled musty and hot. She tiptoed quietly across the room towards the bed.

"Florette?" When there was no response, she called her name out again. "Florette?" She knew her sister, confined to her bed for so long, had difficulties in waking.

Placing the dimming oil lamp on the nearby commode, she leaned down and gently touched Florette's cool brow which before had either been hot and dry or sopping wet at the breaking of one of her frequent bouts of fever.

Now, for the first time since her arrival at The Paramount, Florette's facial expression appeared different. There was a softness Aimée hadn't seen before, not since a different time.

The bitterness and hatred that had consumed Florette Simone for so long, no longer showed on her face.

Aimée saw instead a tender smile resting on her lips "Florette?"

Her eyelids fluttered. "I will be leaving you soon."

"What are you saying? You cannot leave me."

"I have no desire to continue. I've been no good." Florette's eyes filled with tears. "Forgive me, Amethyst Rose, for my hatred, my abusiveness, my viciousness towards you. Please tell me you will." She searched for restitution on Aimée's face with her eyes.

Aimée held her breath then could only shake her head as her eyes welled up with tears. "But I have only wanted to be close to you. I don't blame you for all that happened between us. I only want you to get better. Florette—I *need* you to get well! Please."

Aimée's body jerked and trembled. The tears began pouring down her cheeks and onto the covers. "Don't you know...I—I love you."

"I know you do. And yet I've been terrible to you. I made you not only afraid of me but of men." She shook her head back and forth. "But you...and Papa—both were no different. He taught you what love truly is. It is better this way."

Florette stopped to catch her breath, each one taking a greater effort. "Do something for me, will you?"

Aimée's lips trembled. "What can I do?"

"David, our brother...I need you to tell David...write him, tell him...tell him I *forgive* him." Her voice trailed off.

Aimée was confused. "Forgive him? I don't understand. Why should David need forgiveness from you? Listen to me...Florette, you cannot *die*! No more death! I need you! You are all I have left! David needs you, too."

Florette opened her eyes again and gazed at her.

"You *must* write to David for me...please, Aimée; it's important." She tugged at her sleeve.

"Aimée," she cried, "I'm so sorry I didn't like your name. It's' not true. I love your name. I merely said that."

"Oh, Florette."

"You must listen. There is more!"

"More?"

Aimée struggled to hold back her weeping...to remember all her sister was telling her.

"Thank the soldier for me, too. I need you to do that."

"Thank—the Yankee?" She shook her head. "But I—I cannot."

"The lieutenant...You must. It was he who told me how I could make my life right with God. You absolutely *must* thank him for me—thank him for showing me the way."

Aimée opened her eyes wide in surprise. "Florette, what are you saying?"

She took her hand and reached up to wipe her little sister's cheek then let it fall back down. "Just thank him. He was a godsend for me."

"*He was?*" she whispered

"He was."

"*Oh dear,* you really want me to talk to—" Aimée whispered again.

"Neither he, nor Papa nor even Mama, once condemned me, my life. 'Tis so important to have a *forgiving* heart, Aimée, and not to condemn others...to be thankful about things like the Lord has forgiven us. If you did, you did not do it openly."

Aimée watched her sister in awe.

"Think about it, my sweet sister. God has pardoned my heinous lifestyle; He loves me just as I am. I never would have known that without the help of that Yankee officer."

Aimée watched as Florette slowly shut her eyes. Her lashes twitched. Then she opened her eyes again. She seemed to gaze about without focus, as if her mind was somewhere else.

With great effort, she reached with her frail hand and cupped Aimée's into it. "No tears...promise me?" Florette looked at her, and then turned her head away slowly.

The sudden stillness in the room was unearthly— almost frightening. Then...when Aimée bent down closer to where Florette turned and slowly rested the side of her face against the pillow, she realized, with great sadness, Florette was gone.

"*I do love you, my dear sister,*" she whispered, letting out a soft moan as she brought the coverlet up to Florette's chin and bent down to brush her lips against her cooling cheek.

Chapter Eleven

It was Lulu's sudden presence that awakened Aimée hours later. The oil lit lamp in Florette's room had long since burned down and was dry to the core.

"Come with me, Miss Aimée. I found you asleep here with you sister. I'm gonna put you to your bed."

Aimée let the servant place her arm around her waist and pull her off the bed like a rag doll, so she could lead her out of the quiet chamber.

She felt the snug hold of Lulu's arm around her as Lulu silently led her out of the room and down the hall, into the spare room on the second floor.

Though it was morning, light had not yet welcomed death's silence.

It was not a time to think about anything—not the past, the present, not even the future.

Lulu waited until she sank back into what looked like a blackened sleep where no dreams or thoughts would invade her heart.

"You rest now, Miss Aimée," she whispered, as she stepped out of the room. "This ain't no time to think about nothin'. You gots plenty of time for that. In the meantime the Good Lord and His angels, they be here with you till I come back."

* * * *

The sun shined bright through Aimée's window a few hours later by the time, she finally half awakened. It was not yet half past ten. In a couple of weeks, she would see the entrance of a colder October, but right now, the humidity felt stifling.

She recalled the experience of the night before too well, holding on to Florette's hand, watching her breathe her last breath.

She had not been around to see her parents die. She was too late to save Christopher for he was the first to go.

Never again, would she hold his chubby little hand or tousle his curly red hair.

One by one, her friends and loved ones — even her adversaries — were falling from her grasp.

Now Florette.

There was no one left save David.

David?

Aimée did not know her elder brother. Not well. Perhaps it was time.

Unable to rise from her own fatigue, she felt more desolate than ever. Would she be able to take part in another burial of a loved one?

For the next couple of hours, she fell in and out of erratic sleep until the downstairs clock sounded the noon hour, and she again opened her eyes to the knocking at the door. She watched as the door slowly pushed open.

She saw the glowing silver hair of her aunt, who was elegantly clad, standing at the threshold with her sparkling eyes and affectionate smile.

"May I come in?"

"Please do, Tante."

"I received word in a note from Lulu this morning," she said with great tenderness. "It is good you taught her to read and write, darlin' so I would know this quickly."

"I'm so glad you came."

Fran smiled. "I'll not linger. Though I leave you now, I don't want you to fret; I will take care of things." Backing up she shut the door softly and was gone again but not before Aimée knew she probably saw her quiet, weary tears streaming.

Perhaps it was just as well.

* * * *

Nina spoke quietly yet held an undertone of cold contempt as she glared at the old woman when she saw her pass by her. "How long did you say you were planning to stay, Mrs. Simpson?"

With tightened lips, Fran gazed back at her briefly. "I didn't."

As promised, she took charge of the first floor of The Paramount, moving around quietly so her niece would not be disturbed.

"I have things to do, Mrs. Simpson," interrupted Nina, who followed her from room to room. "I would like to know what I can do to help."

"Nothing," said Fran, her eyes meeting hers. "Don't mind me." She took her pencil and wrote something down on a tablet.

Nina gritted her teeth.

* * * *

Aimée held on to the banister and worked her way down the stairs. Her ears perked up at the voices below.

"And I won't take no for an answer, Miss Burdett," she heard her aunt order the woman.

Then she caught sight of Nina Burdett disappearing into the library.

"Hello Tante," she said.

Her aunt spotted her descending. "You are up, child?"

"I needed to rise," She said.

"Well, dear, I've dispatched my personal lawyer, Herman Withers, to help with matters," she declared. "I doubt Florette had access to one. This was her place, and if there is a will around here, I'm sure he can locate it."

"Do we need a lawyer?" asked Aimée.

She nodded towards the door of the library. "We need one darlin'. *She* went in there with Mr. Proctor. Neither are too happy about my decision-making around here. Don't you worry. Everything is going to be fine."

"I don't *want* to remain here. I want to go with you," said Aimée flatly. "I'm not interested in what these people have chosen to do for a living. Even if Florette wanted to give me this house, which would not be proper and which I highly doubt, I wouldn't feel right staying nor taking over her enterprise."

"I understand," said her aunt. "And we'll get you out of here soon, but you cannot leave this place in their hands until I know the details. It is important we respond correctly. And if there is compensation to which you or perhaps your brother is entitled, we must look into that."

Aimée's aunt squeezed her shoulder then she added, "Don't you fret. Your tante will take care of it."

She turned to see Nina and Beauregard walk out of the library as the two exchanged words.

"Excuse me, Rosette?" said Nina.

Looking over at the woman warily, Aimée twitched, her lashes lowered. "What is it?"

"About The Paramount...if you are quibbling over what to do about this place, your worry is needless, a waste of time. Simone conveyed to me her wishes. She said I was to take charge if anything should happen to her. I was to employ you, which I shall, and what with the continued cleaning and such, you can see you will have ample chores; the rest, simply leave to me. It's pretty clear-cut." She watched Aimée closely.

"Oh...," she added, "there will be times when I will require you to fill in for one of the others...as you did in my stead while I was gone. Your presence, I'm told, being Simone's sister, should bring in a tidy profit once we resume business."

Aimée shook her head. "You'll not have me!"

Nina swiftly turned around and started back towards the library. "Oh, yes," she stopped and swung back around. "Simone also suggested Mr. Proctor take over the financial management of the place, not you, Mrs. Simpson," she said, glancing over at Fran. "He is well suited for the position. So you see, ladies," she grinned at both, "neither of you have a thing to concern yourself with."

Aimée's eyes lit up as she started to speak again when her aunt held up her hand and leaned over to whisper in her ear.

"Don't worry, child. God will protect you. I'll get you out of here soon. Mr. Withers will know what to do."

* * * *

Aimée was relieved when she heard Mr. Proctor suggest Nina give her some time alone to grieve her sister. At the same time for days, she waited for Tante Fran's return.

She had nothing to say to the woman below, and though she wasn't yet sure about Beauregard, he at least seemed to understand her sadness.

But her grieving time would not last for long.

Where is Tante?

Twice on the fifth morning Nina came and pushed her way into her small chamber.

Aimée stood up quickly, watching the open doorway. She held her breath. "What do you want from me, Nina? Why are you locking me in my chamber this way? I demand to know."

Nina lifted a brow. "There are keys in the doors of all my girls, especially yours. Besides, right now, I need you here, Rosette," she snarled casting a quick glance toward the bed. "It will be time soon for you to join the living, Rosette. You don't expect to spend the rest of your days in this room mourning the dead, do you? You are taking up precious space that can be of value to our clients!"

"That is what you expect?" said Aimée, trying to think fast.

Nina faced her squarely. "I will expect to see you below in less than an hour hence, Rosette. I will make the cook prepare something for you. You are withering away to nothing."

"I'm not hungry," Aimée snapped. "I don't wish to eat anything you prepare."

Nina pointed to the pitcher and basin on the small commode. "Wash yourself down in the cold water I had your slave deliver up while you were napping, and you will eat whether you like it or not."

Aimée glanced toward the table then across at the wall "I have no slaves, Nina. Where is Lulu?"

"You need not be expecting what's her name, Lulu, to be in often to help you," she said. "She's busy with some of my newer girls. I've decided to make use of her my own way. No more playing favorites here, regardless of who you think you are. It will do you well to remember Simone's dead and isn't coming back, and you will leave when I say you can leave."

Aimée started to protest but instead spun back around to stare after the woman as she walked out, closing the door behind her.

A few minutes later, she heard a quiet knock. "Lulu?"

"You up yet, Miss Aimée?" Lulu whispered through the wall. "I needs to talk."

Aimée could hear the choke in her voice. "Come around, Lulu, but do be careful. Nina just went down the steps."

The door creaked open, and Lulu hurried in, her large brown eyes streaked with red; puffy circles built up beneath her lower lashes.

"She is treating you badly, isn't she?" Aimée searched her face. "How did you get in without a key?"

"Her left the key in the door."

Aimée pulled her close and gave her a hug.

"Just whipped once, but I's ok. Miss Aimée, this place…I feels like both you and me, we's in the gaul!"

"Tante was supposed to be back by now with news from her attorney, honey, but I'm tired of waiting for her. I think I will make plans to get us out of here. I don't care how we do it! How does that sound?"

Lulu's eyes widened. "Yas'm, Miss Aimée. You thinks you can do it?"

She rubbed her chin. "Just give me some time to think this through."

"I been trying to get a note to Misses Fran like her told me to, but they ain't much letting me walk out to the stable so I can see Abel and get the messages out! Then yesterday, I was wanting to walk down to my church so I could talk to my Lord, and that Mr. Proccor man, he mocked at me and told me no siree," cried Lulu.

"Here take my hanky," said Aimée. "Wipe your eyes.

"That man, he say they ain't no God what I can talk at, Miss Aimée, and to quit being dim-witted! That's the word! Miss Aimée, what's that word, dim-witted?"

"'Tis nothing. Nothing at all, honey. I should have listened to you long ago. Oh, Lulu, rest assured, you are not dim-witted. You are a bright girl."

"I gots to be able to talk at my Jesus." Lulu's chest heaved at the release of her sobs.

Aimée walked her over to her bed and sat her down. "Can't you do that right here, talk to...?" she asked. "Why, I've seen you talk to your God in the quiet of a dark corner and in the middle of a rainstorm. You never let that bother you. Didn't you tell me you could do that?"

"Oh, yas'm, I can do that," assured Lulu, nodding. "That's not what I means." She pulled Aimée down beside her on the bed and looked her in the eyes. "Miss Aimée, I is wanting *and* needing, something bad, to talk at my *Jesus* with my believin' fambly. Miss Aimée, there ain't nothin' like talkin' at the good Lord where two or more is collected and agreein'."

She thought about what Lulu said. She didn't have that connection her servant spoke of so lovingly. She had no friends...not like that. She had no loving relationship of her own with God. It was difficult to understand what Lulu was talking about...that way.

Touching her fingers to Lulu's shoulder, Aimée leaned in and gently kissed her servant on the cheek. She reached up to wipe the corner of a teary eye with the edge of her sleeve. "When I get us out of this place, I'll make sure you can get to your people. I promise."

"That's right, Miss Aimée," said Lulu, rising from the bed. "That ole' Mr. Proccor, he ain't gonna stop me from singing! I shouldn'ta' doubted. What were I thinkin'? He won't stop you neither, Miss Aimée, when the time comes. The good Lord, He won't let him! You'll see."

"Yes, and I promise I'll get us out of this forsaken place soon, honey. Mark my words."

* * * *

The activities Nina had set for the next evening were fused in Aimée's mind even though nightfall would not descend for hours. Aimée found could think of little else. Little else but her own thoughts about how to get herself and Lulu away from The Paramount without getting caught. There had to be a way.

Nina came to inform her just before noon a customer was coming for her later in the afternoon to take her for a ride into the country away from the signs of war.

"Give your client whatever he demands, Rosette, and I expect you to wear your best. He has requested you specifically!"

"Did he say *why* he wanted *me*?" Aimée asked. "It makes no sense. And I told you before I'm not interested, Nina! Has Beauregard gone to town and begun advertising me? Is that what the two of you have gone and done?"

Aimée felt Nina's eyes bore into hers. "Just be ready when the time comes." With an abrupt turn, she walked out and turned the lock.

* * * *.

To Aimée's greater surprise, Nina made a change of orders and sent Lulu up to give her a hand with dressing.

"It's almost time, Miss Aimée," hollered Lulu through the door. "I can come to help you with your paying customer." She rushed into the room, seeing her mistress facing the wall.

"Come on, Miss Aimée." She walked her over to her wardrobe.

"High paying customer, is it?" said Aimée, closing her eyes and shaking her head.

Lulu nodded.

She clenched her hands then opened her eyes and reached in her armoire. "It's gonta to be okay, Miss Aimée. I done did lotsa prayin' God's on our side."

"Get the red and the black with the bolero jacket. I don't know; I don't care."

Aimée busied herself in front of the mirror. She felt as if she was almost in another world as she watched herself pull on her full red skirt that bragged with ruffles and black ribbon trim along the hem.

What was she doing?

"Why not wear one of my favorites? Who cares…anymore? I am going for a ride in the country. Who knows what will happen after that?"

She glanced over at Lulu, suddenly — barely able to contain herself. "Why did I not think of this before? Perhaps it will be my chance!"

"What, Miss Aimée?"

"It could be my chance!"

Lulu's eyes lit up. "Well, you may be right, and I can also say this," she said, smiling and nodding. "Your man, he'll be whistlin' Dixie when he sees you in that pretty dress, Miss Aimée!"

"My man?"

Lulu spoke not another word but returned to work quietly.

Aimée watched as, in the next hour, Lulu flitted around her like a butterfly.

Once Aimée was dressed, Lulu pinned back her hair, leaving looped braids on each side then grinned again from ear to ear at the results but still said nothing.

"You keep bouncing around like a fairy princess, Lulu Jean. You cannot be excited about this rendezvous. Aren't you worried about me going off with this gentleman coming to fetch me?"

"Ah, yas'm, I for sure is," she mumbled. Then, with a fidget, she turned away in a hurry and walked over to replace Aimée's brush on the vanity table. Finishing up with the toilette, Lulu assisted her with her black braided linen bodice and plaid jacket.

"Do you know something I don't?" Aimée shook her.

"Oh, it ain't nothin'. I best be leavin'. Don't you worry," said Lulu, hurrying to the door. Just before shutting it, she leaned back in, fiddling with her hands, holding back a giggle. "Miss Aimée, like I said, the good Lord, He been hearin' all the chatter I been sending His way; I can tell you that."

* * * *

Aimée stood in front of her chair and continued eyeing her reflection.

Will the man be gentle with me? Lord, if you are up there—make him not be mean to me nor harm me. Perhaps there truly will be a way I can escape from out of his clutches. At least I won't be locked away in this place.

She glanced over at the door just as Lulu stepped back into the room. "Back so soon?"

"Miss Aimée, Doris says that man, him here. I come to give you your last inspection. You don't want to keep the boy waiting." She smiled.

Aimée frowned. "I don't care."

"Ah, Miss Aimée, that war—him gonna take to you right quick. Come on now," she said, hustling her along.

"I am not interested in anyone taking to me *right quick*, Lulu, and I don't care if he *must* wait! Quit fussing! Why do you hurry me along so?"

Aimée straightened her full skirts one more time and pulled herself toward the door. Up until now, she had been fortunate enough to feel somewhat protected, even with Mr. Proctor.

She shook her head and sighed.

Today Nina was attempting to change all that.

By the time Aimée reached the foot of the stairs, her initial fears returned. Turning slowly to glance back, she looked up to see Lulu still observing her. Lulu nodded as she turned again and moved on towards the parlor.

She anxiously glanced up.

He was facing the window. The tall, impeccably built officer dressed in his Union blues even from the rear exuded a commanding air of self-confidence. With his legs standing apart and his hands clasped together behind his back, she could not see his face but did catch sight of the wide brimmed hat sitting on the edge of the table beside him.

The smell of Nina's familiar pungent perfume as the woman walked up behind her gave her a start. "Treat your guest kindly, Rosette," she whispered. She took her fingers and sharply pinched Aimée's ear lobe.

"Ouch!" she shook her away. "Stop it! I also don't recall you mentioning the customer would be a Yankee soldier." Aimée fumed, yanking herself away. "I prefer not going for a ride with anyone right now if you don't mind, especially any Yankee," she finished.

Nina was blatantly disregarding her whispering comments but she said them anyway.

"Say hello...now," Nina admonished again. The odors of intoxicants seeped through the woman's pores and heavily clashed with her stale perfume.

Aimée did her best not to gag.

When the officer spun around and looked down at her with a grin, she almost lost her footing.

At first she felt the awkward pause between them.

"Not you! I—I cannot believe 'tis you!"

Nina stepped in front of her. "What is this? Rosette," she stated coldly, her teeth clenched. "We do *not* postulate with our customers. The fine officer here," she pointed, "has come requesting *you* specifically and has paid a pretty penny on your behalf to have you accompany him this afternoon! You will not let him down...now, *will you*?"

With an abrupt pull with her free hand, she grabbed Aimée by the elbow and led her to the Yankee.

"My apologies, Captain," said Nina mellifluently. "Rosette is fairly new with us...not yet accustomed to our ways. She is a bit *timid*. Perhaps you can go easy with her...this first time?"

"No problem," replied the captain, still grinning. "I've been looking forward to this—outing, with—Rosette here. I've heard...good things! Later this evening, I vow I shall return her *right* to where she belongs."

Aimée watched him with awe. The expression on his face at that moment was as if he was clearly smitten by her, and yet she knew that was utterly ridiculous. Who was he trying to fool?

As she watched him peruse her from head to toe, once again, it was as if he gazed at her with eyes in heavy contemplation over something.

What did he want with her now?

"You are looking forward? Marvelous," replied Nina, clasping her fingers together, glancing over at the panic-stricken Aimée then back at the officer. She lifted a brow.

Perhaps she's surprised an officer of the Union would choose a woman of innocence, over all her others who are much more experienced. What do I care when I know I shall seek some way of escape once I get alone with the man?

"Your gentleman awaits your greeting," she reproached Aimée with a jerking nod.

Aimée nodded reluctantly then continued to glare at the captain. She had no desire to greet him in any other way than she had done already. Instead, all she could think of was cinders flying through the air, the smell of singed garments, and destruction—all which flashed again through her mind. All because of men like the one who stood before her.

With negating fortitude, she stiffly extended her hand out for his kiss of greeting, expecting it to be sloppy and brief.

It was not what she expected.

When his gentle lips lingered, as well as the look he gave her, a strange chill went up her spine, and she jerked her hand away. She could feel his eyes pull hers into his, as she looked back at him again with surprise.

"Don't!"

"May I at least take your arm ... Rosette?" he asked with caressing ease, reaching for her elbow. "I must say you look exquisite this afternoon."

His smile melted every sense she had left in her body.

She nodded reluctantly, but the longer she gazed back at him the harder it was becoming to turn away.

Fight it, Aimée! She argued with her mind.
What was it about him that wrenched at her heart?
What is wrong with me!

* * * *

"My carriage awaits us outside," Palmer added warmly, guiding her towards the door, watching the rippling of her back. He leaned in as closely as he dared, as the two walked out the front portal and down the front steps.

Although there was hardly a breath of wind in the air, the Lebrún woman's aloofness felt like the dead of winter to him. Even the dahlias along the walkway appeared to turn frigid and gave a slight droop as he watched her whisk past and onto the carriage.

It was a lost cause trying to make small talk. Palmer could see quickly the girl had nothing to say and was vowing to keep it that way.

When he held up his navy and green-plaid riding blanket to invite a covering for her barely exposed ankles, she only shook her head.

Though he spoke a few words, hoping to break the frigidity, the stubborn woman refused to acknowledge his existence. Although she looked intensely interested in the scenery or some such thing as she stared out the window, he knew she was in truth focused on absolutely nothing.

As a believing man, Palmer realized his approach at coming to The Paramount to help out his cousin PJ was not something he could comfortably discuss with Uncle Henry, PJ's father. Uncle Henry being the town preacher and Palmer's uncle besides would have highly disapproved of such a gesture, regardless of the captain's reasoning.

Even though Palmer's purpose for helping out Philip and his mission was highly principled, in truth Palmer knew he was no different from most men. Palmer was as curious as the next red-blooded male to see what went on over at *The French Quarter* when it came to a woman. A number of his officer friends spoke of the goings on at *The French Quarter* more often than not.

After talking with Philip about his purpose there with Aunt Beryl and Mrs. Simpson, Palmer jumped at the idea everyone had for him to make his own personal appearance.

Simply turn up as a customer and make contact with the girl they had said. Was it not going to be for her protection in the end? Since he only had a couple of days left of his furlough, now was as good a time as any.

What he had not realized when the plans were made was that *the girl* he was to pick up was the same person, who had occupied his mind nearly every night since that morning back in Vicksburg!

If Aimée Lebrún had known *he* was the client coming to take her away from The Paramount that afternoon, she might never have come down the stairs to meet him.

Yet, Palmer knew nothing ever happened by chance. It was amazing how he just happened to have run into her servant that same morning he was to come by. He was truly grateful to God he had been able to send warning ahead of his intentions.

Whatever happened next between the two of them, God only knew.

Chapter Twelve

He turned and gazed over at her creamy soft face again while she faced the window. "I realize you wish not to converse. Let me merely say I hope you won't misunderstand the meaning of all this...Ro—sette."

She mumbled something incoherent and continued staring out.

"You do talk then," Palmer said. "I thought I remembered you had a voice...a sweet one at that—in its unyielding sort of way." He sat back against his padded seat and grinned mischievously.

"What's that supposed to mean?" She turned and glared. "How dare you accuse me of being unyielding! Maybe you'd like to tell me why you're doing this...why you keep interfering into my life."

"You'll understand soon why I came to collect you," said Palmer. "I dare say I don't think you will hate me overmuch for this little rendezvous when you soon hear of my ingenious offer."

"Offer?" She narrowed her eyes and looked down. "As long as I sit here next to you I don't think I have much of a choice whether I can listen or not listen to whatever your silly offer may be, now do I?" Pulling at the ruffles of her skirt, she looked up again. "Go ahead, sir. I'm all ears—just one thing."

"Oh?"

"When you return me to *wherever it is you think I am supposed to be* later this evening, I'm asking you this once *not* to...-not to..."

"Not to what?" Palmer laughed at her with his eyes.

"Quit laughing at me, Captain. I'm asking you not to...to invite yourself into my chamber...and not to...not to touch me."

* * * *

Aimée wanted desperately to loathe the Yankee's handsome lopsided grin and the deep crevices in both his cheeks, the dimpled chin, which sank into oblivion when he smiled. She wanted to hate the twitching of his adorable mustache.

Her eyes burned. She closed them, tried to think then opened them again as she awaited his response to her strange appeal.

He merely peered back at her with that same annoying and comfortable expression on his face.

"Maybe I am asking the impossible, and perhaps my request seems foolhardy."

Most assuredly he probably was aghast by what she was asking. After all, where had he come to fetch her…where, indeed?

How much had he offered to pay for her, and what was it one did with one at *that place*?

Yet she remained sober for Aimée's request was deadly serious. And although she knew it was a dangerous gamble to request such a thing of the man, this man, she figured what more could be the harm? He already had her in his clutches.

Maybe, just maybe he would extend her a small portion of grace…just this once.

* * * *

"Believe it or not, I've no plans to lay a hand on you, Miss Lebrún, Rosette, Amethyst Rose, by whatever name you wished to be called. Not one," Palmer answered barely audible. "'Twas not my intention for collecting you." He stopped short of any further explanation.

"After all you and your band of ruffians did to my family—to my home, you expect me to believe that? Why, sir, could you not just leave me to die with the rest of my family? I'll never understand it. I've no doubt the soldiers knew where I was hiding."

"I cannot speak for your family for I was not there…and I would not boast of dying with the rest, if I were you."

Her eyes glowed. "I don't know what you want with me."

"You will."

She turned silent and swallowed hard. Folding her hands squarely in her lap, she shut her eyes as if she wanted to sleep..

"Remember this, young one," replied Palmer. "If a burning hand cannot handle a flame, how can the body handle death?"

She glanced back up. "Huh?"

"When it comes to dying, all I know is it must not have been your time, the day you lost the ones you loved. But do not now wish it upon yourself, not when you cannot even handle the little difficulties of life thrown your way."

Lifting her chin higher, Aimée pursed her soft lips together and faced him squarely. "I don't understand all that gibberish, sir, but I know I can handle you. In the meantime, you can at least tell me where you are taking me." He said nothing, and his silence made Aimée afraid, deathly afraid. So much so, in the quiet of her heart, she even thought about resorting to the desperate attempt at prayer again. Should she bother? Perhaps if she listened more intently, God would actually speak to her this time.

Aimée edged her body away from the officer and closed her eyes again. She decided to heed God's voice like never before.

This time she waited for what seemed like forever...but as she tarried, there was, as before, nothing—or was there? In the stillness, had she, perhaps, heard something this time?

It seemed in the recesses of her mind, she sensed she did hear a still small voice...or something.

Was it God? Was He trying to speak with her—was He perhaps trying to reach her?

She had always wanted to hear heaven speak. Others had made that claim. If it was He, what was He saying? Indeed, and what had the captain meant by *a burning hand handling a flame*?

The sound of the horse's hoofs along the road droned in her ears. Shutting her eyes as tighter, thinking it might help her hear better, she perked up her ears and listened again.

Then it came—just a short phrase...ever so softly. Yet she heard it all right. Aimée was certain of it.

Be still...and know...that I am God.

A sudden hush went through her.

Then she heard it again!

Be still...and know...that I am God.

Along the recess of her neck, Aimée felt her face flush. A warm glow of euphoria suddenly spread down to her heart

She opened her eyes to discover a single teardrop sliding from the corner of her eye slowly down her hot cheek, falling into the open palm of her hand as a tiny warm puddle.

She closed her fingers around the elfin drop. When she held it to her heart, she could feel it melt back to dryness.

Aimée knew it now. She knew the truth. Heaven *was* real, and God was in it. But she would never remain satisfied with only one whispered phrase from His mouth.

There *had* to be more.

Maybe later that night, after the captain rid himself of her, or she of him, she would try again. She would listen as carefully as she had only moments ago.

Maybe then, she would hear that voice again.

Maybe then, God would explain about what the captain meant when he spoke of the hand handling the burning flame.

* * * *

Palmer could not stop studying Aimée's lovely face...even when she looked away. Concerned he had probably frightened the poor girl, he wondered if he should have told her what he was doing.

Still, he felt it was best to hold his peace until the two of them got closer to their destination. There was always the chance she might attempt to flee from the carriage window. Yet, it was only right she should know in part his purpose.

Hadn't prayer with all the family shown it was the honorable thing to do? The girl's agreement to it, however, was going to be highly questionable.

Everyone agreed, as far as Aimée Lebrún was concerned, it was an ideal plan, and what they decided would be for her own protection.

Would she realize that?

Some might even say what Palmer was doing was admirable. He didn't know about that necessarily.

She wasn't a woman of faith for one thing he had a sense; and she was vehemently against all he stood for besides. He certainly would never marry the girl outright, and he didn't even know if he liked the girl that much!

On second thought, it was better he didn't tell her why he had her with him…not yet, anyway.

* * * *

As the horses led the carriage round the final bend and came to a stop, Aimée heard their snorts of excitement and took a peek out the window.

"Why, this is Tante's home!" she said with a start. "You are taking me to my aunt's? How is it you know her?" Her eyes lit up as she stared at the captain.

Without thinking, Aimée reached across and gave the captain a hug then caught herself and quickly pulled away, her face turning crimson. "I—I'm sorry. I—I didn't mean that." She cleared her throat and leaned back stiffly. "I—I don't get it."

"All in good time, Amethyst Rose." Palmer grinned. "After we get inside, you'll no longer be in the dark about all this."

Palmer got out of the carriage and swung around to take hold of her waist. "Do you mind?" he asked softly.

Shaking her head, she placed her hand in the captain's, allowing him to help her down the step and onto the road. "Are you acquainted with my aunt?"

166

He started to speak, but the front door of the Simpson house flew open, and Millie ran out, smiling.

"Miss Aimée! There you is! We be sure glad to see you again." She pulled back and bowed her head as the captain came forward and led Aimée through the portal.

"Safe and sound as promised," he said with a salute.

Aimée stepped into the hallway, feeling a sense of calm sweep through her. Maybe everything would be okay now.

But what about Lulu?

"Hello, Millie," she replied. "Where's Tante?"

"I go get her. Her be as happy as an oyster pearl when her sees you," she said, hurrying off towards the back of the house.

Aimée gazed up confused, seeing the captain's nod. "My aunt knew I was coming? I still don't understand."

Did Lulu know, too? She had been smiling when I left.

She stood quietly taking in the fragrance of her aunt's vases of flowers and the clean scents of freshened and polished woodwork around the hall. She could hear the swish of her aunt's skirts grow louder as she drew in closer.

A moment later Beryl walked in from the library beside Tante.

Bowing his head slightly, the captain stepped back, and leaned against the wall. "I'll let your aunt explain it all."

"Aimée, darlin', I knew the good officer would get you here, as he promised." She hugged her tightly and kissed her on both cheeks. "We have much to discuss and some decisions to make...but quickly."

Tante Fran stepped back and looked over at Palmer, extending both of her hands. "Captain," she said softly, taking his warm leather-like hand between the two of hers. "You are a precious gem...both you and your cousin. How can I thank you?"

"No trouble at all, ma'am. Of course, I had to finagle my way into getting this little lady to come with me willingly. That's where the wonderful Lulu stepped in."

167

Aimée's eyes widened as she continued to listen.

Looking down at Aimée, he puckered his brow.. "This one can be tenacious."

"A trait picked up from her mother's side," laughed Fran.

"Then Lulu was in on this!" said Aimée.

He nodded. "If you two will excuse me, I'll go have words with PJ around back. Told him I'd let him know when I arrived." He looked over at Fran. "Do remember there's little time to spare." He moved past Aimée, bowing then turned towards the hall. "Miss Lebrún."

Aimée glared at him then looked over at her aunt. "Cousin? Who is PJ?"

"Come sit with Beryl and me in the parlor, darlin'. Tea?"

"Yes, please," Aimée replied. "Who's PJ?"

"We must talk, Amethyst Rose; time, indeed, is of the essence, I'm afraid."

"So you see," Fran finished explaining, "we had to think of the best way to get you out of that dreadful place as quickly as we could. Captain Jordan was kind enough to make the offer after hearing of your situation while he was at the hospital visiting his cousin. Don't you think it was an excellent idea?"

"The captain thought of what? Who was at the hospital with whom?"

"With me, Amethyst Rose, while I visited my nephew, PJ," said Beryl.

"PJ, the captain's cousin, darlin'."

"PJ?" Aimée argued, setting her cup down. "Who's PJ?"

Fran grinned. "Amethyst Rose, listen. Captain Jordan is your friend, just as the good lieutenant is your friend."

Beryl laughed. "You remember Philip. We also call Philip, PJ, dear. Philip and Palmer are cousins, the nephews I spoke to you about when you first arrived at your aunt's. Do you remember now?"

Aimée's mouth thinned with annoyance as she stared at them both. "The lieutenant--Philip is the cousin of the captain, who confronted me back in Vicksburg and again here in New Orleans! Oh, gracious me, Tante." Her face turned scarlet as she started to rise. "Why didn't anyone let me in on any of this earlier?"

"Listen, Amethyst Rose," reasoned Fran, rising again from her own chair and guiding her niece back down into her seat. "If it were not for the Jordans here, you might still be over in that dreaded bordello."

"Why didn't *you* come back, Tante?"

"I have been doing what I can with Mr. Withers to get that place closed down and to get you out of there as quickly as possible. You are tied to The Paramount in more ways than you realize, thanks to your sister. That Burdette woman wanted you there because you are the only one who can release it into her hands!"

"I don't understand," said Aimée. She found herself checking back into the wing where the captain had headed. "And you were using the captain and Philip to do it?"

"Can you not see that Burdett woman just wants to use you to her own end? Darlin', you must learn to trust!"

A hot tear rolled down Aimée's cheek.

"I want you to listen. Our plan has been to get you here first," Fran went on, "then out of New Orleans. The captain was able to accomplish that by rescuing you. Don't you see? No one else could have succeeded as well as he. Otherwise, Miss Burdette might try to find a way to get you back there."

"Why? What does it matter now that I'm gone? All I need to do is get Lulu out of there, Tante Fran!" Aimée was confused. "If Nina Burdette is going to take over Florette's place anyway, of what use am I? Why should I even care?"

"Oh, you should care, all right. You are of great value to her, Amethyst Rose," admonished her aunt.

"Mr. Withers has successfully accessed a copy of Florette's will."

"What is that to me?"

Fran pursed her lips. "Ask Miss Burdette! When Florette's marriage ended, she made *you* benefactor of her property."

A heaviness built in Aimée's chest. "But that cannot be! Florette loathed me…before!" she exclaimed, shaking her head in disbelief.

"Apparently she had plans to teach you all there was to know about the business. Then the day you stole away to be with me, she met up with a friend and the two of them went to see her attorney, and the deed was done. Soon after, she took ill and was never able to contact her counselor to change the will again. You see, darlin', The Paramount by all technicalities belongs to you! Nina Burdette can't get the property back *without* you!"

Aimée stared at her aunt as she leaned back against the settee and scratched her head.

"Let me see, did I remember everything?" she said.

Gracious sakes! "What am I going to do with that revolting place, Tante Fran?" She covered her face with her hands. She couldn't stay at her aunt's…not if Nina was going to try to come and get her.

"I can't believe this is happening to me," she whispered as her aunt rambled on.

* * * *

"…and then you shall be secure until the war is over darlin'," went on Tante, "and no one shall find you there."

"What's that you said?" asked Aimée, perking up.

"I said, 'tis the only way until you can return to Vicksburg to reassess your home at *Shadow Grove*…unless of course David returns or we can contact him."

"What is the only way?"

"Have you not been listening, darlin'? 'Tis not that I am so much on one side of the idea or the other," Fran went on, "We must consider *everything* for the purpose of your safety."

"You are going much too fast." Aimée stood again. "How was it you planned to keep me safe, Tante?"

"It is the best plan," reasoned Fran, holding up both hands.

"What is the best plan?"

"Yes, and we've even arranged for Lulu. She and Abel are sneaking away early in the morning. They'll be here to help."

Aimée sighed. She wished she had been listening then she would not be confused about whatever it was Tante Fran was talking about. But so often her tante tended to ramble. "Could you explain it again?"

"Can you think of a better solution?"

"Oh, Tante, but where shall I go?" asked Aimée.

"She's been trying to tell you, you will be coming with me," said Palmer, walking into the room.

Aimée fixed her gaze on the captain. "What do you mean with you?"

They all turned and stared at her.

"Aimée, were you not listening?" asked Beryl. "My family's large piece of property up in Northern Virginia is the best place to go. They will conceal you. Palmer will take you there, and you will be safe. You will have Lulu with you. Those folks at The Paramount would not think of going that far north."

Aimée labored to speak. She chewed on her lower lip then finally faced the officer.

"I am to go up into Yankee territory with *you*?" She slanted her head.

"That's right."

"Okay, Sir, tell me this. How do you propose getting *me*, a southern woman, up North? Don't begin to assume I would accept an invitation or proposal to become your *mistress*! My life is worth more to me than that, Captain, and I certainly don't plan to join the ranks of your Union Army!" She started to walk off.

171

"Not a proposal as my mistress," he said with a smile, pulling Aimée back and swinging her around. "Far be it from me to do such a thing."

"Then what, pray tell?" Aimée leaned her head to the side to avoid his eyes.

"You will travel north with me…as…"

"Well, as what?" she asked again, arms on her hips.

"My cousin and I have decided you will go—as my bride, Miss Lebrún."

Aimée could feel the stiffening of her body, the turmoil in her stomach, and the blood rushing to her face.

His mouth twitched in slight amusement. "Ma'am, you don't have to be embarrassed. You won't actually *wed* me! You will just *temporarily* take the Jordan name. Indeed, we will not go through a true betrothal, and thank the heavens for that!" he whispered. "Once we arrive at *Pencil Ridge*, I won't even be around."

With her mouth agape, Aimée looked around the room then gazed up at the man who now was literally taking over her life.

"I don't want to do this Tante! I just can't. " Her eyes darted around the room.

"But Aimée, darlin' you won't be actually doing it!" Aimée saw the pleading stare on her aunt's face.

"Madam, will you yield?" asked the captain. "You really haven't much choice, you know."

Aimée felt like a fugitive entering into the outlandish wishes of an aunt at the whims of a handsome Yankee. Would she never find her way back to Vicksburg? She wasn't getting closer to *Shadow Grove*! With each passing day, she was being taken farther from home than ever.

* * * *

"We've turned Aimée's world upside down," said Philip moments before nightfall when Palmer returned to the house and the Jordans met in the Simpson library.

"It would appear Miss Lebrún's world has been in a dither for a long while. Gram will be good for her, don't you agree, Aunt Beryl? said Palmer.

"If anyone can ease the girl's mind, everyone knows Mattie Jordan can," said Aunt Beryl. "Mother has always had a way about her. I wouldn't worry overmuch."

"Nor should you, PJ. That girl has spirit. She'll survive."

* * * *

Everyone around the house was full of activity, busily deciding Aimée's future—everyone but Aimée herself.

She instead found herself sitting mutely in Tante Fran's Parlor, staring blankly at a wall. She glanced up just as Joseph and Abel came down the steps with her trunks. Now and then, she would catch sight of the two cousins through the window as they worked out front.

Now that she saw Philip and Palmer beside each other she, was amazed at the resemblance between the two men. Though not immediately related and not that close in age, both could easily pass for brothers. Aimée wondered how she could have missed it.

Heaving a sigh, she rose and worked her way up the steps to her chamber then sat down at her window seat. Just before removing her boots, she glanced out the window and stared at the stars beginning to line the sky. A shooting star sped through the firmament in the clear evening skies.

God was up behind those stars somewhere; she knew that now. It was as perfect a time as any to talk to Him again. She bowed her head, as she had done earlier. Words that before were far from her suddenly came tumbling out.

"Nina must be wondering when I'm going to return, Father God. Am I doing the right thing by leaving with the captain? Please, Father, help me know the answer, and I will do what you say. Speak to me as you did earlier today. Amen."

Wasn't it true the captain had offered to come to her assistance if she needed it? Could she perhaps count this as one of those times?

The room remained silent.

Aimée waited.

Nothing happened, but she was determined.

She'd heard God speak once. She wanted to hear His voice again. She needed to hear an answer now.

She would not leave her room this time until she did.

Crouching down further on her seat, she tried to think of nothing but Him. She glanced across the room and saw her aunt's book of scriptures.

Aimée got up, walked over to pick it up, and leafed through the pages until she found the Psalms. She'd heard of them before. Perhaps she would find something there. Perhaps heaven could speak to her right there.

...he is their strength in the time of trouble. And the Lord shall help them...

"*Father God,*" she prayed again, "*Will you give me strength in my troubles?*"

She continued, this time with her eyes wide-open. "*I want to believe in you – like Lulu – like Tante Fran. Will you help me?*"

Aimée somehow knew God would. Somehow He *would* rescue her, keep her safe from people like Nina Burdette.

Would He also deliver her from the captain? Or was He sending her the captain as her help? That she didn't yet have the answer to.

* * * *

The journey began calmly enough.

Captain Jordan lit the oil lamp hanging near the window and offered Aimée a covering for her legs as the cooling night air brought in a slight October chill.

She shook her head at first.

As the night progressed, he watched, as she seemed to have a more difficult time keeping her eyes open. Her lids grew heavier as he watched her lashes flutter and her eyes slowly blink shut.

Her hair appeared to grow disheveled the harder she tried to hold her head up, so much so, that she nodded off the third time, unconsciously allowing herself to incline onto Palmer's shoulder.

174

The moment she laid her head softly against his the crook of his neck, he heard her let out a deep sigh. He sucked in his breath.

Looking down at what he could see of her coppery curls as she rested beneath his chin, he grinned. He smelled the perfumed fragrance of her hair and shut his eyes for a split second.

Taking a deeper whiff, he memorized the scents of the beautiful young woman beside him, who while sleeping, reached up and placed her hand on his chest. He heard her sigh again.

Palmer wanted to take his other hand and place it across hers, but he dared not. He couldn't forget his pledge not to touch her. Now she was making that promise for him close to impossible.

As the carriage rolled along, occasionally hitting pocks in the road, the oil lamp swung more freely.

She tucked in closer.

Palmer would not have slept if his life depended on it. He wanted the moment to last forever, and yet, at the same time, he prayed Abel up front would soon turn into the next inn, so he could awaken the girl and get her into a room of her own.

He needed a breath of fresh air. He had to get away.

Nuzzling his chin once along the softness of Aimée's sweet-scented hair again, he lingered there a few more seconds.

He was going to have to pray harder for the Lord to give him strength. He had to remember the girl beside him was not a believer, and in that frame of mind and heart, she would never be the right person for his life.

Pulling himself away from her abruptly, he closed his eyes again.

PJ should have been in his shoes right now! Not him. Maybe he could have fared better with this budding flower.

Mrs. Simpson, Aunt Beryl, all of them had it wrong.

Palmer swallowed hard, stiffened his back, and tried to stretch. Maybe if he cut out his eyes so he would no longer have to look at her and maybe if he discarded a portion of his nose so he would no longer take in her lovely fragrance, it would help.

This trip, this so-called project to save Amethyst Rose Lebrún, was not going to be easy at all!

What had he gotten himself into?

* * * *

Chapter Thirteen

Shenandoah Valley, Virginia

Palmer stepped down from the carriage and lifted Aimée out, while Lulu followed behind, setting her down on the road. He slipped a band around the third finger of her left hand though she'd hardly been awake.

"What's with this?" she asked, yawning.

"You must not forget, Amethyst Rose, that for now, you are my new bride. Just a little reminder. Do you understand?"

She gazed up.

"We are going in to eat and to get you a good night's sleep before we arrive at my grandparent's. It's a respectable inn I'm told."

"Whatever you say."

He headed toward the door keeping her close by his side. "Don't forget to smile."

"I shan't forget."

As he opened the door, he caught sight of a plump lass in the corner humming some Irish tune as she wiped off the far table. The hall was empty, so she must have been doing it to occupy herself. The lass did not see them come in.

Palmer had heard her name was Agnes O'Reilley and that she had the best inn in the valley. But by the looks of the empty tables around the room and what with the war and all, it was most likely times for the poor girl had not been that good lately.

On a couple of her walls Miss O'Reilley had a few carved signs. Palmer nodded as he took a minute to read them.

"Ye gotta go on no matter what...Times can be troublesome for sure."

"Ne'er be no quitter."

"Ne'er let nobody take away yer means o' livin'."

Smart lass, he thought to himself, to hang onto such strong beliefs.

"You are open for business, aren't you, miss?" Palmer looked over to her and called out.

"Oh my! I didn't hear you folks come in!" She glanced back and exclaimed, fixing her apron and straightening her long black braids. "Top o' the evenin' — come on in — you might even find you a seat!" Her belly rolled as she sauntered over, laughing joyfully, her eyes twinkling.

"Nice place you have here," said Palmer.

"You come to *The Leprechaun Inn*, my beloved Danny's place before he took sick and died. Now it be mine. I does my best to keep it scrubbed clean." She kept staring at the young couple.

Palmer moved his hand to the middle of Aimée's back.

"You're taller than most, ain't ye, sir?" she said with a grin, "If ye don't mind my saying, most certainly a beautiful spectacle before *my* eyes, standing there in your rich uniform."

"We've been riding a long way, miss."

Then her eyes darted over to the lass beside him. "And you, girl, I'm thinkin', you could be a princess — a Southern belle, maybe? What you doing up in these parts with a Yankee officer? A fresh new bride and groom, perchance?" Her eyes came in to study her closer. "Why you're as pretty as a picture, that you are!"

Palmer glanced down. "Don't be shy."

"Thank you," said Aimée.

"If you was to have a crown on your head, I could wager a pot of gold you would be perfect for the royal court — one of Old King Solomon's daughters, no doubt."

Aimée smiled and blushed.

"Come with me. I'll seat you at my best table." Agnes placed her arm in the crook of the officer's and walked the couple over to the far corner.

"We'll be needing a bite to eat and a couple of rooms if you have them," stated Palmer.

"Been told about your place. You must be Agnes."

"Right you are, sir," she replied with her largest smile and a continuous bob. "I got a pot o' my best stew boiling in the back, and I kneaded out some dough for *briosca* this morning. You'll be wanting some. You'll have to be 'scusing the fact I ain't got much salt around the place. The soldier boys ain't brought me 'round none for a bit. But I found some grand seasonings out back in the fields, a few herbs n' such, so the bread won't be so plain. In fact, I've got some piping hot right now! Can you folks smell the loaves?"

She lifted her nostrils to take a long whiff. "Mmm Hmm."

"Smells wonderful," Aimée said.

"I could eat me a horse, mister soldier man," said Lulu from behind.

"Come, Amethyst, my dear." He turned and stated solicitously to his *bride* guiding her into her chair. "Let's get you seated. Careful now. Come on Lulu."

Palmer felt the eyes of the innkeeper on them all, closely watching every move they made. He leaned in. "Excuse me, dearest?"

Aimée stared up at him but said nothing.

"You look ravishing, as always." He inclined his face down toward hers. With his hand pulling her chin closer towards him, he met her lips and tenderly kissed her.

Her eyes widened in alarm.

"Say nothing," he whispered as he slowly released her and caressed her cheek, noticing the shocked look on her face and her eyes as big as saucers. "Remember, she must think we are married." Resting his own cheek briefly against the softness of Aimée's sweet-scented hair, he lingered there a second more, closed his eyes, and sighed.

As he sat at the table looking at her now, he could not resist staring. She looked so young and as innocent as a foal, timid, and quite uncertain of herself.

Whether or not she was, he did not know for sure. He had to be careful with her.

Palmer would have thoroughly enjoyed kissing her again, for the memory of his lips upon hers had been warm and sweet…but he dared not.

Instead he sucked in his breath and just watched her. After all, he had to remember he was fighting his own battles.

Lulu sat across from the table and grinned.

* * * *

Aimée held her hands together and twisted the foreign object round on her finger. She wished it was not there. Yet she knew 'twas a necessity to wear the thing for the game she had to play. Did she have any other choice?

He won't make me sleep in the same room, will he? Thank the Lord she at least had her Lulu.

The man was going to tell the world she was his bride! But she was a proper girl. The Lord knew it, but did the Lord tell the captain yet? God would not let her down. Would he?

When she watched the captain snuggle in closer beside her at the table, Aimée caught her breath. She gave him a suspicious glare before gazing down at her ring again. She had to put in an effort to respond sweetly — the innocent bride.

"Yes, beloved," she purred, forming her lips into a rose, pulling free from his grip, at the same time hoping the innkeeper would not turn back around and notice.

Moments later, she did.

"Whilst you folks get comfy, I'll just run to the cellar and get some of my cider what I fixed up last winter," she said. "It's been keeping cool. There's also homemade apple butter down there for your bread," she added, hurrying towards the back door. "I'll return in a few…"

Aimée turned her head and watched her leave then swung back toward the captain.

"I'm trying my best."

"Much obliged," he said not taking his eyes of her. "We anxiously wait."

They both glanced up a short while later to see the innkeeper return.

"The lassie looks a wee bit tired, don't she, cap?" she commented, after she came out of the kitchen. "I ain't heard much more than a peep since she come in—not from the back, not that I been listening' or nothin'. Too hungry to speak?" She set their platters of bread and bowls of hot stew down in front of them and watched them closely.

"I'm just tired is all." Aimée yawned.

"We're both tired," said Palmer. "Anxious to get to bed."

Aimée blinked and swallowed. What would he say next?

"Just to be letting you know, honey, I got the perfect room for the both of you about ready, and will finish that up while you enjoy your fixins'. 'Tis a fine room up at the top o' the stairs. Best bridal suite in the place, even if it is the only one I got. Right clean, even if I do say so meself. Ain't got no bugs nor nothin'. I'm always careful 'bout them things.

"Oh, and for the lassie here," she turned to say to the captain, "I gots my copper tub. Keep it shiny clean, I do. Would you like that, sweetheart?" she finished, looking back at Aimée.

Aimée blushed, as she stared across the clapboard table at Palmer. Had she not moments ago prayed they would not have to have the same room?

Where would he have her do her bathing?

Lulu! Do something!

"Woops! The wee lass is turnin' scarlet! You folks are newer than I expected!" declared Agnes.

Aimée's knees shook beneath the table.

"Mister Soldier…"

Palmer's head shot up. "I think, Agnes, it would be better if we had separate rooms. You see…" he hesitated,

"My bride is in—well, she's in the family way." He paused.

Aimée moved restlessly in her chair, a gasp escaped her.

"Just the early stages you understand," Palmer continued with a chuckle. "We must be extra careful...mustn't we, my sweet?" With that, he extended a lingering wink beside him and reached his hand over to pat hers.

Aimée felt suddenly certain she was about to lose her supper.

She looked up to see the innkeeper raise her eyebrow and laugh. "I got just what the doctor ordered. There's a door 'twixt my two finest rooms, in case you be wantin' to pop in for a wee visit or to say a special night-night later...and even a place for your fine servant to be nearby."

It sounded like a good-natured scoff. "I'm wagerin', princess, you have a hankering for that tub, am I right, dearie?"

Aimée nodded. "I'd like that very much. A bath sounds wonderful."

Agnes nodded then turned and bounced back toward the kitchen, shaking the floor as she walked. Hopefully, mused Aimée, there would be a key for her door

* * * *

The next morning came early, and Palmer could see even then the O'Reilley woman would waste no time following them out with biscuits, cold meat, and left overs for the servants.

He turned to help Aimée with her cape. Pulling it around her more securely to ward off the nip in the air, he hesitated only seconds with his arms on her soft shoulders.

"Don't forget," he reminded her.

She slowly pulled away with a nod. "I haven't forgotten."

To avoid his touch, she rushed over to give the Agnes a quick hug. "You and your place are wonderful, truly wonderful, Agnes. I'm ever-so-appreciative of the scents for my bath."

"Ah, 'twas nothin'," she said with a grin.

"Are you ready, angel? We must be going." Palmer held out his hand.

"I guess this it," she replied.

Palmer decided to leave well before dawn to get a good start on the road. He was in no frame of mind to be stopped, not even by one of his own. Having *her* in the room next to him the night before and realizing what he'd gotten himself into was trouble enough.

Would Pop and Gram at *Pencil Ridge* understand once he got her there? It had been only right to come to the lady's aid, as any good God-fearing man would have done.

Did his dispatched letter stating the time of their arrival arrive in time to warn them? They would need to know she was a high-spirited thing. They would also need to know she at least responded with a hint of compliance.

But did she truly?

Truth be told what Pop and Gram needed to know most was they were about to take on the job of protectors for the poor girl from a sordid lifestyle and possible life of ruin.

It was only right.

Once the war was over, he would simply take Aimée back off their hands and send her back to her aunt's, and the sooner the better.

In the meantime, he needed to get back to his own life. There was his coming promotion to Major and his scheduled tour of Washington to finish out his time. Then there was also Cornelia Smithy to consider. He still had *that woman* with which to contend.

Palmer had almost forgotten about what was he going to do about *her*.

* * * *

Signs of recent fighting surrounded the carriage showing Virginia had been hit hard.

As Aimée sensed the devastation, tears rolled down her cheeks. To avoid the captain's face, she fixed her eyes on the land around her.

I cannot let him see me like this. I cannot let him know these things bother me. But what would he care about how I feel inside? The captain knows nothing about me.

She felt his tap on her shoulder.

No.

Aimée refused to look his way.

"It's closing in on the noon hour," he said, as the coach pulled up to another inn. "I thought you might want to freshen up. We'll be arriving at *Pencil Ridge* in less than an hour."

"I'm fine, thank you," she muttered quietly continuing to gaze out. Was that a grumble she heard?

Aimée heard the captain unlatch the door to get out. When he reached in to help her out, she started to turn. He took a second glance at the puffy redness in her eyes. "You've been weeping."

"No, I haven't. I'm fine." A sourness spilled over in her voice.

"Well, you can stay or come; I will leave you to yourself. Agnes left us some biscuits and meat. I'm hungry and besides, Abel needs to rest the horses. Lulu can stay here with you if you like."

"It matters not to me what she does either at the moment."

She heard him sigh heavily. "I'm sure you can feel the chill I warned you about earlier," he said. "It happens when you get on these northern roads. " He paused. "So stay then."

He sounded different she thought. Aimée could hear the change. A cool impersonal tone. It cut like a knife as it sliced through the stiffness in the air. She could see it as he stared into her eyes.

Did he truly feel that way? Was it because of the way she had treated him?

Then he started to turn away.

He turned back. "If you change your mind…"

Aimée tried not to frown. "Captain…if you don't mind."

"Whatever. By the way, Ma'am, I can see the brick I gave you earlier helped greatly to keep at least your feet *warm*."

* * * *

"Truce?"

Why had he acted so inane and over nothing? She was the immature one, not he.

"My grandparents will take good care of you," said Palmer, stepping up into the carriage to join her. "I thought you would appreciate knowing that. The folks are in their eighties now, and I'm pretty certain *Pencil Ridge* has been well protected."

She refused to acknowledge.

"I see you aren't speaking again," he drawled. "But you have to admit, I've remained fair. I haven't touched you, and I've left you to yourself, just as you asked."

"No, you haven't," she turned, "and yes, you've left me to myself often enough," she mumbled back. "Just remember, I only have to speak to you in public."

He looked down at her fidgeting hands.

"Being a *so-called* bride is leaving a terrible taste in your mouth, is it?"

"At the moment—yes…it is."

"I see."

"I really have nothing more to say at this point." Aimée lowered her head.

"As you wish, then, Miss Lebrún," he answered with gritted teeth. "But I guarantee, you will."

* * * *

Aimée gazed out the carriage window at the vast property surrounding her. It had to be the Jordan estate. She craned her neck to get a better view.

Although it appeared secluded, it looked inviting at the same time. Stone fencing surrounded several outbuildings ahead, all still in tact, and horses grazed in the scenic pasturelands.

Up beyond a generous barn, a meadow full of wet clover grass covered the terrain where several head of steer looked to be enjoying the new growth of green from what could have been a recent rain.

Even the large manse, which stood facing a clump of trees beyond several smaller cabins, seemed ready to welcome any company.

The place was colossal. *As beautiful as Shadow Grove before the fire,* thought Aimée, as the image focused in her memory.

How could this lovely piece of land have evaded the shattering effects of the horrendous war? This home's thick walls of stone appeared to have remained intact even to the surrounding porches.

Wasn't this northern area also the homeland to General Lee, who was said to live just a few hundred miles north up by the border? Had she not heard back at the inn that only recently there'd been some of the worst fighting ever there in the valley? Indeed, how could *Pencil Ridge* have escaped it all? It almost didn't make sense.

Aimée glanced over at the captain who gazed towards his grandparents' place with pride.

He loves it here. Perhaps it is because he now knows his family is unharmed, that their home was spared. Naturally, I would feel the same, if I too was returning home to a protected land. But I am not, nor shall I ever again.

Perhaps it made a difference his grandparents had two grandsons who fought for the north, which was fortunate for them.

But it was her home, and her land that was destroyed, not theirs. She had lost everything! They had lost nothing. She looked around again.

If I must pretend to be the captain's endearing bride I certainly don't have to be thrilled to be here!

* * * *

"That woman standing on the porch is my gram," Palmer pointed out. "I don't know if you can see her from here."

"I do see her," said Aimée.

He nodded. "The mistress of *Pencil Ridge*. Her name is Mattie. We call her Gram. Call her what you wish. You'll like her. I look forward to introducing you." He smiled then turned back away.

After he waved, he saw her lift her arm and wave back from the porch with a huge smile on her face.

They soon drove up closer and stopped.

"Will you allow me?" He asked after stepping out.

Aimée extended her arm.

Palmer took her by the waist, pulled her down then quickly let go. "I'll be right back." Leaving her standing alone by Lulu, he turned, ran up to Gram, and gave her a generous hug.

"Gram!" he said. "Did you perchance receive my letter? You look as full of beans as ever! And you'd better be healthy!"

She laughed. "Well, I am still as round as an over-fed filly, Polly boy, as you can see. My white cotton hair is too thin. I've got way too many freckles and far too many sunspots on my arm. I couldn't be healthier, and that's not going to change! What letter?"

He stepped back. "I had hoped…"

"Haven't seen any letter. She giggled, her middle rolling with her laughter. "Let me have a look at you." She took her hands and pulled him down, cupping his face between them.

"Looking mighty good. About time, you got yourself here, Polly boy. We've been wondering when you would get up this way. Who's your girl?" She glanced in Aimée's direction.

"Welcome, son," interrupted Palmer senior from behind her, his arm out for a firm handshake. "You brought us a guest?" Covering his brow to shield the sun, he looked out towards the carriage to get a better look.

"My girl? Wait. I explained in my letter, Pop. I was hoping it would reach you ahead of us. It would've explained everything better than…"

"You have something you need to tell us?"

Palmer shook his head. "Nothing unbecoming, Pop. Amethyst Rose is her name—she goes by Aimée. No secrets—from the two of you, anyway…let me go get her."

Palmer senior looked harder. "Are you sure you don't want to fill us in first?"

"You're always coming up with something novel," squawked Gram. "It's been too quiet around here, anyway…since the fighting stopped."

"I'll explain the rest once I get the girl settled in. She's had a long trip."

Palmer turned to head back towards the carriage. When he looked ahead to smile at Aimée, she turned away. Shaking his head once he reached her, he breathed only two words.

"Be civil."

Without another word, he quietly walked her towards the house.

"I'd like you to meet Amethyst Rose…Aimée," he stated when they reached the bottom of the porch.

Palmer watched his grandparents observe the bewildered young woman's blushing cheeks then him, then her again.

She looked even more beautiful when the afternoon sun beat down on her crimson face, causing her freckles to pop out more prominently.

"Aimée, I'd like you to meet my grandparents."

Eyes full of gentleness gazed back at her. "It's nice to meet you both," she answered softly. "I hope you will forgive my intrusion."

They were kind as he expected. "Any friend of our grandson is a friend of ours. Come in and make yourself at home!"

As Palmer guided her inside, he breathed a sigh of relief. But he found it difficult taking his eyes off the young woman he had just brought home.

* * * *

Shadows flitted across the ceiling in the room where Aimée rested. When she opened her eyes, it took her a moment to remember where she was. She watched the fire crackle in the fireplace, throwing off traces of light along the wall. She put her arms behind her head and watched the activity drearily.

Her mind wandered back to weeks, even years past, and all the changes that had gone on in her life, to all through which she had been. Though she was usually a woman of high spirits, she had changed.

The person lying in her bed was a long way off from the one time flickering flame of Vicksburg, Mississippi. What about the frivolous, mischievous, foolhardy tomboy years? Her life had since become so serious.

Part of her longed for those carefree days again.

As first light continued in, Aimée drifted off into daydreams of actually *being* wedded to the man who slept in the room down the hall.

To be Palmer Jordan's bride…

Would it bother her so much being married to a Yankee officer? And would Papa approve of such a thing?

She couldn't for the life of her understand why something like that would cross her mind at a time like this.

Oddly, she did not shudder in her illusion, as she might have before. Even the fact that he was a soldier did not seem to matter as much anymore.

Perhaps it was because of his nice family, who had treated her so kindly, who acted as if her arrival had been planned for months—as if she truly *was* his new bride.

Perhaps it was because she had no one else…anymore.

Maybe it was the land. *Pencil Ridge* was indeed breathtaking. Aimée had overheard Gram call the place her little heaven on earth. Away from the dregs of war, it was easy to dream about what it would be like to live there permanently.

Why do I lay here dreaming of impossibilities?

A lump filled Aimée's throat as she thought of her own war-torn home and beloved family back at *Shadow Grove* – all gone now.

She rose from her bed and walked over to the window to gaze out then walked back over to crawl back beneath the covers.

What am I doing here?

It was light enough to see clearly around the room now. Over on the bureau table she spied what looked like an old prayer book and walked over to gingerly pick it up.

On the inside front page of the leather-bound journal sketched in youthful penmanship across the top were the following words, *"The year of our Lord, 1795."*

If it belonged to Mattie Jordan, she would have written those words back when she was a child. The name Matilda Louise (Mattie) Duchy appeared inside the front cover with a special mark leading to the rear of the book.

Aimée leafed through the pages, careful not to disturb her private writings. The reference she found looked familiar.

"He was in the world, and the world was made by him, and the world knew him not. He came unto his own, and his own received him not."

It was the same scripture she'd read back at Tante Fran's. She read on.

"But as many as received him, to them gave he power to become the sons of God, even to them that believe on his name…."

Then Aimée noticed the handwritten comment at the bottom of the back page.

"Today, at the age of ten and five, I have given my heart to Jesus. The dapper Palmer Jordan just asked daddy for my hand.

I said YES! This is the grandest day of my life! Signed: Mattie Duchy, June 1, 1799."

Aimée's heart felt light. A smile crossed her face as she closed the book then carefully replaced it on the bureau. When she walked back to her bed, instead of climbing back in, she knelt down on the floor beside it, feeling the warmth of the fire beside her.

"Dear God," she prayed, her eyes closed, her head bowed down on the bed, *"I want you to have my heart, too. I want to believe on your name as I just read. I want to be your child."*

With her head still bowed, Aimée fell asleep in the same position, a sense of unexplainable peace in her heart and mind.

Chapter Fourteen

Palmer smiled and listened to his gram as she rambled.

"The good Lord has seen fit to take good care of us during war time, Polly," she announced Sunday morning in the parlor. She'd called him Polly since he was a youngster.

"Perhaps it is because PJ and I are serving on the side of the Union."

"I'd rather think it's the good Lord who's doing the protecting," she scolded. "Don't you go trying to take credit for the things God does."

"The Lord orders our steps, I know." Palmer leaned down to give her a lengthy smooch on both her cheeks. "You always have your priorities in order," he finished with a laugh.

As he turned to look over at Pop, their expressions met, eye-to-eye, neither with a smile, both with a firm nod.

"With that, I guess I shall go get myself ready for church. I'll see you both in a while," he said, heading out of the room. "If you see the girl, tell her I'll be down shortly. She might be a little fearful this morning."

Gram nodded. "Don't worry, Polly. I'm thinking God's ordered that girls steps, too!"

* * * *

The sitting room was empty of life when Aimée walked into the room but for the sound of footsteps behind her.

"We're going to church shortly," said the captain curtly. "Don't feel as if you must join us. We shall return after lunch. You can find yourself something in the kitchen if you hunger."

When Aimée tugged at his arm then pulled away, she hoped he wouldn't notice her trembling. "Would you mind too much if I joined you? I only have to change."

She had not been kind before, especially at the inn. Why should he think she'd act any differently now?

"It matters not a whit to me what you choose to do." He started to walk off, slightly tugging away, so her hand fell from his arm and down to her side. "It's up to you. We leave in less than an hour."

She watched as he walked away.

Please care.

At the door, he turned but it looked as if he was avoiding her face.

"And since everyone is at breakfast, you should probably get yourself something to eat before then. I'll have one of our servants inform Lulu so she can go up to your chamber and help you dress if you like."

"Thank you," said Aimée quietly.

When she watched him hasten out the front door and slam it shut, leaving her to stare after him, she could only close her eyes.

How was she supposed to feel? She'd been the one who had been rude to him first. Now he was. Did she truly want to attend services with the man and his family?

Her stomach now sour, Aimée gazed down the empty hall and slowly headed up the stairs back to her room to wait for Lulu.

"What you be wearin' for the preachin'?" asked Lulu, walking in right behind her. "I hurried over soon as I heard you was attendin' with the soldier man."

"Apparently news travels fast around this place. Did the captain send one of servants your way? He was awfully quick."

"Oh no, Miss Aimée. The warrior man, him come told me hisself. Him seem awful excited to me."

Aimée glanced up with a surprised look on her face.

* * * *

When Aimée joined the Jordan family and they walked into the sanctuary, a few families twisted around curiously.

No one observed her and the uniformed Yankee captain beside her — no one that is, except the one woman sitting in the first pew, front row, center-left.

Aimée got a closer view.

The woman's dirty blonde tresses were liberally adorned with flowers and jewelry in her chignon. Gold chenille netting loosely held her curls in tact. It seemed strangely inappropriate for the parishioner to be in such fancy attire during wartime even in church.

Other than her, the sanctuary held only a sprinkling in its congregation; men, mostly aged, with great sadness on their faces, which showed by their wrinkled brows and turned down mouths.

Aimée took only a curious glance the woman's way then followed Gram to find the family pew. Once seated with Palmer at her right, she edged away so she wouldn't touch him until the rest of the family scooted her in closer to him.

Though they didn't speak, she immediately noticed the nervous twitch in his jaw.

He cannot stand even the nearness of my touch. She bent her head away quickly. She glanced up front to see the reverend walk from a wooden bench up to the pulpit in his tattered robe and watched as he opened his book of scriptures.

His wife hobbled across the platform behind him, with her cane and took her place on the chair in front of the piano. After a few ripples across the keyboard, she began the first hymn.

As the music echoed throughout the high-ceilinged hall, everyone stood and began singing as loudly as anything Aimée had ever heard.

Aimée closed her eyes, willing her ears to take in every word. She could hear the haunting voice of the captain as he belted out his words of praise the loudest, his deep baritone voice.

Aimée held her breath. Tears flowed down her cheeks as she listened to the melodious name of Jesus being sung.

Oh, Lord indeed, You continue to show me how real you are becoming to me.

At the end of the singing, the reverend directed the congregation back to their seats and began to preach. When he finished, several affirmative nods and a few soft amens swept across the room. Then he prayed.

It would be the first time in Aimée's life she herself had uttered the name of the Lord in a public place. Even in that small crowd, His presence to her was compelling. Yet, she would never be able to tell the captain all that had been happening to her lately. Especially due to all the times she'd been so discourteous to the man...and far too many times.

* * * *

Following the service, Gram Jordan proudly pulled Aimée around the fellowship hall as if she was a small child in front of several of her own friends.

"Don't worry, Polly," Gram whispered as she walked by him standing in the corner. "No one will know the difference. Did you tell Louisa yet?"

He shook his head as he stood in the corner with his arms folded. His brows narrowed.

Gram knew she was not making things easy at all. She also knew what she was doing.

"This here is Palmer's bride, Amethyst Rose, Louisa and Martha," she stated demurely when she walked up to a table full of women. "I thought you both would like to meet her."

"Isn't she a beauty, Amanda?" she said. She turned to Aimée and grinned mischievously.

So many of the women in the valley had daughters who had hoped one day to themselves be added to the family of Jordan. Gram had known it for years. Each one looked over in the corner at her grandson in dismay. He had, after all, been the true catch of Shenandoah Valley.

But now, young Palmer had gone off and wed a stranger.

Certainly, there was still Philip Jordan the cousin from Ohio. She knew they would still talk about him. He, too, was a prize for any girl who did not mind playing second fiddle to the ministry. He was a Jordan and as handsome as the elder.

Gram would be sure to later reassure several there was still time.

She searched the room for Cornelia Smithy. Finally spying her at the end of the dessert table, she saw the woman had already cornered Polly.

* * * *

Palmer greeted them both with a ready smile. He pulled Aimée in close beside him then placed his arm across her shoulders before she could stiffen.

"My bride, Amethyst Rose, Cornelia. Aimée, meet an old, old friend of mine."

She straightened her body and smiled, but the return smile was anything but welcoming.

With a glare, Cornelia stared first at her then at Palmer then back at Aimée. Her mouth dropped. "So when did this happen, Palmer darling? I thought..."

His gram grinned and started to turn. "I was just about to come and introduce your bride myself. I'm glad you were here to doing the honors."

Gram hurried away leaving Palmer to handle the women, and Aimée at his arm for the first time...but not for the last.

* * * *

It was late the next morning by the time Captain Jordan got around to looking at the property one more time. In more ways than one, he was ready to go.

Placing his boot in the stirrup, he lifted his leg over his horse. He still had his mind on her. His mind was always on her.

Steering the stallion towards the house, he looked around until he caught sight of Aimée, standing quietly in the shadows.

"Come here."

When she came closer, their eyes locked.

Virginia's wind in its briskness had emptied the trees completely of their leaves and left a coolness that invited the soon-coming winter. "What is it?" she asked softly, holding her cloak close around her.

"Take care of the folks for me. If you do nothing else, at least make them *think* you are grateful for them taking you in." He was not smiling.

"I don't mean to sound boorish," he confessed. "It is just difficult to know your thoughts from one minute to the next. I've never before met anyone as temperamental as you."

He held up his hand as she went to speak.

"Not that I don't understand, mind you. You've been through much, and I know you don't think much of me right now. It's—"

"Captain Jordan," she replied, "I'm most grateful for their hospitality, and I shall have no problem in showing my appreciation. You need not concern yourself over the matter. I—I need to tell you—"

"Enough then."

After reaching up to tip his hat, Palmer abruptly swung his arm around and gave the Lebrún woman a quick nod of the head then turned and rode away swiftly.

He had to leave now before he changed his mind and said what was truly on his heart.

The extent of his good bye was as chilling as the morning itself.

* * * *

Did he hate her so very much?

Aimée had wanted to tell him, but she could see he would not have been interested. She did not want to have him on her mind. Not again. She figured he obviously felt the same way about her as he did before.

Now that he would be away, perhaps it would make life easier.

* * * *

"Okay, young lady, are you ready to tell me?" she heard Gram ask her several days later.

"Tell you?" Aimée asked, lifting her eyes from her book.

"Come now." Gram's smile teased. "You've been trying to tell me something for days, Amethyst Rose. You cannot keep these things from me. I've a sixth sense about such things. You want to tell me when you came to believing? Or is it something about Palmer?"

"Believing? Palmer?" Aimée blushed. She had contained her newfound faith by keeping it to herself. She hadn't even shared it with Lulu. About Palmer, she hadn't told a soul.

Religion was such a private thing...wasn't it? What might she comfortably say to Gram about Palmer? "What was it you wanted to talk to me about, Gram?"

"I have watched you the last three Sundays," she said. "Almost from the moment you arrived, you've been glued to every word the reverend speaks. I've even seen you pick up the words to the hymns faster than a jackrabbit can hop! When will you be you ready to tell me?"

Aimée's face relaxed. Gram wasn't thinking about Palmer at all. Just as she opened her mouth to speak, she heard Lulu walk in the front door.

"It's like this," she finally opened her mouth. "I know God is within me. I simply know it," she said with a grin, hearing the shrieking halleluiah coming from the hall.

Aimée turned to the parlor entry.

She saw Lulu's brown eyes grow as big as saucers, and both her hands clapped.

"Come here." Gram drew Aimée in close to her breast and let her cry. "I must say it shows, dear. Palmer should have seen it himself. And does he know you care about him as well?"

Aimée's head shot up. "You can tell?"

"No tears of sadness here, only tears of joy shall fall from your eyes, as it should be."

"I just know'd it!" announced Lulu from behind her. "Yas'm, I did. I could tell by the way you been walkin' around, Miss Aimée. Now I'm hearin' it straight from your mouth!" Lulu turned and ran outside.

Aimée turned back to Gram.

"I need to sit down a spell, honey. Come with me out on the porch. I want to hear all about it. Better yet, follow me up stairs. I want to give you something."

They walked up into Gram's personal sanctuary — where she explained she spent time talking to God, where she and her Palmy had taken separate, but adjoining rooms twenty years earlier.

One of the walls was covered with shelves of books — Gram's personal library.

"You can come in here and find whatever you want to look through and read, Amethyst Rose." She directed towards the books. "But right now, this is what I want to give you."

Reaching up on a high shelf and set back from the rest, she pulled out a small leather-bound Bible. "This was my first book of scriptures. I got it from Palmy when we first wed. I want you to have it."

Just before she handed it to Aimée, she held it to her lips and gave it a kiss. "It has meant the world to me. I gave it to my first daughter-in-law, Anna Ross, the day she married Palmer II, our oldest boy. Anna was your Palmer's mother. She passed away when he was a boy. His father returned it to me."

"My Palmer."

She placed it in Aimée's hands and closed her hands around it. "I won't say anything about that, Aimée, if you prefer. But about your newfound faith, I promised myself the night you arrived, if you came to know God, I would give you one of my greatest treasures. And so I have," she finished.

"I — I don't know what to say, Gram," said Aimée, tears in her eyes.

"I'd rather you didn't say anything, child. If you read it that will be the greatest thanks I could receive.

Will you do that for me?"

"I will. I promise."

"God will bless you, child."

But deep down Aimée could not help worrying. And what Palmer would think when he discovered she now had his mother's treasured Bible?

* * * *

February 1865

It was frigid cold. Except for the spray of mud from yesterday's rain, the wheels of Philip and Aunt Beryl's carriage whipped up the dirt as it rolled northward where the snow-covered grounds blanketed both the roadway and the surrounding fields. As they rounded the bend and *Pencil Ridge* came into view, they both glanced out and smiled.

It felt good to be home.

"I hope you two don't think we're surprised!" declared Gram with a huff when she watched them walk through the door. "I wondered when you'd return," she added playfully a few minutes later, a twinkle shining in her eyes.

"Mama, hush!" said Beryl.

"You run off on me, girl, and left me with a bunch of rebel servants, most who upped and skedaddled, too. Almost everyone left me and your pop holding the bag around here."

Once she said her peace, Gram hurried over, hugged her daughter's neck, and cried on her shoulder.

"It's good to be home, Mama, and it was no trouble at all. You may as well be nice. We're here now. Besides you'll be blubbering in no time."

Gram's daughter stepped back and gave her a lingering look. "You're glad to see Philip and me, I can tell." She hugged her again then looked around. "Where's Pop?"

"Out working with a couple of the field hands; we don't have many left these days. Polly had to go back to the fighting no sooner than he got here."

She saw Philip looking around. "Amethyst Rose is doing well, too. I figured you would ask about her next. She's out back feeding my chickens. Interested?"

"I'll go out and say hello," he said, smiling and giving Gram a huge hug. "In the meantime, how's my favorite girl? You look as young as ever!"

"Ah, quit," she answered, dismissing him, her cheeks growing hot.

He smiled broadly then pinched Gram's cheek as he hurried towards the door.

"Who's this I hear Gram?" yelled Pop coming in from the back of the house. "Is that Beryl's voice…and young PJ's?" His heavily booted feet announced his presence as he crossed the wood floor on his way through the house. "There you two are!"

"Safe and sound," said Gram.

A seldom seen smile crossed his face when he saw his sixty-year-old daughter.

"Sir, I trust all is well?" said Philip to Pop.

"The good Lord has been protecting us.

"And the Lebrún girl; is she fitting in?"

"Go see for yourself. You will be mildly surprised and pleased at the change in the girl," put in Gram.

"Yes, ma'am—I shall do that right now." Without further ado, Philip headed out the door.

* * * *

Philip found his way past the garden to the old barn and saw Aimée out back. She seemed different to him, standing there tossing cracked corn to the chickens.

He watched her in silence as she spoke out each of the chicken's names and bent down to pat their feathered backs. Most came right up to her as if she was an old friend.

Even a few of the other animals in the near pasture lingered close, he noticed. Were they mesmerized by her soft-spoken nature, her sweet spirit?

Amethyst Rose Lebrún –sweet spirit, soft-spoken nature?

Except for that week he had worked with her on The St Honorine, she had not once shown a spirit of *sweetness*, a heart tender, a nature soft-spoken, certainly not around the Yankees.

Was this the same girl?

When he walked towards the protective chicken wire, some dead leaves crumpled beneath his boots. He caught the expression on her face as she glanced up and their eyes met.

"Philip?" She straightened up and tossed the remainder of the corn down on the ground then started over his way. "I had no idea you were here! When did you arrive?" She glanced back down to where she had collected some eggs and gathered them into the fold of her skirt, allowing the tip of her petticoats to be in view.

"It's me all right, Aimée," said Philip.

"You'll have to excuse me while I…" Aimée's cheeks flushed, as she bent around to search for the basket she'd set down earlier.

He watched her in awe.

"I, uh, must look awfully silly, I know," she said with a giggle. "Do you see a little basket somewhere?" she asked, still looking around. "I can't seem to recall where I placed it."

"It's right here on the post." Philip reached for it and handed it over to her. "Need any help?"

"N-no." She laughed and took it with her free hand. "There."

His mouth curved.

Aimée worked the eggs gently into its cradle. "Now." She smoothed down her skirts, just as a couple of leftover kernels of dried corn splattered on the ground, drawing her feathered friends in close around her ankles.

She tried to step carefully over each as she headed for the gate of the pen. "We certainly don't want to break any of these precious eggs, now do we, girls?" she murmured softly to the hens.

"I see you have made a few friends." He lifted a brow.

"Precious, aren't they? They're Grams."

Philip stared at her. "I can imagine. Gram loves her girls. They treating you good? Gram and Pop, I mean."

"It's been wonderfully refreshing here." She stared at him and paused then went watched the chickens again.

"And are you missing your friend Jonathan?"

She glanced up and shook her head. "Not so much. Philip, seeing you…this is such a pleasant surprise! I also see…you aren't wearing a uniform."

"I'm on my way home to Ohio," he said. "Just thought I would say hello before I headed out. I brought my aunt here to visit her folks."

She frowned. "Must you leave so soon? You've only just arrived."

"You want me to stay, Aimée? How different from before." Philip's brow flickered. "May I be so bold as to ask why the change of thought?"

"It's just good to see a smiling face is all," she said, blushing.

"Gram would want me to stay. I have yet to decide. I wanted to see *you* before I made my decision about that, actually."

"Me?"

"Will you walk with me a moment, Aimée?"

* * * *

The two walked slowly back towards the back entrance of the house off the south garden where Pop had built a swing, its seat still damp from the earlier snowfall. It was too cold to sit out, but the garden smelled clean, fresh.

"What did you wish to speak to me about?" Aimée stopped to ask.

"About your sister. I'm sorry about the unfortunate illness which led to her death. I know it has been a while, but I never did get to tell you that."

"'Tis all right. She is at peace now."

"Is she?" he asked.

"Oh yes," said Aimée. "Much more now than she ever was there at that…that place. Florette found her peace with God, Lieutenant Jordan, Philip, and I know you played a great part in that. She wanted me to say a special thank you."

"She did?"

Aimée looked into Philip's tender eyes so like those of his cousin. "I truly *cannot* thank you enough for what you did."

Philip gazed at her and slanted his head. "You say your sister found peace with God?"

"She did." Aimée could only smile, her eyes sparkling as she watched him grin from ear to ear. "She said I was to tell you that. It was you who opened her eyes, Philip. You! "

"It was nothing."

"Oh, no, it was *everything*! But there is more."

"There's more?"

Aimée reached out and clutched his hand. "May I?"

He gulped. "Why, yes."

Since Florette passed on, I too have found peace with God, Lieutenant—Philip," she whispered, "I, too." Aimée stared down at her feet.

"But this is splendid!" he said. "You don't know how happy you have made me!"

"I have?" Aimée cried.

"And I have to greatly apologize for the way I too treated you so unkindly…before," she gazed back up, "so unkindly before I departed New Orleans. I was despicable."

As she watched him look at her in silence she was amazed at the look on his face.

Suddenly in lightning-fast motion, Philip leaped awkwardly forward, grabbing the basket of eggs from her hand. After setting it on the ground, he seized her and pulled her to him. Before she knew it, he had her in his arms and was spinning her around in a circle.

Aimée nervously giggled and tried to draw back.

"Philip! Wh-what is it?"

He was gazing strangely into her eyes.

"*Good grief!* Philip, what *are* you doing? Don't you think you should put me down!"

After slowly setting her back down, he blushed.

"Amethyst Rose, Aimée, I have had you on my mind and in my heart for months now; in fact, I haven't been able to get you out of those thoughts for even one moment."

"You have?" She gulped and heard herself barely whisper in response.

"Oh Amethyst Rose," he rasped. "I—I simply have to kiss you!"

"You do?"

And before Aimée had a chance to fully recover, Philip leaned forward and kissed her fully on her lips while her eyes remained wide open, the rest of her standing in shock.

When she watched him suddenly pulled back, Aimée gasped.

In the next moment he was bending down on one knee before her.

She covered her mouth with her hand. "Oh Philip, what pray tell are you about to do *now*?"

As her eyes met his, shock ran through her.

* * * *

Philip paused for what seemed like forever.

And then the proposal came.

"Would it be too bold for me to ask if, peradventure, you would allow me to court you, Aimée, my darling?" he pleaded. "Please tell me you will say yes. 'Tis my greatest desire! I want to take you with me when I go…when I go west into the mission field. I think—I think I have fallen in love with you."

Philip exhaled a long sigh of contentment and gazed her longingly. When his proffer was complete, he slowly rose, more crimson-faced.

It took a moment for the disbelief of what he had just done to hit him with full force. Never before had Lieutenant Philip Jacobus Jordan sought a close relationship, even clumsily, with *any* woman. Weren't these the very words he had planned to deliver back home to his girl, Mary Ann O'Hare? Now, he had just poured out his heart to another woman.

What have I just done?

He was usually a logical, calculating man. He liked to plan his days. He liked to plan his entire life.

This was not how it was supposed to be. When he saw the look on the face of the woman before him and heard her answer come without pause he recognized his mistake immediately.

* * * *

Chapter Fifteen

"Though I thank you for the lovely kiss and proposal, Philip," said Aimée, smiling gently, "it was exquisitely sweet, I—I would have to say no. I truly apologize"

Aimée again looked down at the cold earth and then back up at his reddened face. She watched his tender eyes. Would he understand if she tried to explain?

"Is it the way I went about it? I cannot explain why I did that."

"No, 'tis not that at all."

"I'm a Yankee soldier, I know."

"'Tis not that either...you see, Philip..." but Aimée could not go on.

She could not tell the lieutenant that deep down, she was in love with someone else against her own wishes. She hated herself for it. The last person in the world she had planned to have feelings for was Captain Palmer Jordan III.

Why does it have to be the captain when he thinks so little of me? Why can't I love Philip, this man of such gentle character?

She already knew the truth deep down.

The mighty warrior from the north had stolen her heart from day one even through her bitterness and hatred...even through her time of wishing herself removed from the earth.

"Does he know it yet, Aimée?"

"He?"

"Yes, he—Palmer."

"Palmer..." she said softly, ingesting the word...drawing out the name.

Philip knew it too, just like Gram.

"Yes, Aimée. How long now?"

"I would prefer not discussing Palmer…if you don't mind."

"I understand perfectly, and I apologize for my forwardness. It was wrong of me to put you on the spot like that. I would like to renew our friendship at least…as we had before. Maybe we should talk about something else…say the details of your conversion…something like that?"

"I would like that."

He ran his fingers through his tousled hair. "I promise I won't bring up my cousin again…unless of course you wish to. Shall we go in?" He touched the small of her back and guided her back to the house towards the parlor. "Let's not speak of *him* again, okay?"

"Let's not."

"Aimée…" He stopped to look again into her face.

Aimée turned and met Philip's eyes.

"If you ever change your mind about…I mean, I just want you to know you can tell me anything. I'll be around if you ever need to talk."

"You are a dear, Philip. But…let's just leave him out of this, shall we?

"Consider it done."

* * * *

"Is it time for tea, Aunt Beryl?" asked Philip as they entered the parlor.

"Aimée, Philip," she said from across the room. "You are just in time." She turned to Aimée. "Aimée, have you heard the news of your aunt? A letter is coming soon."

"No," said Aimée. "Did you see her before you and the lieutenant rode up?"

"I did, and before I left she sent her love, both her and the good Captain Moreau," she said. "He paid your aunt a visit. He even attended church with her a few times."

"Dear Captain Moreau?" exclaimed Aimée with a smile.

"He came to see you at your sister's and ended up at your aunt's. She had him over for Sunday supper, and I was invited to join them," she went on. "He took right to her!"

"A budding romance I think!" Philip said with a laugh.

"It's about time Fran found herself a man to help her prune her roses before spring. She deserves it," Beryl finished.

"Does Captain Moreau know why I'm up here and about the captain and the pretense of a wedding?" Aimée asked.

"He knows it all," answered Philip

"And he understands?"

"Perfectly."

"Suppertime is soon upon us," said Gram at the door. "Pop should be returning soon."

"Let me help you." Aimée got up and headed out of the room.

"I didn't know if we should bring it up while Aimée was here or not, but do you think we should mention anything to Aimée about that Proctor fellow visiting Mrs. Simpson, Aunt Beryl?" asked Philip to Aunt Beryl.

"I haven't said anything yet. I didn't want to spoil her joy. She is so happy here. I guess she will know soon enough whatever he wanted from her aunt. Fran was going to inform the man that Aimée was married and be done with it."

"Was she convincing?" asked Philip.

"I expect to receive a letter from her any day now. I imagine she will update me about their meeting then, It should be quite interesting."

"Philip went back to Ohio, Palmy," said Gram. "He's decided to go west alone." She stood at the door of the library, watching her husband. "But he said he'll come back and see us before he goes."

Gram thought her husband looked too tired from the physical workload of his now neglected ranch with so few field hands left to help him. Washington Irving and his son, Jeb, were the only two field hands he had left who had faithfully stayed on.

She stared at him closer.

He told her it might have been because of Jeb's slow mind that they stayed on. It was all Mr. Irving could do to help him, especially since his wife Ertha had passed away. She'd been a weak woman anyway, always catching whatever ailed everyone else. Everyone at *Pencil Ridge* said the consumption had overtaken her rapidly.

"You feeling okay, Palmy?"

He didn't look up. "Time sure is moving faster these days, ain't it, wife?"

She walked into the room further. "What's up, husband?"

"It's time, that's what." He looked down at a list of names on the paper in front of him and mumbled them out as he tapped the pen on the desk. Scanning his way through the pages of his will one more time, he motioned her toward the desk. He dipped his quill in the inkwell once again to make his final notations. "Will you make sure I don't leave anyone out?"

"Did you remember to cross off your firstborn's name like I told you to last week, Palmy? You never did years ago when he died."

He looked up and scowled.

"I know you," Gram interrupted. "You've been reminiscing about that boy for years, but he's not coming back. You know that. He never once was interested in this place once he found his love for the sea."

"What can I say?" he complained. "The boy had a real character flaw, not normally a Jordan trait, of course."

"And God took him and then his wife, Anna," Gram said. "I sometimes wonder if she didn't die of a broken heart."

"I don't like to think about it."

"Maybe if we had not ended up with Polly, you would not have discovered *his* love for ranching. He adores this place, and you know it. Did you read his letter?" asked Gram.

Pop shook his head. He glanced down beside his old blotter and spotted the envelope. "Here it is." With a deep yawn, he picked it up and opened it. "Polly's on his way here it says. Did you know he was coming? In fact, the post date was three weeks ago. I suspect he'll be arriving anytime."

"I knew." She smiled.

"Good, because it's time I have that talk with the boy, officially."

"Yes, husband."

"This place has to be handed down soon."

Gram walked over to her balding husband and rubbed his shoulders. She'd seen his exhaustion and the unsteady pace in his walk during the last several months. He also could no longer stand as ramrod straight as in the past.

"Do you think he'll be ready to take over and well, put us out to pasture, so to speak?"

He laughed his deep-throated chuckle and reached up to smooth back what was left of his white thinning hair. "I'm ready, aren't you?"

"I've been ready for a long, long time–probably ever since this old war began."

* * * *

When Palmer came in through the front door, Lulu caught sight of him first. "If it ain't the mighty warrior man!" she hollered from across the room. "Welcome home!"

"Miss Aimée," he heard her turn to yell up the stairwell, "your warrior, that other one, him here!" She looked back at him and with her smiling eyes nodded. "Fightin' over yet?"

"Just about, Lulu," he muttered quietly. "In the meantime, I could use some hot water and some warm breakfast, if there's anything in the house to eat. Haven't eaten for two days; is the cook about?"

"Ain't no cook no more. She run off with the rest. But somebody will cook you up somethin'. Ain't much to pick from."

"Anything'll do."

Palmer still felt the effects of the brisk winds, which left him chilled to the bone. He'd been anxious to get back to *Pencil Ridge*—the only home he truly loved.

He knew many other soldiers who were on their way home now as well, as things concerning the war were finally winding down.

He appeared tired, and after a closer observation, Lulu came in to see he was limping and his arm was in a sling. "How come you's all banged up?"

Palmer shrugged. "Well, I am a bit, aren't I, but I have to tell you, I'm much better this morning than I was a week ago." He turned to see Gram and Pop standing in the foyer.

"It's Polly all right!" she said. "We got your correspondence, son, but weren't sure when you'd be arriving. Is it all over? Hey! What's happened here?" Gram hurried over and examined his arm.

"You said nothing about being injured in your post," stated his grandfather, giving him a big hug and leading him into the parlor. "You have some news, I see."

Palmer gave them both a wide smile. "I was wounded up north three weeks back," he replied. "Found myself in the middle of a skirmish. Not too many were hurt but enough to release about twenty of us. The war is supposed to end soon, I'm told, so I'm not concerned about the shoulder or foot. They'll heal up, soon enough. Just relieved to be here…finally."

"What's Lincoln going to do?"

"We should be hearing something soon. A few things to work out still, I understand."

"We remember him every night in our prayers. Maybe we'll know more by Sunday," said Gram. "Pastor tells us everything soon as he hears!"

"Did Henry and Elizabeth know you were coming here instead of going home?"

"Uncle Henry knew," said Palmer. "Besides, this is home to me not Ohio. You know that, Pop."

"We know. In fact there's something I want to discuss with you about that very thing this morning."

Gram rose. "I'll leave you two then."

"If I could get something in my stomach, Pop, I could more easily carry on a conversation. You don't mind if I eat first. I'm starving."

"I'll meet you in there," said Gram from the hallway.

Palmer sat in the kitchen a few minutes later and wolfed down five scrambled eggs, helping himself to the fresh bread baked from the day prior, savoring each fresh cut slice. "How'd you come up with these eggs and bread? I thought we had little to eat."

Gram stood by the counter, turned, and smiled. "We've not lost a chicken one, and I save each and every egg. My cellar has all kinds of food. That's how we're able to help the neighbors. I tell you, God is watching over us!"

"The bread? You can't be keeping that in the cellar! I know how much flour cost these days."

"Amethyst Rose baked that," she said before she headed to the door. "Just some flour I hung on to from before."

"How is the girl, anyway? Didn't run off, huh? I have to say I am somewhat surprised." He gave a slight chuckle. "Didn't know the waif could actually cook. All I ever saw in her was…oh, never mind," he mumbled.

"You may be surprised," declared Pop at the door.

"Why? What have you two done…tame her?" With a laugh, Palmer went on. "Is she still upset about our spurious marriage contract, or has she settled in around here as the effervescent *Mrs. Jordan* for all the neighbors to see…at least for the time being?"

He laughed again. "She shouldn't have to play the game much longer now that we are away from those scoundrels down in New Orleans. I'm sure she'll be relieved to hear that. By now, she must be ready to go off on her own, what with the war winding down. It'd probably be for the best...for me...for all of us," he trailed off.

His grandmother scowled, then spoke up. "Who's the charitable here? After all, weren't you the one who brought her up here?"

Palmer looked up. "What's that?"

"I don't think you disfavor the girl so much as you are pretending, now do you, Polly?" She held up her hand.

"What's that?" He stopped chewing.

"By the way, young man, PJ was here. He and the girl spent a good deal of time together...talking."

"Oh?"

"Too bad you missed him. He's gone up to Ohio to see your sister Annabelle and his folks. He didn't say for sure when he was returning."

Walking back to take Palmer's empty dish, she turned and spoke again with just a hint of sarcasm, "But he's thinking about *who* he will take West with him. They had an interesting conversation I must say, Polly. *You* should've been here."

Palmer arched one of his brows and stared after his grandmother. "If you mean him and her together, I think the lad and I should have a bit of chat soon." He scratched his neck.

"I need to speak with you, son." Pop glowered at Gram, changing the subject. "Are you ready to talk some business, Palmer, or do you need to rest that foot some more? Seems to me the wife here is about to insert hers where it need not be."

She shrugged her shoulders.

"I'll be okay. Let me finish washing up, Pop, and get the rest of this grime off me."

"Your gram will have Lulu get you some water on for a lengthy soak later. I need you to come with me. Besides, if I don't get you out of here soon, somebody in the kitchen here is going to stick her nose where maybe it shouldn't be. Isn't that right, wife?"

Palmer gazed at them both. "Uh oh."

Gram moved quickly out of sight.

The two men rose and headed towards Pop's study.

Palmer started to turn at the sound of soft steps at the bottom of the stairs.

* * * *

Although Lulu had brushed out Aimée's tresses, she was the only one who knew how to fasten them up the way Aimée liked them.

Now, Aimée wished she had finished her job before running out. It was considered improper to be walking around the house without her hair pinned up and no slippers on one's feet, but at least no one was around to see. Maybe she could slip through the house unaware… if she hurried

Stopping short at the bottom of the stairs, she watched as the door of the study shut behind the two men, she hurried to the door of the kitchen to see if Lulu was in there.

"Lulu," she called out as loudly as she dared, "are you in there? I need hot water in the big tub. I also need you to finish my hair. Hurry back upstairs and help me."

"Oh, my." Her servant came running in from the back and pulled back the door of the pantry to see her.

"I'm comin', Miss Aimée, fast as I can. I weren't in the kitchen. You get yourself back up them steps before somebody sees you there with your hair tricklin' down your back and your feets stickin' out. You just missed the men from the study and this ain't like standin' back at them docks! My, My!"

"I'm going. But hurry with you! Where have you been?"

Aimée turned back as Lulu rushed back and finished pouring the heated water into some buckets then ran over and grabbed some drying towels and a homemade bar of soap. She then hurried to Mr. Jordan's study while the water sat in the tub steaming.

"Is you in there Mr. Captain Sodure Man?' she hollered through the door. "Your water, I got it ready."

Not waiting for his answer, she turned and clipped up the stairs towards Miss Aimée's room.

* * * *

Palmer eyed his grandfather. He looked overtired.

"Give me a few minutes to gather up the paper work I need," he stated.

"No rush." Palmer closed his eyes briefly and thought drearily about the steaming water waiting for him. He sighed.

As he waited, the thoughts lingering on his mind from the past sped forward as they had so many times over the last several weeks.

How long would he and Aimée play the marital game? He hadn't planned to continue the charade once he arrived at *Pencil Ridge*. By now, she would surely be wanting to leave.

One thing that kept surfacing was his ceaseless interest in the woman which was driving him wild. Angry with himself about it all, he had to admit, she had been in his thoughts for weeks, no, not weeks, rather months—since the first day he saw her in her filthy rags, bare of foot, and smelling tart.

Every morning, every evening, the girl tiptoed back into the recesses of his mind—almost every time he spoke his prayers. Constantly she surfaced, and she was affecting his judgment.

It was good the grandparents took her in the way they did. If miracles were to happen, maybe a little of his grandmother might rub off on the tenacious girl. Maybe she'd even become approachable...someday.

It didn't matter, though. He'd fallen in love with Amethyst Rose Lebrún just the way she was.

"That's the problem," he nodded.

"What's that?" asked Pop, finishing up. "I saw your lips move but didn't catch the comment."

"Uh, no, no, I didn't say anything. I'm just sitting here thinking." Palmer took his right hand and rubbed at the scruff of his growing beard along his chin. "I, uh, need to give myself a shave. Will this take long?"

216

"Nope. I'm about ready to sign the ranch over to your care, that's all."

Palmer stared long and hard at his grandfather. "What did you say? You aren't ill are you, Pop?"

"No, but it's time, son. Let's get to it. The place, this place, it is to be yours."

The eyes of the younger Palmer widened as he looked on at his beloved. "I—I am indeed honored, *Grandfather*, I am even surprised. I don't know what to say. I was not expecting this! Not now."

"You have already made known your care and love for *Pencil Ridge* just by your actions over the years. Your father knew how much you were a part of this place. That's why he brought you here as much as he did. Your Uncle Henry doesn't want it, nor does your cousin. Neither have been much love for ranching. Henry's perfectly content with his ministry and the Ohio property. You know PJ is going into the mission field and wants to head out west. I spoke to him and your sister already.

"Aunt Beryl?"

"She would like to continue to maintain her townhouse down in Louisiana and have a place to stay up here when she feels like it. I've already spoken to her, too. She's not interested in the responsibilities of an entire plantation. Looks like you were the only one who didn't know."

"I'm speechless."

"Besides, there's plenty to the Jordan Estate— enough to go around for all!" He opened his inkwell and handed Palmer the quill. "Shall we sign then?"

* * * *

"He's here?" Aimée bit her lip. "I had no idea."

"Oh, yes, Miss Aimée, as big as life. I held off telling you 'till afta' you took your sudsin'. You gonna tell your warrior man about your happy heart?" Lulu looped up her tresses around her ears.

217

"That man is not *my* warrior man. He does not want to be. I doubt the good captain would be interested in anything about me. The man hates me."

Lulu stood behind her mistress and shook her head, her eyes on Aimée's back through the mirror. "I knows how you feels about the good captain, Miss Aimée. You may be su'prised about the sodure man and his ways! Sides! Good Christians, they don't hates nobody!"

Aimée sat quiet. Watching Lulu help to groom her, she thought about what the girl had just said. More often than not, her Lulu was wiser beyond her years.

Maybe the captain did not *hate* her so much, but she knew good and well he certainly was not partial to her! But that was her own fault.

How many times had she reminded herself the captain had not exactly forced her into the silly farce of a marriage? She had accompanied him North all by herself.

Still, what was she going to do now? And how or when was she ever going to get home to *Shadow Grove*? She couldn't stay at *Pencil Ridge* forever.

Would she even get to see her papa's land again? Even if it was charred? It seemed as if she was now a million miles away from Vicksburg. It might as well have been a million years.

"Ever'thing is going to be all right Miss Aimée," Lulu reassured her, "I just knows it."

A solitary tear rolled down Aimée's cheek. "We'll see, Lulu." She reached for her hanky and wiped her cheek.

"We'll see."

* * * *

By the time Aimée found her way down the stairs to the Parlor, she realized lunch had long past. Gram was already taking afternoon tea.

"I wondered what had become of you. Did you take ill, child?"

"I needed some time, Gram. It had nothing to do with you. By this summer, it will be two years for my

218

family. Once again, I realize how much I miss them. I apologize for missing lunch."

"You've nothing for which to apologize. I understand why you've chosen not to discuss them. I'm also sure you understand days like this will arise now and again. Eventually, they will fade. Even I still have moments of sadness concerning my eldest son, Palmer. We called him Palmer Jr.", said Gram. "After years of his being gone I must say, my husband and I have been fortunate in comparison to many."

She patted the chair next to her. "Come over here, and join me. I had Lulu bring in an extra cup and saucer in case you want some tea."

"I would like that," Aimee said.

"I expect the men will be returning in an hour or so." Gram poured the liquid. "Milk? Sugar?"

"Please. Have they been gone long?"

"Drink up dear, while I pour you some more and we'll continue to chat."

"Left before noon to inspect some of the grounds. Honestly, I don't know how young Palmer can get around with that maimed foot."

"The captain…wounded? I had no idea."

"Oh, yes, quite, so," she declared, raising a brow, adding a lilt in her voice and a twinkle in her eye. "Perhaps he's home for good now. That means," she continued, "It means you will be seeing a great deal of each other." She turned her head away.

"I had no idea. What happened?"

"Oh, I'm sure he'll want to tell you that himself. 'Tis such a pity. This war and all. I think we have all had enough of this fighting and fussing. Don't you agree?"

Aimée nodded slowly. "What was it like here before the conflict began?"

"'Twas a country near as beautiful as heaven," she said. "You would have loved it, Amethyst Rose."

"I love it now."

"Virginia is a green lush land, like no other. 'Tis not so bad right now…in places…but in so many others…"

Aimée agreed. "Back home as well. Vicksburg endured the worst I think."

"I have never been to your homeland, but I've heard nice things about your Mississippi. Our first son found his bride down that way. Maybe someday I can get down there for a visit. Then again, perhaps not. I'm eighty now, much too old for all that."

"You look magnificent—not a day over five and sixty!" Aimée smiled.

"Such a tease you are!" Gram laughed.

"Not at all! I wish you could have met my family. I also have an older brother, David, who resides in France. I have not seen him in years. He was several years older than the sister who passed away."

"Your older brother—he's been gone a long time?"

"I was considerably young when he left. My family comes from France, and there is land over there. I was told he went to help my Grandpère until his death."

"I'd love to hear more about it sometime." Gram leaned in to pour them both another cup of tea. "So when will you tell Polly?" She asked finally, changing the subject.

"Tell Polly?"

"Polly—the boy," Gram replied, laughing. "When are you going to tell my grandson you've lately had your sights for him like we spoke about the other day and that you are now a woman of faith...like the rest of us? He needs to know. It would make all the difference dear."

Aimée reddened. "I—I certainly do not intend, well, that is not exactly..., oh, Gram." She sighed.

"Yes?" Gram held up her chin.

"I don't know if he would be at all interested in the fact that I—that I care," Aimée covered her face then looked up into Gram's eyes. "And I don't think it would matter to him that I am now a believer. I—I hadn't really thought about doing any true confessions with the man."

"Perhaps 'tis just as well." Gram's brows lifted. She took Aimée's hands and placed them between her own. "You're planning to disappear from our lives soon, anyway, I understand. You wouldn't want to entangle yourself with someone for whom you have so much animosity, right?"

"Animosity?"

Gram fixed her eyes on her. "Well, isn't that what you have mostly shown him lately?"

Aimée had never known anyone quite like Mattie Jordan before.

"Here," Aimée stood. She reached out her arm. "Let me take the tray back to the kitchen for you, Gram." She desperately wanted to change the subject. "I just remembered I had something I needed to do up in my room. You will forgive me, but I cannot join you for needlework this afternoon. Call me down to help you with supper?"

"I'll call. You go now, and Aimée…"

Aimée stopped.

"Forgive me for intruding, dear. 'Tis an unfortunate habit, difficult to break for an old woman such as I."

Aimée leaned down and gave her a hug. "You have nothing for which to apologize, sweetheart." With a smile, she left the room.

Why was it when she was around people, apologies were always in order for some reason?

Chapter Sixteen

After unlacing her boots and kicking them off, Aimée plopped on her bed. She leaned back against her pillow and stared up at the textured ceiling with her hands behind her head, watching the shadows from the tree limbs outside the window sway slightly from the breeze. She was more tired than she thought, though she hadn't done a thing.

She moved her head from side to side her mind on a million things…three men to be exact.

Why couldn't Philip have been enough to satisfy her heart? Why was it, her heart instead rended for the one the only Captain Jordan when she kept trying to convince herself she did not care?

And then there was Jonathan! Why in the world did he have to die! Would it have made any difference to her if he were now alive?

Aimée yawned.

All three young men who'd occupied her life over the last few years swirled through her head.

Jonathan Dewey — the charmer…the one she had not once developed a love for. She had actually been willing to be his bride… for her father's sake.

In all the years, Aimée had known him and his family, not once had any of *them* mentioned God or heaven in a respectful sort of way. Was it only his boyish charm which drew her girlish-interest? 'Twould never have been enough! She knew that now.

Poor Jonathan. Indeed, it was sad he had to die.

What about kind, loveable, generous Philip — the man who introduced her sister to the forgiveness of God? He was certainly a good man. His life was set, his future laid out. He was one who knew exactly what he wanted.

He wanted her.

But Philip you weren't enough for me.

He didn't have what she wanted.

She shook her head.

When her mind strayed to Palmer Jordan—the handsome, valiant, unshakable captain who'd been there right from the start…watching her from not only the first harbor in Vicksburg, but in New Orlean's as well. Everywhere she turned God had placed him in her path.

How could she miss him with those dimpled cheeks and moon-like eyes of liquid hazel?

She could still hear that whispered phrase he'd called out to her that first morning. The one that came to her ears during that most difficult time of her life.

"God speed to you, ma'am." Ever-so-clearly she'd heard him say it, but she'd never told him so. In the fog of that capricious dawn, Aimée remembered well one man's simple regard for her to have success on her early journey. She knew now the man meant spiritual success.

Back then, she had refused to acknowledge him.

She desperately wanted to be noticed by him now. Would it matter to him that her feelings for him had changed?

Would it make a difference if she told him about her faith?

Or would Palmer forever have no use for her after the way she'd treated him.

* * * *

While Aimée rested in her chamber, Gram made her own plans by inviting the Smithys over for supper as a surprise.

"Is Palmer the reason you have invited the Smithys over, Mama?" Beryl asked as she peeled the potatoes. She glanced over at her skeptically. "You're scheming again, aren't you?"

"Me, scheming?" Gram's eyes twinkled.

"Well, it's the first time the Smithys and their daughter, Cornelia, have been invited to join us here. I've heard the rumors about Cornelia and her hankering for Palmer. So what are you doing, Mama?"

"Not a thing. Polly hasn't turned an eye that woman's way. Maybe I enjoy the company of Genevieve, her mother," reasoned Gram. "I thought Aimée and Palmy would enjoy their company as well."

Beryl glanced over at her. "Perhaps. I don't know them much myself, but I know of Cornelia mostly through talk from the others. What is she—the ripe old age of five and twenty now? I've also heard that most of this community has a hard time…well, never mind."

"Can't a soul do a kind deed now and then?" asked Gram.

"Just being courteous then, are you, Mama? I really think you should have told Aimée." Beryl shook her head.

"Did someone mention my name?" Aimée called out from the door of the kitchen. She walked over to where Gram stood checking on her meat.

"I was just waiting for Lulu to get back from the carriage house. I would've sent for you." Gram glanced over at Beryl and frowned. "We have company coming for supper."

* * * *

Aimée couldn't help but frown when Lulu walked in. What was that girl doing never being around anymore?

"You folks lookin' for me?" she hollered from the hall. "Well, here I is."

For the last few weeks, Aimée had a slight fear in the back of her mind Lulu might soon be leaving her. After all, the girl had lately become scarcer, after having gotten friendlier with the stableman. Were the two of them about to take off like all the rest?

"It no longer matters, Lulu," she said. "I'm downstairs now, but my room needs tidying up."

"Yas'm, 'n then I'm hopin' we could talk some."

The look on Lulu's face confirmed Aimée's fears.

She is leaving me. I'm sure of it.

"I can talk with you after supper tonight, Lulu; how's that?"

"Yas'm," she mumbled, walking off.

Aimée watched her go back out the back door and head for the barn instead of up to her room as directed.

She must be planning to leave!

* * * *

As she received her guests at the dinner table, Gram saw how Aimée shined, until the garrulous Cornelia Smithy, who sat at Palmer's right, took over the conversation. From then on, it remained uncomfortably quiet in the rest of the dining room.

She frowned as Cornelia's chair scraped the floor when she slid her dining chair in closer to the captain, leaning in against him, making it difficult for him to lift his utensil with his good arm.

That wasn't my plan at all!

Gram lowered her head and lifted her eyes as Polly glanced over at her with question. She wanted to say she was sorry, but it was too late now.

Across from both Cornelia and Palmer, Gram could see the girl's father, Desmond, attempting to gain the attention of his daughter to correct her.

The young woman was becoming an embarrassment to him. She ignored him. As the meal progressed, if she was not chatting about nothing, she had an argumentative opinion about everything.

Genevieve, the woman's mother, on the other hand, glanced over at her husband with disapproval.

Gram wished now she had not been so presumptuous to think it was a good idea to invite the family over.

Poor Palmer, she mused.

As she observed the expressions on each face of the Smithy family one more time and then toward young Aimée, she noted how Cornelia's aging face had spawned a look of jealousy or so it certainly seemed.

And by the Smithy woman's plethora of wrinkles, Gram was also noting perhaps for the first time, Cornelia certainly was moving further and further away from marriageable age.

No wonder the family is desperate for the girl!
More than likely her relationship with Palmer had been discussed in the Smithy home more often than not and what was going to be done about her.

Gram knew the Smithys wanted to get their daughter married off soon and it was Palmer Jordan she wanted.

It all came down to finances. The Smithys were broke!

Gram had hoped this dinner, and Cornelia seeing Polly with Amethyst Rose would take care of any false hopes and dreams.

But now that she watched the two of them from across the table she saw that she couldn't have been more mistaken.

Me and my bright ideas.
Gram suddenly lost her appetite.

* * * *

Palmer pushed back his chair and stood up. "Shall we leave the women?"

"Sounds good," Pop said. "I'll have Lulu bring us some of Gram's blackberry cordial she made a while back and hid in the cellar. We can depart for my study, men."

All three men rose and stepped away from the table to wait for the women to leave for the parlor.

"Mrs. Jordan?" said Mr. Smithy. He turned back toward Aimée. "I enjoyed our enlightening conversation." Smiling at her gently, he added, "From your brief description of your father, Mr. Lebrún sounded like a genuine sort. I would have enjoyed meeting the chap. He must've been extremely proud of his daughter."

Palmer walked over without warning and touched the small of her back. "I never had the privilege of meeting her family, did I, my sweet?" His breath warmed her neck.

"No."

"Excuse me," Genevieve interrupted, stepping forward to glower at her husband. The gurgling sound of her throat drew attention her way. "You should've been more involved with the conversations of the rest of us, instead of occupying all your time with this poor girl. You've upset her, Desmond, bringing up her dead father. The man's dead. Can you not see you've sapped the girl of all color?"

She pointed at Aimee's draining face. "Any woman could see she's beginning to look sickly. Let the dead bury the dead, I always say. Don't you agree, Palmer, darling?"

Palmer leaned in. "Excuse me, Mrs. Smithy. Aimée is just fine, if you don't mind."

The older woman frowned and bent down to tap Palmer's bride on the shoulder as if to attempt to show comfort.

"What do you know young man!"

"I said…Aimée is just fine, folks," said Palmer again patting her hand.

"Go on now," Genevieve Smithy threw her head back, ordering everyone out of the area, swinging her arm towards the door. "We women have things to talk about that concern you little. This girl needs some air."

Hurrying over by her side, Cornelia said, "Mama, I, too, noticed Daddy was ignoring the rest of us at dinner. 'Twas extremely rude of him."

"Go in the parlor and sit down and shut up, Cornelia."

"Yes, Mama."

Palmer leaned down and whispered in Aimée's ear. "You can stay here with the others, Aimée, or if you prefer I will even take you out for a breath of fresh air. I can't guarantee which of these women is the lesser of the two evils to be around to be honest with you."

She gritted her teeth. "Thanks for the warning. I might as well stay and face the music."

* * * *

The warmth of the parlor was almost too much or perhaps it was the present company.

227

After Aimée played a couple of tunes on the pianoforte at Gram's request, she prayed silently the evening would speed by. She soon noted the Smithy women were not at all interested in her musical abilities, let alone her melody choices.

Aimée rose from the piano bench to return to her chair, noting with surprise Palmer was standing at the door listening.

"Impressive!" He clapped his hands. "Perhaps you will bless us another tune and your gracious talents. I had no idea!"

She blushed.

He stepped back into the study and shut the door behind him.

Aimée heard a throat clearing across from her.

"Perhaps he was searching for you, Cornelia," said Genevieve. "Did you want to go and see?"

"No, Mama," she replied, frowning. "He was here for her! How come you never taught me the pianoforte?"

"You wouldn't sit still long enough to learn!"

Cornelia turned back to Aimée. "With a bit more practice, you may someday actually be good."

"You are too kind." Aimée returned with an acerbic smile.

"By the way, didn't you have a young man back in Alabama or the Appalachian Mountains of Georgia or from wherever it is you hail?" Cornelia snickered. "How did you happen to snatch up my Palmer?"

Aimée was in no mood to discuss Jonathan *or* the captain.

"By the way," Cornelia went on, her brows narrowing, "You might as well explain it all tonight, anyway. I've done my best to hold it in. I haven't even told Mama. Do you want to tell the truth, Amethyst Rose, or shall I?"

"Shall you what?" queried Aimée. "I don't know what's on your mind."

"Cornelia?" Genevieve's eyes were wide.

Cornelia's jaw twitched. She lifted her chin to speak again. "I happen to know this woman and Palmer are not married at all as they would have us believe!"

Genevieve's eyes bulged as she slowly looked first Aimée's way then towards Gram.

"Why the pompous game, *Miss Lebrún*, for that is your *true* name, and how long must you continue to live this farce here at *Pencil Ridge*? What is this…this game you play, intruding on the Jordan family? Don't you think it rather childish, if not the least bit scandalous?" Cornelia snorted.

Gram started too speak, until Aimée's hand flew up to hold her off. There were too many questions, too much probing, but all three women deserved an answer.

Aimée hesitated at first then spoke. "It's not that difficult to explain. There was someone else—back home in Vicksburg, Mississippi, my home. We were to be wed. The banns were written; the date was set."

"What happened?" probed Cornelia, "Did the man reject you?" She snickered again.

"Apparently he must have," put in Genevieve.

"'Twas not that way at all. My betrothed was ordered to report to his post a couple of days before we were to say our vows, but soon after he left, he became missing-in-action," said Aimée. "His family got word he was in all probability killed, as were so many others."

She paused. "Indeed this *is* a time of war! After a space of time, they held his funeral and returned to their home country."

Aimée reached into her sewing basket for her sampler and studied her stitches. It was difficult to go on. "I was…I was in an environment that—that could've become, let me say, detrimental to my health. That's when the captain came along. Palmer removed me from that dreadful place in which I found myself. He rescued me…"

Aimée refused to say anymore.

"He was a foreigner!" Genevieve whispered just loud enough for everyone to hear.

"Not like that!" Aimée contradicted.

"What environment could have been so *dreadful*?" asked Cornelia. "And he *rescued* you? It sounds intriguing. You say your betrothed came from a family of foreigners?" She shuddered. "From some distant continent perhaps? 'Tis uncanny you would be drawn to an *foreigne*."

"Cornelia," her mother said, "don't press the issue. He was probably all the girl could catch. Just be glad your Palmer didn't find himself missing-in-action, too. Could have easily happened to him and then where would you be? Look at the poor soul now, all maimed up as he is. Hopefully, he won't stay a cripple!"

"Genevieve!" Gram shouted," watching Aimée.

"'Tis a pity our men up and disappearing from us when they should be minding us at home is all I can say! And yes, Gram, cripple! That's all we need around here…more of them! They'll not be able to do anything, and we'll be stuck with all the work!"

Aimée watched as Cornelia crossed her bird thin legs and began to pout as her mother continued spouting off. Would the spiteful woman probe further, want more information than Aimée was willing to give?

"At least I have Desmond at home," Cornelia's mother said with a scowl. "I wouldn't allow them to take him, though I'm certain they would have.

"The Army wanted anyone with two legs and a pair of baggy trousers, Mama, even Daddy's."

"Well, I told them Desmond was deathly ill," said Genevieve.

"Genevieve," cried Gram, "you didn't! Perhaps Desmond might have *wanted* to serve with the others. They would have found something for him to do. If it weren't for our soldiers, why, I don't know where we'd be today…I tell you, I just don't know. Mark my words, Genevieve Smithy, we'd probably all be long gone by now. We certainly wouldn't be safe in our homes."

"Poppycock!" Genevieve spouted off. "What do you know?"

Aimée heard Aunt Beryl over in the corner clear her throat. She'd been quiet all evening. "What made you think Palmer and Aimée were not husband and wife, Cornelia?" She finally inserted.

She had asked the question on Aimée's mind.

"It was that slave talking to that ignorant stable hand, and, no, I was not listening in. I just *happened* to be going by the other day. I was coming to see the family, and she spoke loud enough for the world to hear, and that's the truth."

Exasperated, Aimée put her stitching back in the basket and rose suddenly to head towards the door. "If you'll excuse me."

She turned her head while the others stared after her. "My apologies, Gram, Aunt Beryl, I have developed a horrendous headache."

After a brief glance at Cornelia, she turned to walk out of the room.

* * * *

Aimée looked up from her writing desk when she heard the tap on her door. Lulu had finally come.

"Miss Aimée?"

"Come in, Lulu. It's open. I'm ready for you to comb out my hair."

Her maidservant entered slowly. In all of her ten and eight short years, she'd never once shown a hint of shyness towards her. Never once had she been frightened of her, nor once had she been hesitant to talk with Aimée about subjects important.

Tonight Aimée wasn't so sure.

"I got somethin' to say — Miss Aimée," she hemmed and hawed, wiggling her left leg. "You be wantin' me to fix your hair, so maybe I should before I says somethin'."

"Talk *as* you brush…as you always do. Come over here and don't dawdle."

"Miss Aimée?"

"You already said my name. What is it? Nothing surprises me, anymore — truly nothing! If it is about your slip of the tongue about Palmer and myself—I already know."

"It ain't that. I seen Miss Corny when I was talkin' at Abel, but she was snoopin' out to the stable is why. I wasn't sure what she done heard. I was going to tell you but then they all come to the house before I could get to you. But that ain't it. It be somethin' else."

"Such as when you are leaving?"

Lulu set the brush down on the table and stood behind Aimée stiffly. "Leavin'? Is I leavin', Miss Aimée?"

"Well, aren't you? Isn't that what this is all about?"

"No," she whispered.

Aimée blinked her eyes and creased her brows. "You aren't?"

"No!"

Rising from her chair, Aimée turned and looked at her. "Come with me. Let's sit down on the bed. We'll chat."

"I don't want to get your bed all crumpled. I ain't clean as you. I shouldn't be sittin' on your sleepin' stuff."

"Nonsense...now sit down!"

Lulu barely placed the weight of her body on the covers.

After plopping her down on the far edge, Aimée took a seat alongside her and placed her arm around the woman's shoulders.

"It's Abel," reasoned Lulu, "He be needin' me. He don't got no one. He don't talk and don't hear much. We worked it out, and we be wantin' to get wed."

Lulu studied Aimée's face. "We be wantin' you and your warrior man to come, 'cept I knows you prob'ly ain't feeling right coming down to our meetin' house with us who's different from you. But could you, Miss Aimée?"

Aimée pulled Lulu in and embraced her. "God bless you and Abel! You've been keeping secrets from me!"

Lulu shook her head. "No! I walk out to the barn in plain sight every day a good girl."

"No, no," said Aimée with another laugh. "I meant I didn't know both you and Abel had sights for each other! I do have to admit; lately I was beginning to wonder what was going on out there. I thought you were going to leave me."

"You be fambly." Lulu grinned wide. "Maybe one day me and Abel can get our own little place, instead of in the back of the barn where he is now. Don't need much…just somethin' over our head, so's we can have us a fambly, too."

Aimée continued laughing. "I'll see what I can do when I get you back home to *Shadow Grove*. How's that? In the meantime, could you finish with my hair? It needs the braid, so I can get some sleep for church tomorrow."

She gave her another hug. "Come time for that wedding, I would love to attend, Lulu. I cannot speak for the captain. Just tell me when, and I'll get myself there."

* * * *

All around, the melting snow left puddles. Spring had poked through from the cold of winter, leaving the scent of bursting buds in front of Pop and Gram's home. It felt good that morning.

Abel brought the carriage around for the family and waited by the door to assist anyone who would need help from the house. It would be the second Sunday Aimée would attend church with the family since Palmer had returned home, and everyone was excited.

The war had finally ended!

Since Reverend Goodman was known to receive the freshest news about everything and usually passed it on when it arrived, the entire community flocked to the church to hear the details.

The entire morning Aimée carried her new Bible close to her heart. Being careful not to harm it in any way, she still hesitated in opening it too much. She knew it was time she started reading it.

She wanted to locate the scriptures she'd come across while at her aunt's that played such a great part in opening her eyes…her heart…her soul. Perhaps, she could ask Palmer where she might find them. Then again, it would probably be best to ask anyone but him.

The family sat down along the Jordan bench, and several sets of eyes turned and were glued on the captain and his scandalous *bride,* thanks to Genevieve and Cornelia Smithy.

Aimée saw the raised eyebrows the moment they walked into the church.

Cornelia swung around on her bench and smiled at Palmer, in hopes Palmer would veer his head her way.

"Miss Smithy appears to be trying to gain your attention, Captain." Aimée nudged her head toward the girl.

"I'm not interested in *her.*" Palmer pointed at her Bible in her lap. "I'm surprised to see that always with you. Why do you carry it around when you probably don't read it?" he remarked, changing the subject.

Aimée curved toward him. "But it was—"

"In fact, why do you bother attending service at all? I don't understand it."

Aimée said nothing, but in response, picked the book back up and held it close.

"Who are you trying to fool? God is either real or He is not. What evidence have you given He is remotely of interest to you?"

Aimée tilted her face toward his and suppressed a sigh. "Is that all, Captain Jordan?"

* * * *

Something told him he had gone too far. Suddenly he felt like a heel. Palmer waited for her to face him again, so he could say something more, but it was too late.

When she didn't a few moments later, he attempted to put his mind on other things, grateful the good reverend had stood up and was walking to the podium to commence speaking. Just the same, his mind lingered on the woman sitting beside him longer than it should.

There had to be a way to get the girl back home and out of his life soon. It was the best way. After all, the war was over, why keep her there?

When the pianist began the notes of her selected hymn, the congregation stood to sing, and Palmer, who usually jumped right in, stood silently listening to the Aimée's voice.

He felt the presence of God speaking softly to his heart, telling him to forgive the girl and to be patient. How could he do that when she had not even thanked him once for assisting her all the times he had? God only knew how patient he had been up until now.

He listened to the news shared by Reverend Goodman as he lifted his flabby stub of a finger to draw the congregation's attention towards him when the music came to a poetic stop.

Everyone sat up straight to listen.

"As you know, people, on April 9th up in Richmond, almost to the day the first shot was fired back in '61, the war made its end as it began. I'm told the town evacuated; the good General Lee surrendered to General Grant."

The congregation waited together in hushed silence as the baldheaded, round-bellied Reverend Goodman before continuing. "There has been much sorrow and grief in all of our hearts lately, what with the recent news of the president's assassination. And yet you all have been strangely silent about that since they still have not located the assassin. I need you to listen to me my people."

Goodman lifted his chin. "For though we rejoice the battle has ended, together we mourn the passing of our beloved Mr. Lincoln, weeping for the loss of a great man."

The reverend reached up with his knuckle to wipe a tear from his eye. "I tell you this, my people, and I hope only to have to say it once. While we pray for the searchers, we must also remember this about the ending of the war…it's time for us to lay down our own arms of bitterness towards those who fought against us, especially for our brothers and sisters who love the Lord." The pastor stopped and moved his eyes across the congregation.

Swallowing his own tears, Palmer refused to acknowledge Aimée's as the reverend finished.

"Though you may sometimes feel as if you are drowning in the deepest of sorrows over your own personal losses, will you become scorched by the heat of life's fires that come against you? What does the Good Book say, folks? God is still with you and will see you through. Do not lose your trust in Him to see you through the difficult times. It is time to begin to show love, compassion, and forgive again. Shall we pray?"

Palmer's muscles tensed. *Love, compassion, and forgiveness, Lord. You know my heart. I think we have some talking to do in the days ahead.*

Chapter Seventeen

The family rode home in silence until Palmer heard Pop grunt. "Did you want to say something Pop?"

"What will you do now, son?"

"Now I have mended, I need to report back to Washington. I am due my promotion to Major. A lot of us officers have waited long and hard for this, and right now that's the most important thing on my mind. "

"Is it?"

"Unless they don't want me to return at all with this limp."

"I'd just as soon you were here with us."

Palmer took a sidelong glance at Aimée who he could tell had been listening while the others dozed. After the reverend had shared the news, Palmer remembered the other words he'd shared from the Book of Isaiah which had hit him hard.

The South had lost a difficult war. Palmer wondered if the girl would eventually be able to forgive and forget it all. After studying Aimée with a slight bit of sympathy, he shut his eyes.

He did not want to think about it now. He did not want to think about *her*.

The problem was he did...constantly.

* * * *

"My orders came!" announced Palmer at the breakfast table three days later. "As I thought, I'll be leaving in the morning for Washington. My promotion came in as I expected."

"Will you be gone long?" asked Gram.

"Can't say." He glanced up and nodded as Aimée entered the room. She walked behind him and sat down on the furthest chair at the table.

"You must go?" she asked softly.

"I am leaving."

"I—I wanted to speak to you about something."

"If you're desirous for me to get you back to New Orleans, I shan't let you down. I will do as I vowed when I return from Washington."

"I wasn't thinking about that," she mumbled.

His gram watched them both. "If you both will excuse me," she blathered, getting up and walking towards the hall, "I'll just make myself scarce. Talk nice, you two," she finished, and she was gone. When she disappeared, they both stared at the entryway, avoiding each other.

"What is it then?" Palmer asked, turning her way.

"I wanted to tell you, and with you leaving and all, I know I must for sure tell you now," Aimée replied rather sheepishly.

"What could you have to tell me now after all these months? You've chosen to speak nary a kind word to me since I brought you here."

"I know," she went on. "I feel the need first to apologize to you for my impoliteness. I've acted bitterly and unforgiving while you've been more than fair to me. I—I wanted to ask if you would forgive me."

Palmer sat there and stared at her, startled, his mind refusing at first to register the significance of her words.

His eyes probed hers with question. She indeed had the bluest of eyes he had ever seen. Funny, he thought, how he had not noted that so much before. At the moment, he could see they were thickly shaded by glistening lashes from an earlier session of tears.

"Why now?"

"I overheard your conversation a few moments ago. We've lost our president, and the South has lost the dreadful war to the Union. I feel, after what the reverend spoke about last Sunday, it is time to make amends. It's about so many things."

When she opened her mouth to speak further, nothing proceeded.

"Is this sputtering to try to get me to take you back to your aunt's and forget my trip north?"

"Didn't you hear what the pastor said?"

"I heard the message," Palmer answered defensively. "Not five months ago you were ready to give up your life, but I brought you here. You are correct I have tried to be fair to you and kind. But you have had your own agenda."

"I haven't," she stubbornly replied.

"Didn't you just accuse me of not listening to the sermon last Sunday? I remember it...He spoke of..." Palmer stood up and walked around the table.

He knew, but in truth, his mind had also wandered on his feelings about Aimée. He had not wanted to dwell much on anything the pastor said...not when it came to the part about love, compassion, and forgiveness.

As Palmer stood dangerously close to her and he breathed in the scent of her hair, his senses reeled as if short-circuited. He had to pull back immediately.

If she only knew how he *truly* felt about her.

She glowered at him and scooted her chair closer to the table to avoid contact of his body at her backside. "That wasn't my intention at all!"

"Amethyst Rose," he said again, emphasizing her name, "'twas not six months ago I took you away from that brothel, no thanks to your sister. I did that to *help* you. Have you shown your appreciation even once?"

A look of exasperation spread across her face. She spread out her hands. "I'm trying to do so now." Aimée blinked back her tears. "I came here this morning to apologize to you, Captain Jordan! I can see my apology has not been remotely accepted!"

Glancing up at the wrinkle of his brow caused her only to frown more. "I need to go home--not to my Aunt's but home! I want to go to Vicksburg. Can you not see you have everything--Everything! I have nothing; I have no one!"

Palmer wanted to say something, but she touched her hand to his lips to stop him. He blinked slowly. The mere touch of her hand sent a warm shiver through him.

"Even though this is Virginia, *you and your people* have still won the war!"

Tears poured down her cheeks. She stood up, accidentally brushing up against him, giving her cause to further tremble. "Please move out of my way. You *don't* even recall the minister's wonderful words. Worse yet you are—you are Palmer Jordan!"

"What is that supposed to mean?"

"You have been no friend to me like your cousin Philip. And you—you...why you are nothing like—like...oh never mind."

"Like who, Amethyst Rose?"

"Like—like, well, like Jonathan! That's who!" She ran out of the room.

"Where are you going?"

"As far away from you as possible!" She was already heading up the stairs. Moments later the door of her room slammed behind her.

* * * *

After watching her leave, Palmer sat down on the nearest chair and looked down on the table where Aimée left behind her handkerchief. He absentmindedly picked it up and rubbed it against his cheek, taking in her fragrance of lavender. He sighed then made a mental note to himself. He would be sure to get the handkerchief back to her...someday.

In the meantime, surely she would not miss it. Giving it a slight caress, he brought it to his nostrils one more time, taking another whiff of her lovely scent. It was only a whisper of the one who'd just run away, but it was ...something.

What am I doing?

After placing it in his shirt pocket, he got up and walked out of the room and out the portal.

"Women!" he growled. "They are fickle and confusing! First, the lady despises me due to the color of my uniform. Then she throws out something about Philip and friendship! Then she tells me she's sorry and for what? At the same time, she spews more venom at me about who knows what again...and Jonathan? Who the heck is Jonathan?"

He brooded on, forgetting his first impulse to turn back to the house and chase up the stairs after her. Palmer sucked in his breath then shook his head. Right now a walk was more important. Anything to clear his head and keep him from falling further under Aimée's spell.

"So what am I to do about her, God? You know my heart. You know I'm desperately in love with her! Now, what exactly do you want me to do about it? I need a woman of faith by my side, God. And Jonathan...I ask again, Lord, who indeed is this man, Jonathan? And what am I supposed to do about him?"

* * * *

Aimée lingered in her chamber most of the afternoon. Her appetite long gone, she excused herself from dinner to nurse the headache she was sure to develop.

She had poured her heart out to the man she did not want to love then instantly felt his rejection which she knew she probably deserved. But did she truly...still?

Why does he hate me so, God? Am I so bad?

A war of emotions raged within her. She hadn't even been able to tell him about her newfound faith, hoping he might've been pleased. In all likelihood, he would not have cared, anyway.

Aimée had fallen in love with everyone and everything at the Jordan's place — the animals, Gram, Pop, Philip, even her new church family.

More than anything, she loved Palmer Jordan, the man who wanted nothing to do with her.

By the time, she found her way down to the dining room table for breakfast where Pop, Gram, and Beryl were about to finish, the dawn sky had already become mottled with rain clouds streaking and tinting. It was impossible not to notice the captain's empty chair.

"He's gone, dear...left early this morning," said Gram. "It is only us now. How about some flapjacks? We saved you some." She pushed the plate of cakes in front of her, avoiding the pointed stare. "I had some homemade molasses hidden down in the cellar, enough to spark up breakfast. You must be hungry. You didn't come down last night for supper again."

"Was feeling out of sorts," Aimée mumbled as her eyes darted back across the table again towards the empty chair.

"Don't worry. Polly shall return soon to take you to your aunt's."

Aimée smiled. "To *Shadow Grove* you mean."

"Yes. Yes. Trust him. Can you try?"

"I will try, truly I will." Even with her smile of acknowledgement, she did not dare tell the Jordans she had decided the night before to work out her own way home.

* * * *

New Orleans
May 1865

Beauregard practiced the words he planned to say one more time before he tapped on the Simpson woman's door for a second visit. He hadn't gotten very far with the woman the last time.

Proper English always sounded so much more convincing. "I say," he rehearsed quietly with his back to the closed door, "I do hope you will forgive my intrusion again, Mrs. Simpson, but I wanted to gather a bit more information… for the sake of your esteemed niece." He had the words memorized well.

"You wants to know about Miss Aimée?" Millie asked, as she stood at the entry with the door wide open. It was obvious she'd seen and heard him through the window and had hurriedly opened the door, calling the mistress over just ahead of him.

Fran Simpson stepped in front of her and smiled.

Beauregard's words caught quickly in his throat, as he swung around in surprise. "Well, well…and how are you this fine spring afternoon, Mrs. Simpson?" he asked, a nervous twitch flicking in his jaw. "I was about to knock, and there you are already available to greet me." He smiled loosely.

"And you were speaking to whom on my porch?"

"I—I, well, no one, exactly, madam," he said. "You see, I came across your sla—servant earlier to let her know I wanted to speak to you again."

"I was told you were coming around."

"I do hope you will invite me in…such a tingle in the spring air, do you not agree?"

Avoiding a frown, she returned, stepping back, "I was about to, Mr. Proctor. Let Millie take your hat…you can join me in the drawing room, and we shall have a brief chat. I am rather busy, but I have set aside a few moments for you."

Fran walked ahead of him, her eyes narrowed, her chin pointed. "I understand you wished to speak to me…about Amethyst Rose." She motioned for him to sit down.

* * * *

She replied with care after hearing what he had to say…all of little value.

"And you are certain about all this?" Beauregard stood, his face blotchy. His nostrils flared.

"I told you the last time Amethyst Rose is married now, Mr. Proctor. I thought you would have understood me from before. "

"Surely," he replied, "but this cannot be. She cannot have gained interest in another like I said before. You must be mistaken. As I tried to explain the last time, the two of us were well on our way to…" Beuregard stopped.

He licked his lower lip then continued. "I say…for a while, the young lady showed more than a slight endearing to me, you understand, Mrs. Simpson…me, the honorable Beauregard T. Proctor. She expressed no interest whatsoever in anyone of the opposite sex *other* than me from what I observed at The Paramount."

Fran's eyes narrowed.

"You see, I thought before it was a mistake. 'Twas only right to allow the young lady time to think things through. Indeed, I thought she'd return to me. Thus, with patience, I waited." His voice went quiet, yet held an undertone of cold contempt.

Proctor quickly stood back up and hastened to leave the room. "I venture to say I must be going." Before he walked out, he twisted a knee around and gazed back at the woman a speculative look on his face.

She could see he was still not at all convinced about her tale.

* * * *

"I'll find her and bring her back, married or not," he told Nina later that afternoon. "I have ways of convincing her. Watch and see."

"It's your own fault you didn't pursue Rosette more aggressively. Why couldn't you at least pin the old lady down to her whereabouts?" she said.

"The news caught me by such surprise; I'll have to admit, though I still doubt the verity of it."

"There is still unfinished business at The Paramount, and Rosette is a part of it."

Proctor nodded. "Now that I finally have a little coin in my purse it should help. I couldn't go searching anywhere while I was broke!"

"Well, you are not broke now. Have you thought about how you will get her back here?" Nina eyed him.

He twisted his mustache. "The good looks and charms of one Beauregard T. Proctor naturally!"

"I doubt that will work this time," she said, shaking her head. "I have a better way." She walked toward the nearby table.

Proctor followed her and watched her pick something up. "What's that? Give it to me." He noted the gleam in her eye as she swung around. "What is it?"

"I saved some of the tonics. This is one of the powders the doctor used to help the others sleep."

"Give it over."

"If you need it to get Rosette back here, do it. Just drop some in her tea or brandy."

Proctor shook his head. "I don't think she drinks brandy, but if I find her I can get it in tea easy enough. I'll head North and inquire at a few inns. I'm sure to collect information along the way. It helps that the war is over. How many Yankee officers in the last several months might have been riding around with Southern Belles at their side in the middle of a war when it was going on, I ask you?"

* * * *

It would be a good visit. Jonathan had planned it for weeks. He took a deep breath and knocked then turned his head and smiled at the sound of the door opening.

"How do you do? Might I speak to the lady of the house? I believe she is titled Mrs. Francis Simpson."

The servant gazed at the thin and somewhat disheveled man with bearded face as he stood looking down at her. "Her name is Misses Simpson," she said. "This be her house."

"My name is Jonathan Langston Dewey. I doubt she will recognize the name, but you may announce me just the same."

"Wait here," she replied, shutting the door in his face.

"We gots company, again, miss. There be a man wants to see you, Miss Franny. It ain't your cap'n friend. What you wantin' me to do?"

"It's not Mr. Proctor again, is it?"

"No, miss."

"Is it Captain Moreau?" she asked, checking her hair in the hallway mirror.

"No, he say his name be Dewey, sumpin' like that, miss. You sure you don't want me to send him away?"

"Invite the gentleman in, Millie, of course," she said, walking toward the door. "The name sounds familiar to me from somewhere. Take the gentleman into the parlor; I'll be there directly."

When she walked into the room, Mr. Dewey was studying the small framed image of her husband and her on the mantle of the fireplace. "How do you do?" she asked, extending her hand. When he drew closer and she noted his face, she studied his cheekbones and alert and steady eyes.

"Mrs. Simpson, let me introduce myself. My name is Jonathon Langston Dewey. I am the grandson of Baron Edwin Dewey and the former Baroness Lydia Campton of Rame-Cornwall. I hope you will excuse my appearance. I just noticed in your looking glass I am now much too lean, and my hair is greatly in need of a trim. I hope my looks and attire do not frighten you overmuch."

She smiled in return. "Go on."

Jonathan reached up and caressed his face. "You are also taking note of my whiskers, I see!" He frowned at his own image in the mirror. "I am in need of a trim."

"That is true, sir."

"...and yes, my trousers and shirt have become much too large for my frame."

Fran nodded. "I have many questions, yes. What can I do for you, sir?"

"The truth is, madam, I am trying to discover the whereabouts of my fiancé, Amethyst Rose Lebrún, your great niece, I believe. I realize this is abrupt and would have forewarned you of my visit," he went on, "but I didn't know I was coming till just the other week. I knew a post would not arrive before my person."

"Jonathan Dewey...of Vicksburg, Mississippi?" Fran's eyes widened as she touched her chin. "Now I recall where I heard the name. Please, do sit down."

"Thank you, Madam. Then you have heard of me and my family."

"Of course! But...but everyone thought you were dead!" Fran moved to the chair across from him.

"No, as you can jolly well see, I am very much alive. I was missing-in-action," he continued, "but I am full of life...now." He looked down at himself, "a bit on the gaunt side, perhaps," he chuckled. "I am usually not so thin. I have not been well fed for over a year and a half."

"Allow me to ring Jasmine for some refreshment, Mr. Dewey." She picked up the bell on the table next to her chair. "And you are searching for Amethyst Rose."

"I am. Her brother, David, mentioned she might be here. You see, Mrs. Simpson, Miss Lebrún and I are to be married, and now I have discovered my parents have returned to England. I hope to get our wedding underway, so I can journey there myself, accompanied by my bride. You can be sure the family will be surprised, too. I've heard the entire town presumed me dead."

"David? You saw David? And you mentioned a wedding," Fran repeated the words slowly.

"You must've been told of our betrothal."

"Why, yes, but you see, Mr. Dewey," she paused.

"Yes?"

"Since you were reported dead, and it has been nigh onto two years, Amethyst Rose has since wed!"

His face paled. "Wed, you say?"

"You also mentioned David," Fran said, interrupting. "You spoke with him?"

He ignored her. "What's this you say; she has wed another?" he interrupted, rising. "I must see her."

Fran held up her hand to give the man pause. "Perhaps you could first tell me the circumstances which led to your disappearance," she stated cautiously. "Sit back down, Mr. Dewey—may I call you Jonathan? I'm sure Aimée will want to know you're alive. I must hear about David, too. After that I will tell you where she is."

* * * *

When he was finished telling his unusual story and lengthy excuse for his disappearance, he gave her a nod and a grin. "Quite a story, what?"

He held out his leg, giving it a shake. "I am fit as a fiddle, as they say, but an accomplished rider I am not. 'Twas an unfortunate fall off that horse, I dare say...though great timing for the Union soldiers, who snatched me up. At least I was not left for dead. When they released me, I returned to Vicksburg and came upon David, who had returned to the states. I found him restoring *Shadow Grove*. Unfortunately, my home across the river was beyond salvation."

He watched her as she listened intently. "You've probably heard much of the rest of the post war news."

"I have. Did you view your marked grave where they placed your empty casket?"

"I did!" Jonathan said. "The folks gave me a nice stone!"

She patted Jonathan's knee and got up. "I would love to help you out, Mr. Dewey, monetarily as well. At least it will be enough to aid you in your travel. And if you will wait a few minutes, I shall get Amethyst Rose's address for you."

When Mrs. Simpson left the room, Jonathan walked to the mirror, lifted a brow, and smiled again. So far, his task had been easy. Twice, he had convinced family members of the missing-in-action story. Twice, he had been offered financial aid.

If things continued as planned, it should be no problem at all winning over Aimée and letting her know his family lost everything from the war. Even if it was too late to wed the girl, if all went well, he could at least make her feel guilty enough to offer him enough money to get him back to England.

* * * *

It took several days for Jonathan to pass through Louisiana and Mississippi then up through Tennessee. The roads were still in disarray, much traveled now.

He passed by several people who, like him, were searching for loved ones after years away at service or time spent in prison. Just off the road ahead, he found the place a few had mentioned along the way. *The First Inn* was nestled in a grove of old trees and apparently was more crowded than it had been in years.

As he entered the dining hall in search of an empty table in the far corner, he came across a space occupied by only one customer, looking as if he had held his chair long enough judging by the empty cider jug sitting in front of him. The man he saw there was about to sidle off his chair. He was mumbling something to himself as Jonathan walked over.

"There's no place else to sit. Perhaps you could make way for a hungry stranger?"

The other patron slowly lifted his head. "Whas' that?" he slurred then reached up to wipe the slobber off the oozing corner of his lips.

"I say, would you mind if I sit down?" Jonathan repeated, taking a seat across from him without permission. "The name here is Jonathan Langston Dewey, at your service."

"Be my guest," the drunkard returned shakily. Reaching across the table, he shook the stranger's hand with his own clammy one. "You came jus' as the right time, stranger. I could use someone to talk to."

* * * *

"The name here is the Honorable Beauregard T. Proctor," said the inebriated man emphasizing with great zest the letter *T*. "Won't you join me in a drink?" He looked at his empty cider jug and turned to motion for service from the buxom maid across the room

"No thanks," said the other. "I need to put some nourishment into my belly right now…not that foul-looking liquid. I have not eaten and must build my strength before I get back on the road. I still have a distance to travel."

"Where you headed, *ami*?" asked Beauregard, slipping into his native tongue. He tried hard to keep his focus. He did not normally take in so much strong drink, but losing his horse and running out of money along with not knowing the exact location of his destination had frustrated him.

He wasn't even certain how he was going to pay the Innkeeper. He had earlier convinced the scantily dressed attendant, who was glad for the attention, he would pay his bill upon his departure. The wench had been more than pleased to wait after the two of them had their quick tryst in one of the upstairs room.

Probably because when they were finished, Beauregard produced a valueless but sparkly necklace, and with amorous touches, clasped it around her neck.

"Up north...the Shenandoah Valley," said the man across from him. "Up around—"

"You don't say!" he interrupted. "I, too, am headed in that direction, but my decrepit horse, the dastardly old mule, broke her shoe then went lame on me. I had to shoot the thing. Left her along the road somewhere. Unfortunately, I'm stuck."

"Sorry to hear that old chap. You spoke French earlier...a visitor to the colonies, perchance?"

"It is only part of my heritage. There is also English."

"'Tis no shame, my friend. I'm going to a place called *Pencil Ridge* myself," said Jonathan. "Perhaps you would like to travel along with me, Mr. Proctor. I knew some Proctors in Bath, I recall. I could give you a lift part of the way. My carriage is just outside. I could use the company."

"Shenandoah Valley to *Pencil Ridge*? Why not? Call me Beauregard. Do." Though Beauregard did not know the exact whereabouts of Amethyst Rose, he knew if he inquired of enough people along the way, he was sure to find the Jordan plantation.

"I suspect the place I'm going will be along the way. It shouldn't be too difficult to find someone who is familiar with the name Jordan. Yes, Bath. I have a grandfather from Bath. Then we are old friends, aren't we?"

"Did you say Jordan?" Jonathan asked, suddenly. "How extraordinary! *Pencil Ridge is* the Jordan place!"

Proctor's bloodshot eyes lit up.

"'Tis a small world, indeed!" said Jonathan.

"Indeed, it is. Unfortunately, someone stole my purse, and I've nothing with which to offer you pay for a ride, Mr. Dewer."

"Dewey, sir, but do not worry about funding. I am a man of means. You being part French and part English must have recognized the name! I'm grandson to the Baron Edwin Dewey and the former Baroness Lydia Campton of Rame-Cornwall!"

Beauregard raised one eyebrow. "I've heard the name."

"There you see. You have nothing about which to worry!"

Though still slightly intoxicated, he had enough faculties to begin working his brain quickly at the news.

"Care to join me in a bite to eat Proctor, Beauregard? It would clear your–head somewhat, and you can catch some shut-eye once we get on the road. I will be glad to assist you, and you can repay me later. Have your run up a tidy bill?"

He nodded slowly! "But no food for me, if you don't mind...my insides are burning. I daresay I need to sleep off this liquid first." His return smile was overly generous.

"Just leave things to me, old chap," said Jonathan.

Beauregard reached out his hand again to shake on it. "You are simply too too kind, Mr. Dewer."

"Dewey. Jonathan Langston Dewey of Rame-Cornwall, remember?"

"Oh, that's right," he slurred, leaning his head on the table. "If you don't mind, Mr. Dewey...I think I'll just rest my head here a second until you pay my bill for me then and say it's time to go."

Chapter Eighteen

Shenandoah Valley, Virginia

Aimée wasn't at all surprised the longer she stayed at the Jordans the more difficult it was becoming to leave. Too many weeks had passed since she'd seen Palmer, and much to her disappointment, she missed him terribly. She still had not found a simple way to get herself back to Vicksburg on her own, but sitting quietly out on the porch with Beryl, she found she could think of nothing else.

Something would come up soon.

"Miss Lebrún, I thought you were leaving soon."

Oh, hello, Cornelia," said Aimée in surprise, "I didn't see you come up."

Cornelia glanced over at Beryl then back at her. "Did I startle you, dear?" She replied. "My conveyance is over by the carriage house. I thought if Palmer were here, I might run into him. Any word from the darling? We chatted before he left, and I have been waiting anxiously to see him again."

"No. I told you last time you were here."

"When you see him, let him know I stopped by. You are still leaving…before long, I presume."

"Soon, Cornelia."

"Good, good. I'm sure it will bring great relief to the family." Cornelia angled her body back towards the carriage house.

"You feed her ego." Aunt Beryl shook her head.

"Do I? Well, what harm is there? She's a lonely woman. Perhaps the captain would be good for her," said Aimée.

"I think your good captain is a major now, dear. And good for her? It shall never happen. Mark my words," said Aunt Beryl. "To tell you the truth, if there was

252

another man around here, any, mind you, I'm sure the Smithy woman would latch on to him as quickly. All she's interested in is two legs and a pair of fitted trousers, dear, as long as in the pocket of those trousers one happens to have plenty of money to keep her in fine attire. Shall we go in and get some lunch?"

* * * *

The humidity was settling in early for a Virginia summer afternoon. A warm southerly breeze swept up towards the porch. Gram breathed in the sweet air as she and Pop sat quietly on the porch gazing out towards the rolling hills beyond their property. Palmy's work schedule was becoming more and more difficult. Gram could see that now.

"You look tired again, husband. Let me take your tea, and I will go in and get you a pillow."

"Um hmm," he mumbled, opening his eyes only slightly. "I could use a pillow, but I'll be well into my nap by the time you get your legs back out here with one." He started to close his eyes then opened them again and stretched his neck. "Someone's coming." Reaching into his shirt pocket for his spectacles, Pop put them on to get a better look.

"Who is it, husband?"

"It's not Polly's barouche; I don't recognize the driver, the horses, or the conveyance." He scowled.

"Who knows these days with all the traffic lately."

Both stood as Pop leaned against the rail of the front post as the horses pulled the carriage in closer.

They watched as two horses came to a halt and stopped digging their hooves in the loose sod then the driver stepped down to calm the steeds. When the carriage door opened, two men stepped out.

"You going?" said Gram.

"You wait here."

"What can we do for you?" said Pop loud enough for the strangers to hear.

"Is this the Jordan property?"

"This is it. Welcome to *Pencil Ridge*."

"I'm looking for Amethyst Rose," stated a tall skinny man in front. "I understand she's staying with you." He moved in closer, another stranger following close behind.

Gram looked over in at Pop in question.

"Leave it to me. Maybe they are friends of hers."

"Wait here." Pop stepped slowly off the porch and walked up to meet the men. "Who might you be?" he asked. "I'd like you to introduce yourself if you don't mind."

Gram stood frozen in the doorway surveying the two men.

"Jonathan Langston Dewey, sir, ma'am. This man beside me is the honorable Beauregard T. Proctor. I just learned Mr. Proctor here is a friend of Amethyst Rose also. I, on the other hand, was her betrothed until I heard the news of her marriage to your grandson." He eyed them both.

Proctor readied himself to speak by clearing his throat noisily, but Jonathon cut him off. "I shall do the talking, Proctor, if you don't mind."

"Indeed," answered Beauregard, bowing then backing off, an eyebrow lifting in scrutiny. "I am at your service."

Pop scratched his head. "What's that you say? Your betrothed?"

"Betrothed we were or should've been. Now, I understand she has wed another. I need to see her."

Gram hurried off the porch. "Amethyst Rose is not available now, but why don't the two of you come in and I'll bring refreshment," she interjected. "Palmer, why don't you take the men inside?"

"You say she's not here, ma'am?"

She lifted her brow. "Oh, I'm sure she'll turn up."

* * * *

"So you are from Vicksburg, Mr. Dewey?" Gram asked, standing in the parlor after the three sat down with their drinks, and Jonathan began his explanation of how he ended up missing.

"Our families met years ago," he explained. "We had a rousing tobacco plantation. Then after the Northern Armies came and raided us, my parents, who thought I had perished, lost everything and returned to England."

"And you plan to return soon?"

"With my bride was the plan, Mrs. Jordan," he answered pointedly. "I don't see how that's possible now. I would at least like to see the girl."

"Will you both excuse me?" she stammered suddenly. "Palmer?"

"I have it under control. Be on your way."

Gram hurried towards the back of the house and stood at the door of the pantry until she could see Aimée. She smiled.

"Aimée?" Gram started to call out then changed her mind and watched her instead.

She looked as no fashion plate, with her faded pastel dress of simple muslin and her soiled cotton apron, evidently from holding some of the hens and chicks in her lap.

The girl exuded a beauty impossible to obscure. With her winsome smile and laughing eyes, it didn't matter how she was dressed. Even with her large bonnet protecting her from the elements, she'd gained a lot more freckles across her nose since summer began.

Gram had grown to love the girl as her own over the last weeks and months.

What was it that bothered her about those two men back at the house? She just couldn't put her finger on it.

Certainly, if the presence of those two who were there to see Aimée were going to mean trouble for the girl she knew the only thing that would take care of matters was prayer.

And that will only take me a second.

* * * *

Tanned from the rays of an overcast sun, Aimée, who'd just finished gathering eggs, started back towards the house. It was hard to leave the flock that followed her everywhere.

She began to chuckle so much she had to look around to make sure she was not being observed or perhaps be considered off in the head. She giggled harder when she saw Gram's face.

"You have guests," she said to her. "I thought I would tell you before you entered the house."

Aimée's heart skipped a beat. "Guests? The major has returned and who else? I do look a sight," she commented, peeking down at her dress. "I must run up and change."

"It is not the major, but there are two men waiting to see you."

Face flushed, Aimée walked faster, handing her the basket of eggs. "Did they say who they were?"

"The one with whom I spoke called himself Jonathan—"

Before Gram could finish saying the name of the man, she watched some of the eggs fall one by one from Aimée's basket onto the ground.

Aimée's confidence dwindled. "I...I don't understand," she stammered, bending over to try to pick up the broken shells, gooey from the spill. "Jonathan? Jonathan Dewey? But it cannot be."

"Don't fuss about the eggs, dear. There are plenty of others there. Jonathan Langston Dewey, I believe he said his name was, a fine looking Englishman, somewhat charming, though a bit on the gaunt side. Didn't you mention his name a few weeks ago?"

"I did," Aimée whispered, pulling back up, looking confused.

"He said he came to fetch you till he discovered from your aunt that you and Polly had married." She watched her more closely.

"Fetch me," repeated Aimée.

"He was the one with whom you were ...betrothed?" she went on. "Mrs. Simpson did not tell him, it appears. Maybe she figured that was something you would want to do yourself."

"Jonathan Dewey," she repeated again. "He and I were betrothed, yes. But...he died! Well, we thought he died."

"He doesn't look dead to me, dear; as I said before, a little on the thin side, but very much alive," she commented, smiling.

"I shall see him, of course." Then Aimée looked down at her attire once again. "I do need to change. Oh, look at the broken eggs, all over, too! He will wait, won't he?"

"Aimée, I think the young man has been waiting a long time. Did I hear him claim he has been in prison until only recently? I cannot recall now. I don't imagine he will mind waiting a bit longer. You run along. I'll make excuses. In the meantime, stop your fretting about a few broken eggs!"

Aimée nodded and turned to run. What would she do now? What about Major Jordan? How would she tell Jonathan there actually was no real marriage? As usual, her life was about to produce more upheaval. Hurrying past Gram, Aimée stopped for a moment and looked back. "Did you get the name of the man with him?"

"I can't remember," she said.

"Well, please inform Mr. Dewey I'll be down directly!"

"I will. Be off with you then." Gram watched Aimée disappear back into the house.

* * * *

"Amethyst Rose has returned to the house only a moment ago," Gram announced as she arrived in the parlor. "She should be down straight away."

"Jolly good," replied Jonathan, rising to give the older woman his arm.

With a firm jolt, she ignored his gesture. "Sit back down, Mr. Dewey; I'm fine, thank you." Turning her head quickly towards the other visitor, she spoke again. "And you are...?"

"Proctor, ma'am—the Honorable Beauregard T. Proctor. You may have heard the name."

"Yes, that was it…the Honorable Proctor, you said. No, I *don't* recognize the name. Why don't you tell me a about yourself? What is your association with Amethyst Rose…or did you already go through all this whilst I was out back?"

She made it a point to keep her eyes on his face and eyes to see if they started to get shifty.

Pop's interruptive snore caught her attention.

How long had he been sleeping?

"I hope Mr. Jordan has been good company to you gentlemen, while I was gone."

"We've had a good visit, madam," claimed Jonathan. "Mr. Jordan told us all about your plantation. I say, we must have tired him out with all of our chatter. Beauregard here expressed great interest in your acreage and livestock."

"Indeed," Beauregard replied, "I'm always interested in land issues, madam. The Proctors own property in various parts of the country, which, of course, will go to me in the near future. 'Tis a hobby of mine, learning what I can. I will be in the market to purchase up in this locale fairly soon. Mr. Jordan declared he plans to be passing this piece of land on or letting it go or some such thing. An attractive piece of real estate to place on the market — it should take no time at all to sell."

"*Pencil Ridge* is not for sale, Mr. Proctor," corrected Gram quickly, trying to get the man to look her straight in the eye.

"Sell?" Pop piped in, waking up abruptly. "Sell what?"

"I heard no mention of selling," corrected Jonathan. "Perhaps it was, rather, it would be passed down." He gazed over at the other. Then, turning back to Gram, he said, "The two of us only met, recently. In fact, it was during my journey up this way we came upon one another. I had no idea Mr. Proctor, Beauregard here, was in the market to purchase ranch land of any sort."

"Yes," he intruded. "I came across this hungry soul in an inn and was glad to help him out. It has been a real pleasure guiding Jonathan Dewey up your way. Of course, I was not at all sure of his condition, learning of his recent incarceration and for such a lengthy period. He looked rather decrepit and lost, indeed, forlorn at the time of our meeting."

Jonathan stared at the man strangely and ran a hand through his hair. "Wait a minute. That's not exactly how…"

* * * *

Aimée looked at herself in the mirror before heading down the steps. She looked good in her blue and yellow plaid day dress with its snug bodice and fluid bell sleeves, of a soft lemon hue, which gracefully flowed with the movement of her body.

Miracles never ceased when it came to making an appearance before a man. Of course, Lulu had accomplished one of her miracles. Normally, it would have taken her hours to prepare for guests for she had numerous dresses from which to choose. Hours to settle on how she would wear her hair. That afternoon she had made up her mind in seconds.

The rustling sound of Aimée's crinoline brushed against her petticoats as it echoed in the hall. Everyone in the parlor turned. She had not meant to interrupt the guests, or maybe she did, but both stopped to watch her enter, stumbling to rise.

Gram looked over and smiled.

While waltzing into the room, beaming, she could feel a few of her ringlets attempting to escape their netting as they bounced about trying to break free and flow down her back. Thankfully, Lulu had ingeniously fastened them on each side above her ears.

When her eyes fell upon her once-promised betrothed, Jonathan, she had to look again to be certain it was indeed him, as a spark of disappointment filled her heart. There was something missing when she looked at the man. Not only was he gaunt and pale. There was much more missing.

Feelings she might have once had, if any at all, were no longer there. Aimée had never once loved Jonathan Dewey. Certainly, he had always seemed a caring person…a gentleman, truly, although well-known for his frivolity. Many even thought the man utterly charming and quite a catch, in fact…at one time. His family, as her mama had pointed out, had come from old money, and the Dewey name without doubt held honor.

No, it was none of those things that tugged at Aimée's heart today. When she looked at the man now all she saw was complete emptiness.

Managing to keep her dignity, she concealed her thoughts as best she could. Walking towards him, she reached out to give him her hand. "I cannot believe you are still alive; 'tis a miracle!"

When he bent his head down to greet her with a kiss, she turned her head, lifting her hand instead then turned to greet the man beside him. As she did, Aimée nearly lost her breath.

"Beau-Beau — Mr. Proctor?   What are *you* doing here…with — Jonathan?   I do not understand. How did you…find me?" She stepped back as if in a daze.

"Are you okay?" pressed Jonathan, reaching for her before she fell. "Are you that shocked I am alive?"

With Gram and Pop's help, the three eased her into the nearest chair.

"Get Amethyst Rose a stiff brandy," said Jonathan.

Gram walked over and pushed the man out of the way. "No brandy. I'll take care of her." She reached into her sleeve for her clean handkerchief and wiped Aimée's forehead. "My servants, Sarah and Agatha, returned this morning, Aimée. I shall have Sarah bring you some tea with lemon, dear. Would that suit you? I think a small cup would ease your shaking somewhat, don't you?"

Aimée touched Gram's arm. "I will be fine. Tell Sarah no tea."

"You look as if you've seen a ghost!"

"At first I thought I had." Aimée's voice drifted off.

Both visitors laughed nervously.

"It was her shock of seeing me, no doubt," Beauregard interjected quickly. "It would seem I have brought back memories of Miss Lebrún's, excuse me, I mean Mrs. Jordan's dearly departed sister, isn't that right?" He stared into her eyes as she looked up at him.

"I beg everyone's pardon," said Aimée slowly. Motioning for those around her to move away, she sat back against her chair. "I'll be fine. Truly, I will."

"Please, everyone. Jonathan, you are alive! Why did I not hear?"

"It must appear strange," he admitted, "but 'tis not so difficult to understand once I explain it all to you. Shall we begin again then?"

"But wait, folks." He reached into his pocket and pulled out two sealed envelopes. "I almost forgot. While Beauregard and I were in town, we stopped at the post office to inquire of your whereabouts. When your postmaster discovered we were coming this way, he handed me these letters to give to you, Mrs. Jordan."

Gram reached out and collected both letters, addressed to Jordan. "How wonderful!" she exclaimed, "Polly has written us two posts, Pop, and one is just to me! Perhaps now we can find out when he is coming home again for good!" Setting them down on the table beside her, she focused in on the guests again. "Excuse me. Please go on, Mr. Dewey."

Aimée's eyes glanced over at the envelopes, her heart beating louder at the thought of the sender. There would have been no reason for him to have written her after there last few minutes together. Once again she had treated him unkindly. Then again, had the captain been any more the gracious to her?

She did not want to think about Gram's letters from Palmer Jordan. He would not have said a thing about her in them anyway. And there were two men standing in front of her right now she must deal with. Somehow

Beauregard Proctor had located her. That was trouble enough. And Jonathan was alive!

She leaned forward and tried to concentrate on Jonathan's detailed account as he spoke of his tribulation over the last year and a half. The fact he was standing in front of her and had such a story to tell was remarkable in itself. That she had no feelings about any of it was almost certainly a pity.

* * * *

No one would leave Aimée alone. She'd tried every moment she could to avoid speaking to Beauregard to know avail. Each time she left the house with Jonathan, Beauregard followed like a puppy dog right behind. Neither man would allow her out their sight

"Excuse me one moment, my dear," Jonathan said on the second morning as they were about to walk over near the chickens. "He's here again. That Proctor fellow."

Aimée nodded and breathed a sigh of relief. Up until then, nothing had been mentioned about her and Palmer's marriage-of-convenience, but Jonathan would not quit hanging on her.

She turned and watched him walk away. He left her little time to arrange her words, little time to think straight, hardly a moment to pray. Almost from the time she stepped out of the door of her room until the time she returned, he and Beauregard insisted on accompanying her.

I must tell Jonathan the truth but be careful Mr. Proctor does not learn of it. It is because of Nina this absurd marriage farce came about in the first place!

Glancing about her to see she had a rare free moment, Aimée hurried over to the garden swing, sat down, and bowed her head.

* * * *

"Do you mind, old chap?" Jonathan complained, leading Beauregard back towards the house.

"I would like to have some time alone with the girl. We've hardly had a moment to speak without you hanging around."

"My pardon, indeed!" With a mocking gesture, Beauregard leaned over to bow in jest. A sneering grin lingered on his face as he drew back up and turned to walk away.

"Before you go, what was all that rubbish about how you came upon *me* at the inn the other day? You know that's not what took place. Be glad I said nothing in contradiction."

Proctor laughed again. "Just making idle conversation, *jeune*." With that, he walked off.

When Jonathan returned to the garden, he saw Aimée wiping a tear from her cheek. "Are you all right, Aimée?"

She nodded. "I was praying. My prayer time sometimes causes me to weep."

"Your *prayer* time?" Jonathan winced when he mouthed the word again. "*Prayer*?" he vented. "What's that all about?"

"Come sit with me. There are a couple of things I must tell you, Jonathan."

He stared. "Am I hearing what I think I'm hearing?"

"That is the truth of it," she said as the two stared out at the bushes beyond the trellised roses, and she explained how she ended up in Virginia.

"You see, I am not truly married at all." She studied his face as she went on. "It is only for my protection the Jordans having me here. The other truth," she hurried herself along, "is…I have found God, or better yet, He has found me. I have become a woman of faith, now, Jonathan, a Christian."

"Oh?" Jonathan came back. "What you are trying to say is that you have been living up here with a strange man, a Union Officer, knowing you were betrothed to another, while at the same time playing this Christian charade…and all for what?"

Jonathan stood quickly. "I can hardly believe it." He glared at her coolly, his voice tightening with each word. "What has happened to you Aimée?"

"'Tis no charade!"

"No charade, you say? Ha! You have totally dishonored me, my family, and the Lebrún family name, and I shall not forget it—not for a second!" Jonathan retreated the garden, leaving Aimée sitting there staring after him.

She had successfully said what she wanted to say. To her disappointment, however, she had not made him understand. "Jonathan?" she called out his name weakly. "I guess you do not hear me." She looked down at her folded hands and spoke again. "I guess I don't truly care either."

* * * *

It was the next morning at breakfast when the two men walked in, and Gram could no longer hide the worry on her face, especially with the hovering guests, who lingered continuously around her husband.

"I understood Aimée had a headache last night so I'm going to go upstairs to see how she is." Gram hurried out of the room.

"While you check on her, we shall be going out with Mr. Jordan again. Do not fret about him," declared Jonathan as he followed her in the hall, "I'll watch over him closely."

In all the turmoil of the last few days, Gram had forgotten Polly's recent letters, which still sat on the table unopened in the parlor. Just before heading up the stairs, she spied them on the table and hurried into the room to collect them. Before she could pick up the first envelope, the sound of horses' hooves out front rippled through the quietness.

She turned and looked out the front window and could hardly contain herself. As fast as her legs could carry her, she hurried back out the front door and down the porch steps.

It was just what she needed.

Chapter Nineteen

Joseph pulled the two lead horses to a stop and sat stiffly as Philip jumped out of the carriage and noted Gram standing at the bottom of the porch.

He ran over and swooped her up into his arms. "There's my girl!"

"Put me down before you break your back!"

As the two embraced, Philip stepped back and smiled.

"Well, come in. Most of the servants are gone, but I still have Sarah and Agatha. Sarah will bring us some of my blackberry cordial."

Philip glanced across the yard, motioning for Joseph to go ahead and lead the horses over to the carriage house. "Where's Abel?"

"He'll be here. That lad has a sixth sense about him and knows when people come before they even round the bend somehow!"

Just as she finished, they both caught sight of Abel walking down the path towards them.

"Gram, you look tired," said Philip. "Is something amiss?"

"Let me just say you came in the nick of time."

* * * *

"Is *she* still here?" he asked stretching his neck. "And where are Aunt Beryl and Pop?"

Gram leaned in so no servants would hear. "Of course *she* is still here and Beryl, too. Aimée was up in her room reading a letter last I heard. She probably didn't see you arrive. Your grandfather, well that's another story. He is, well, he is just not himself. He's been forgetful too, Philip."

"Pop is ill?"

"He was out earlier with Mr. Dewey and Mr. Proctor looking at the property again."

"Say who?" Philip stood up. "Gram, tell me you didn't say the name Proctor."

"Yes, dear, Aimée's friends from the back home I understand...they have come for a visit and have taken right to Palmy, in fact they are with him constantly." Gram watched the look on Philip's face.

"What's the matter?"

"You cannot mean Beauregard Proctor! It is due to *that* man and his chicaneries Palmer and I decided to bring the girl here!"

Gram went on. "What are you saying, Philip?"

The sound of the front door shutting caught their attention as Pop and Jonathan entered.

Pop peeked into the parlor and smiled. "What's this? Welcome back, my boy! I wondered when you would return, Palmer."

Looking quickly at Gram and then at Pop, Philip replied, "Not Palmer, Pop. It's Philip here...PJ." Hurrying over, he extended his hand then guided the old man into the room. "Come, take a seat. You seem tired."

"We were out walking," explained Jonathan.

"Where is Mr. Proctor?" asked Gram, looking past them.

"He said he needed to go to town, Mrs. Jordan. Your stable hand saddled up a horse for him."

She turned back to Pop. "Are you okay, Palmy? What can we get for you?"

"I don't feel well, mother." Pop leaned against Philip and began shaking.

Gram thinned her lips and nodded towards her grandson. She spoke softly. "Philip, please take your grandfather up to his chamber and help him with his boots and trousers. He—he's never ever called me *Mother* before."

"Don't fret, Gram. Don't. We should get word to the doctor right away."

* * * *

Philip held Gram's hand when she heard the voices of the reverend and the doctor at the door of Palmer's chambers.

"Sorry to have to come under these circumstances," said the doctor. "But it is always good to see you."

Philip shook both men's hands.

Reverend Goodman said, "Lulu and Abel stopped by the church on their way in to town. I had to come."

"He's still sleeping," she said. "Almost all of the family is here."

The reverend nodded at them all then stepped aside and waited for the doctor to do his examination.

Philip shook his head *"Palmy?"* she said softly to her husband. "The doctor and the reverend are here to see you. The reverend wants to pray for you."

"Palmy?" Gram whispered one more time.

Aimée quietly tiptoed in and sat down at the end of the bed.

"Reverend, we're ready now for your prayer."

* * * *

Gram listened to the doctor's orders before he packed up his instruments.

Pop needed some good long bed rest and further tests, especially with him fast losing his retentiveness. Regrettably, the tools the doctor needed were not available to do the task. "I'll have to take him in to the right facility for those tests," he said.

With that information, Gram could hold back her weeping no longer. She turned to Aimée. "I need my Polly. He should be here soon. There are two envelopes addressed to me down in the parlor on the table by the hearth."

"Let me go get them, Gram."

* * * *

He was sitting in the corner when Aimée walked into the room downstairs.

"What are you doing sitting alone in the dark, Jonathan?"

"Thinking." He shrugged.

"It would be nice if you went upstairs and showed some concern for all going on right now. At least paid your respects. I thought you cared about Mr. Jordan."

"What concern is it of mine, Mrs. Jordan, Miss Lebrún, Amethyst Rose, whoever you are?" His jaw twitched.

"It is Miss Lebrún, as it should be. Truth be told, Jonathan Dewey, you've shown me in many ways, 'tis is a good thing the two of us never married. You are showing me you have little heart for anything of real importance."

She gathered more courage as she stood there. "I can no longer abide you, sir. Will you be leaving soon?"

"When I'm ready." His hands clenched at his sides.

Walking further into the room, Aimée replied, "I'm here to pick up Gram's mail, if you don't mind."

She searched the room and spotted the envelopes on the table beside him. Before she could lift them from the table, he snatched them up and glanced at them.

"One is to Mr. and Mrs. Palmer Jordan, I see. The other to Mrs. Palmer Jordan. Why, this couldn't be to you now could it...a note from your scandalous and spurious husband perhaps?" He held them both tighter.

"Neither is addressed to me, Jonathan Dewey! They belong to Gram. Give them to me."

She tried to pull them from his clenched hand.

"Maybe I should open this one and find out to be certain." He laughed and began slowly tearing the side one of the envelopes.

"What are you doing!" she shrieked. "That is government mail! Give them to me!"

He twitched his jaw tightly and rolled his eyes. "Here then," he bellowed, tossing the two envelopes at her. "Take them. What does it matter to me to whom they've been addressed? I will be glad to be out of here soon. I wasted my time coming this far north for the likes of you. A lot of good you're doing me. You have no money anymore."

Clutching the letters to her heart, Aimée backed out of the room, seeing Jonathan Dewey, for the first time.

As she entered the front hall, Aimée heard voices.

"Who is it, Agatha?"

She recognized the voice of Cornelia at the door.

"Hello, Cornelia."

"Amethyst," she said walking in and turning to Agatha. "Let me by, slave, and get back to your chores," she continued, pushing her out of her way. "I heard Mr. Jordan was ill and that you had other guests. I came as soon as I could. I'm sure there must be something I can do to help, or perhaps, I can occupy your guests while you tend the old man...whatever. I'm not prone to reading, but if he would like, I suppose I could chat with him...or something. I'm good at holding hands, if his are not too tactile. I know the old soul holds a tender heart towards me."

"His chamber is full, I'm afraid, Cornelia."

She smiled condescendingly as her eyes darted past Aimée's and into the parlor towards Jonathan. Reaching up, she wrapped a loose curl around her finger. "Is that one of your guests I've been hearing about?"

"This isn't the best time to come for a visit, Cornelia," said Aimée, though she suddenly had an idea. "Perhaps you would like to sit in the parlor with...with my...guest. Wait. Let me take you in and introduce you."

Cornelia peeked into the oval looking glass hanging on the wall and checked her teeth. "Am I presentable?"

"Quite so." Aimée guided her into the room.

As the two of them entered, she watched as Jonathan immediately stood and bowed, and a gleaming smile spread across his face.

Perfect.

"And who might this be?" he said. "I do hope you plan to introduce me to your lady friend!"

With the envelopes clutched tightly in her hand, Aimée hurried back up the stairs, leaving Jonathan and Cornelia to acquaint themselves. Upstairs, the chamber was nearly as quiet as before. She tiptoed up to Gram, and reached for the letters.

"You are just in time," Gram whispered taking them. "The reverend is about to say another prayer. Come join us."

Taking off his spectacles, the doctor wiped his lens with his handkerchief. "Remember, Mattie, a good solid bed rest for you, too."

"But is he going to be okay?" asked Gram.

"It is for God to decide." Gathering up his bag, he turned to leave.

"Will Palmy know me when he wakes up?"

"I cannot answer that." He stopped at the door. "Let that be the least of your worries."

* * * *

"We understand." Philip followed the doctor out.

"You might want to get in touch with your cousin, Philip," the doctor advised from outside the chamber.

"I'll get a wire off to Palmer right away."

Placing his hat on his head, he departed down the hall. "I'll be in touch."

Philip turned back to the chamber.

"And I must get back to the parsonage, myself," said the reverend to them all.

"I'll see you out." Gram got up.

* * * *

Saturday Late Morning

It took much convincing to persuade Gram to come away from Palmer's bed and work on her own much-needed rest.

"You need your strength, Gram, to help Pop when he is better," reasoned Philip. "Aunt Beryl and I are ready to take our own turns at his side. Why don't you take a look at your letters?"

She nodded. "I did earlier. One of these is not mine. It is for Aimée. I'll give it to her or one of you can when she comes up. Has anyone wired Henry or Polly to come? And has there been word from them yet, Philip? I need to see them."

"Nothing yet." Philip stood over by the window and stared out.

"You scoot on out of here now, Gram, and have Sarah fix you up some broth." Without waiting for her response, Philip and Aunt Beryl helped her up from her seat and walked her to the door.

"We will keep your seat warm till you return. Aimée should be returning soon. She's off to support Lulu who is getting married today. She felt it was important for her be there."

Gram nodded but stood motionless in the center of the room.

Philip watched her. "Listen, Gram, if we don't hear anything by Monday morning, I'll wire Palmer again, I promise," he said. "Remember, the doctor is still not sure what the problem is. Pop has simply forgotten all of us. It's been nearly five days now, and his brain is still not functioning correctly."

Gram sighed. "He seems so far away."

* * * *

Downstairs in the hall, Aimée removed her gloves and placed them on the table beside the chair. Taking a breath, she sat down.

All weddings made her weep. Lulu and Abel's that morning had been particularly special.

Lulu had now found meaning for her life with Abel. It was a wonderful feeling...for Lulu...and for Abel. Yet why couldn't it have been her and...

Would God ever bring to her the same happiness that she was now seeing happen with Lulu and Abel that morning? Could she hope to expect that too one day?

Lulu had always been such a good Christian girl. She had always done such noble and upright things. At the appropriate times Lulu knew how to fight the Christian fight! And Lulu had never been selfish!

I want to be like Lulu!

Dear Lord, she prayed. *You have graciously given me peace and so undeservingly. Will you now show me how to go the next step in my Christian faith?*

She looked up the stairs and thought about Pop.

And help Pop, too, God, if it's Your will. And help me to be pleasing to You, like Lulu is. Help me to be someone to make you proud of me. Help me not to be so self-centered anymore.

* * * *

Beauregard had entered the house earlier and found a cozy spot where he could quietly sit, sight unseen by anyone.

The moment *she* walked in his eyes lit up. He could undress her slowly with his eyes should he choose to, slowly, worshipfully.

He glanced at the clock. It was the woman he'd been waiting for. And he was ready. He felt in his pocket. He had the bottle of powder.

Mrs. Jordan, he noticed, whom he had earlier planned to take as his own bride, could not help but exude her familiar look of innocence, even after taking the hand of marriage with that Yankee. She was forever soiled now, but where he was returning, no one would bother to question.

Now he had access to his own carriage and driver, and a heavy purse of money thanks to his stroke of luck at the gambling table in town. He could disappear from the Jordan place without incident, while the rest of the family busied themselves with nursing the old man.

He had enjoyed his three days in town at *Berta's Inn*, those days proving advantageous after borrowing more coin from the Dewey fellow.

Proctor was good at what he did—he knew it. Not only for his skills at the gaming table, but upstairs with that buxom, nearly toothless wench, who required only a small purse for time well spent. Even the wench had been quick with her smile of appreciation for his manly talents.

"Nobody's did that much nice stuff for me before, sweet gov'na," he remembered her saying. "You has a heart of gold, you does." The maid had been close to tears when he had left her.

His heart was a long way from being gold, but what she didn't know certainly couldn't hurt her. He knew he always had a special way with the women.

After slipping out of the parlor quietly, he reached down and touched Aimée's shoulder.

Tilting her head in his direction, she gasped. "Mr. Proctor! What are you doing here?"

Beauregard's eyes widened as he casually inched closer with a cynical grin. "My greatest of pardons, Mrs. Jordan, I did not intend to frighten you. It is simply I came to say my goodbyes."

Disoriented, she blinked. "You are going back to Louisiana?"

"There is nothing more for me here, Mrs. Jordan." Aimée sat up stiffly.

He held his throat. "I have been sitting here a long time waiting. I know you don't think much of me."

Aimée nodded. "There is really nothing to say. If you are going then."

She scratched her chin.

He coughed and continued holding his throat. "Would it be too much to ask to share a quick cup of tea before I head down the road?"

She glanced up and around the hall. "Me, with you? I don't know, Mr. Proctor."

He pursed his lips and glanced up the stairs. "I say, if you'd rather not, no hard feelings. How is Mr. Jordan, the old man, by the way? I did not get a chance to go up to say goodbye. I understand he was feeling poorly before I left the other day."

Aimée narrowed her brow as if to concentrate further. "He's not been well, Mr. Proctor. I haven't been back up yet since my return to the house."

After a pause, he answered. "Yes, well, I do say, I hope the chap is up on his feet in no time. Mrs. Jordan…indeed, if you would rather not have tea with me, I would understand completely. We have had difficult times you and I." He backed up and bowed. "I understand completely. I will take my leave then. "

He turned to walk toward the door, coughing.

Aimée called after him, "Wait. I'm being extremely selfish. I suppose I can at least send you off with that cup for the long road. Really, Mr. Proctor. I *can* do that."

She lifted a brow. "By the way, how were you planning to get yourself back?"

He had to grin to himself, keenly aware of the delicacy of the situation. He did not want to make any mistakes. "I have a carriage that I procured in town at an auction purely by chance. It is most fortunate for me."

"How nice for you." She turned as if in a rush. "Well, let me go find Sarah about that tea, but guaranteed, Mr. Proctor, then you must leave. In the meantime, I'd like to let the others upstairs know I'm back and look in on Pop. I will be only a moment."

"Of course. No problem at all," he grinned, licking his teeth when she started to disappear from his sight.

He felt the bottle again in his pocket. *Yes...*

Just a few sprinkles in her cup would easily see her put to sleep in no time—then picking her up and placing her into the carriage would be easy enough. He leaned casually against the door frame. *It shall all be quite simple.*

* * * *

"Where is Aimée?" asked Philip later.

"Isn't she going to come up to sit with Pop this evening?" Aunt Beryl asked from her chair beside the bed. "I haven't seen her she came up and got Palmer's letter. She went down to send off that Mr. Proctor fellow. I understand he was returning home. She looked relieved that he was going."

"Well, good riddance to the man. Perhaps Aimée is still resting then," said Philip. "When I returned from town, I didn't find her downstairs. Have you seen Gram?"

"The doctor encouraged her to remain in bed. He is worried about her. I'm going downstairs to summons Sarah to prepare a meal since it's getting close to the supper hour. Everything is so disorganized around here now with Pop down. I just wish dad and Palmer would get here soon."

Beryl gave him a warm hug. "The house will run fine. You do fine; never think you do not. Oh," she added, "did Aimée's other guest return yet? I didn't get to talk with either gentlemen."

Philip frowned and pulled back. "I came upon Jonathan out at the carriage house earlier, and believe me, you didn't miss anything by not talking with Proctor while he was here, Aunt Beryl. There's not one good thing that could come from Beauregard T. Proctor. I don't know why Aimée put up with him around here as long as she did."

* * * *

Philip stood at the back door and hung his hat on the hook by the door. Breakfast was late, but the smell of coffee permeated from atop the cook stove in the kitchen.

"Where's Sarah?" He leaned out and asked Agatha, who had stooped to pick up her laundry basket by the clothesline.

"Don't know, Master Philip," she replied, looking up. "Ain't seen her since yesterday, and it ain't like her to go without sayin' nothin'. Last night she don't come down, so Miss Beryl had me put supper on. Her friend Bertha's girl's gonna have her babe soon. Maybe she—" Agatha rambled on, lifting her eyes towards heaven. "Ain't no special nothin' happenin' at the church I don't reckon, not this early in the mornin'."

"Master Philip?" yelled Lulu from the door of Aimée's chambers a few minutes later. "Miss Aimée ain't slept in her bed. Her clothes still hangin'. "

Leaving Agatha to her rambling, Philip shut the door and walked into the hall looking up the stairs.

"Ain't nobody up around this place?" hollered Lulu again from upstairs.

Philip called back. "What is it? Come down here. No need to be yelling through the house."

"There you is!" she replied, shutting Aimée's door and running down the stairs. She shook her head. "My lady's gone… gone!"

"Whaaa?" Philip stepped back.

"Don't blame me none," said Lulu. "I been with my new man. You done told me I could."

"No, no, it's not that," Philip said, feeling queasy in his stomach.

* * * *

Jonathan stretched his limbs as he ambled into the breakfast room where Philip and Aunt Beryl sat.

"I say there, good morning you two. You both look a bit peaked. Did neither of you have a good night's sleep?" No one except him seemed in the mood for jovial conversation.

Without looking over at Jonathan Dewey, Philip glanced towards the kitchen door.

"My aunt and I don't feel like eating, Agatha, but I'm sure Jonathan will. Whenever you are ready, bring something in."

He turned towards him. "I'm sorry?"

"Where are the rest? Indeed, it does look as if you are still all aflutter," said Jonathan. "I feel like talking this morning."

Philip frowned. "Gram is sitting with Pop and won't be down. My aunt and I have something on our mind right now. In the meantime let me ask the Lord to bless *your* meal at least, Jonathan, so you can eat."

Bowing their heads, he and his aunt closed their eyes and silently prayed for Aimée, while Jonathan's jaw twitched nervously.

He'd been dressed and ready to be on his way for hours. While the others at the table wasted the next few minutes summoning their God, he was ready to discuss all that had transpired in his life in the last three days. He wanted to tell them his news.

They finally looked up. "Are you finished?" he said.

Philip nodded and started to rise. "If you will excuse…"

"I shall be moving my things into town. I hope you will not be too disappointed to see me go," he announced loudly.

"You're going to remain in the area for a while then?" asked Philip, sitting back down.

"Not for long. There is no longer anything for me here at *Pencil Ridge*."

Philip eyed him squarely. "Mr. Dewey, were you aware Mr. Proctor was going to take Aimée away from here and that he might take our Sarah along with them? I am not sure if that is what happened, but I have a very good suspicion."

Jonathan huffed. "So that's it! Are you accusing me? Of course I knew nothing!" He stood up stiffly then sat down again and wiped his brow. "Indeed, I did hear rumors in town the chap was going to return south." He shrugged. "I wondered how Proctor might accomplish the task." He eyed them both. "That was before I knew he procured a carriage. He did have money. I know that."

"Why didn't you say something?" asked Philip.

Jonathan's lips twisted cynically. "What was there to say? How was I to know before she would be so simple-minded and go along with the chap? Thanks to the help of others I came to realize the girl is more inept than I realized. I can see that now." He clenched his teeth. "She is an ignorant fool if she complied with the man!"

"Don't say that about my niece," said Beryl, rising to move toward him.

"Wait, Aunt Beryl," said Philip. "Sit down."

"Maybe Mr. Proctor fed her some disgusting line, and she fell for it," she argued, turning back.

Jonathan shot her a penetrating look. "It was Cornelia Smithy and her mother who convinced me a marriage with Miss Amethyst Rose Lebrún would have been a terrible mistake had it in fact taken place."

"And how would they know?" she asked.

Jonathan chuckled and went on. "From what I understand, she wanted to get away from here anyway. Perhaps she asked him to take her! I say good riddance!"

He lifted a brow. "To be sure, I believe she's no different than her sister. Perhaps you knew nothing of the notorious Florette Simone. I knew plenty about that infamous one. Since I've been here, I might add, I have discovered a great deal more about your Aimée, thanks to the bright and witty Cornelia. Cornelia remarked several times how fate had taken its hand in the two of *us* meeting.

"You listened to that woman? What would you or she know?" said Philip. "Cast the blame on me and my cousin, Palmer, and Aimée's aunt, not on Aimée herself. We were trying to protect her from the man!"

Jonathan refused to listen. Without further delay, he stood. "Personally, I'm glad to be rid of the girl. Fortunately, for me, Mr. Beauregard Proctor has made it much easier for me to get her out of my life completely. He has taken her off my hands!"

Before Philip and his aunt could respond, Jonathan found his way out of the room and almost out of hearing distance.

"If you will both will excuse me, I have an appointment with my betrothed. I might as well get a room at the inn this morning rather than later."

"Your betrothed?" Beryl questioned.

"Yes, my bride to be. It was her delightful mother, Mrs. Smithy who suggested we tie the knot soon. I had to agree it was a swimming idea."

* * * *

"Did I hear him say Cornelia Smithy?" Philip asked as soon as the door shut behind him.

"That's what he said—the legendary Cornelia," said Beryl rising again and heading for the hallway. "Who's the inept one?"

Philip shook his head. "Well, at least when Palmer returns home he will no longer have to worry about that woman hounding him anymore!"

278

"No, he won't."

"Well, I don't care one whit about Cornelia Smithy, Aunt Beryl...nor do I think Palmer will, either. Our concern is with where Aimée is and Pop and Gram upstairs."

"Are you going to go after her?" asked Beryl.

He stopped midstride. "If Palmer doesn't, indeed I will. I hate leaving this in the air, but I can't do anything with Pop ill this way and Gram as she is. I don't think Pop will be with us much longer."

"Nor I." She gazed back at him in silence.

"Palmer and my father should arrive soon. In the meantime, we'd better get upstairs to relieve Gram."

Chapter Twenty

Sunday Afternoon

Gram had Philip send for the doctor who arrived the same time as Henry.

"I'm glad you made it, Henry," she said.

"Has Pop awakened at all?"

Gram shook her head and sat down quietly in her corner holding her bible in her lap. Her eyes were swollen from too many tears.

"I know where Palmy is going, and I know once he arrives there, he will no longer be in pain, no longer weary. But I will miss him so. I don't want him to think I am fretting." Her voice broke.

"Mother," said Henry. "Pop understands. He's been through the thick of it. You remember his favorite verses? Have you been reading him some of those?"

"Will you, Henry? I cannot."

"I know them by heart."

"You can be certain," The doctor cut in, "even if he *appears* unconscious, he may well not be. The good Lord often allows people to keep their faculties, even when we might think they do not. Let's assume he hears everything you speak, son."

"Beryl, you hold Pop's left hand, and Mother, you take his right...that's good," Henry soon began his recital.

Everyone in the room watched as Pop's face slowly regained some of its color. A single tear escaped his right eye, and his lips parted. Everyone stood in awe for he had not awakened in days.

The doctor nodded at Gram. "Appears to me, that is what your husband has been waiting for."

Moments later Gram felt a groping squeeze upon her hand.

She lifted her head. "He squeezed my hand, doctor."

"Squeeze back, Mattie," he said.

Although the moment brought a hush to the entire group, slowly Palmy's touch again went limp, and Pop's face leaned to the side.

The doctor shook his head. "I'm sorry. He is gone."

"Palmy?" Gram bent down and wept softly, "Good bye, my husband. It won't be too long before I'll see you again."

* * * *

Palmer walked in to the house and removed his hat. Though he was exhausted from the long ride, he was grateful to be home again, hopefully to stay this time.

"You're finally here." Uncle Henry worked his way down to the bottom of the stairs.

"Is Pop any better?"

"Your grandfather is gone, son."

Palmer ran his fingers through his hair. "Gone?"

"Yesterday, son."

He closed his eyes and took a deep breath. "Give me a minute, Uncle Henry..."

"Oh Lord, I did not get to say my good bye."

He shook his head, took another unsteady breath and then turned to his uncle.

Uncle Henry touched his shoulder.

"Uncle Henry, I did my best to get here as soon as I could. I so wanted to be here." he said when he finally lifted his head. Palmer turned in, and he and his uncle embraced.

"You're here, boy. That's all that matters. You're here."

Palmer rubbed his eyes. "Where is everyone ?"

"Come with me. I'll take you to them. Services have to be arranged. I'm sure you'd like to be involved."

* * * *

Palmer saw Lulu's smile as soon as she heard him call out her name.

"They said you come back, Warrior Man. Was it a nice funeral, and is you stayin' now?"

"It was a pleasant service, Lulu. I heard congratulations are in order for you," he said walking up.

She blushed. "Yessuh, Abel, him's a good man. You too, Master Palmer, and Misses Mattie Gram, she give us a real stick house for us to make a fambly for the weddin' present. When is you gonna go get Miss Aimée and bring her back where her belongs so you can make a fambly like you supposed to?"

"That's what I came to talk to you about. You haven't changed a bit, have you!"

"Nope."

"I have a couple of questions, Lulu. You didn't see her leave I understand." Palmer looked at her as the two turned to walk up the road towards the main house.

Lulu stopped and grabbed his arm. "No sir. I only knows what I knows."

"And what's that?"

"You don't know much of nothin'. Nobody told you—not Misses Mattie Gram? Not about Miss Aimée and her Jesus God?"

"Her what?"

"That's what I's sayin'," giggled Lulu, biting her lower lip.

Palmer leaned back in surprise. "Tell me about this Jesus God stuff, Lulu. I'm all ears.

She pushed at him and laughed. "Only if you's gonna do somethin' about it."

"Oh, I'm planning on doing something."

"Miss Aimée, her's in love with bein' a believer now, and plus hers in love with her warrior man but yous ain't with her. And—and that Mister Proccer, I think him steal her and take her down to that nasty place that's what I thinks!" She shook her head. "I'm not thinking her went of her own 'cord!"

Palmer stiffened and took her arm. "Her what, and I what?"

She placed her hands on her hips. "Her own 'cord! And if you don't go get her...me n' Abel, we'll go ourselves and steal our Miss Aimée back up this way ourselves! That's what!"

"You'll do no such thing, Lulu Jean!"

* * * *

"You are leaving then, Palmer?" asked Philip.

"As soon as Abel preps the horses and Aunt Beryl finishes packing. Aunt Beryl wants to get back to Louisiana and needs an escort. I volunteered my services."

Beryl walked in the room shaking her head. "I'm ready to go. Was that your excuse, Palmer? Why don't you tell the truth? With Mama choosing to go to Ohio with Henry tomorrow for an extended visit to see Annie and the others, I'm no longer needed here anyway," she said.

Philip's vexation was evident. "Well, Palm, if you weren't going to go after the girl, I *would* have! I've been biting at the bit to anyway. We all know where he's taken her."

"I need to return home anyway," said Beryl. "And Mama wants to go and meet her great granddaughter. I've missed my townhouse and need to get back to see Fran."

"It looks as if we are all heading out then. Palmer. Agatha and the other hired hands can hold things together here until you return."

Palmer walked over to the window.

"What are you going to do after you get her? Do we hear wedding bells?"

Palmer turned around and gave him a frown. Even with Aimée being a believer now, he didn't figure it changed her bitterness toward him. It was difficult to believe what Lulu had said about the warrior man and love.

To her he was still very much a Yankee; and in the South, that bitterness ran as deep and wide as the mighty Mississippi.

* * * *

New Orleans

By the time Aimée came awake in the carriage it was much too late.

Her breathing was shallow. Something was terribly wrong. Her bones ached, and she found it difficult to move. She tried licking her lips, but her mouth felt like old paper, dry and dusty, and every time she attempted to speak, her throat wanted to close up.

It was hard lifting her head. When she was able to get her focus back, she was thankful to see a familiar face sitting across from her as little by little, warmth crept back into her body.

"Sarah?"

"I'm here, miss," she said, looking as if she'd been crying.

When she turned her head, the man asleep sitting beside her was none other than Beauregard T. Proctor.

She ran her fingers through her hair. "What exactly happened, Sarah?" she whispered. "How did we get here?"

"That stupid man done put something in your tea back at the master's house. You been out more'n a couple of days, miss. I ain't sure how long. I was to help him find the doctor and here we is. I's just been sick about it. Now I's gonna get fired. I never got to tell nobody I left the house!"

Aimée reached across the aisle. "Don't worry." She placed her other hand on her head. "I feel faint and my stomach feels weak."

"You ain't eat nothin' miss."

"Where are we?" she asked, looking around. "It is so dark."

"On our way to New Orleans."

Aimée pointed to the man. "Has *he* been sleeping long?"

"Yas'm. And I think we's close. We done stop already twice."

Aimée leaned back on her seat. The only thing to taking her mind off her troubles now was the noisy rattling of the wheels along the old road, which caused her eyelids to grow heavy again.

* * * *

"Wake up," said Proctor a short time later. "We've arrived at our destination. I'm going to get you inside."

She tried unsuccessfully in her weakness to pull away. It was impossible to see through the fog outside the window. It was difficult to focus more than a couple of feet ahead or behind.

"Where's Sarah?" she asked, glancing around.

"Already within. You are where you belong now. Come along." He reached across her to unlatch the door. "Let me get past you to help you down."

Aimée saw the front door of the house open up and Nina standing at the porch watching. She could just see the dim light from the inside of the dark foyer. It was clear where she was then.

Pulling back as tautly as she was able, she tried to fix her body against her seat and away from Beauregard. "I am *not* going in there with you, Mr. Proctor! I don't *want* to be at this place!"

"What you want does not matter, Mrs. Jordan. It's what we need that matters. Now, come with me; let me help you down." Proctor, much stronger, drew Aimée into his grip and refused to let go.

* * * *

"I will not stay here, Nina," said Aimée, struggling to stand, as they both pulled her inside and shut the door. "I want to go to home." She tried to pull away. "And where's Sarah?"

"Shut your mouth, wench," said Nina. "You will get to leave in due time."

Both pulled her arms behind her and dragged her up the stairs.

"Let me go!"

They pushed her into a chamber, Beauregard slipping in behind her. "You knew it was only a matter of time before we got you back."

"You can't lock me up this way, Mr. Proctor! Someone will come for me."

"No one will come. Why should they? All we need from you, my sweet," he slobbered, "is a simple signature on a piece of paper so this place will be released to us. Then we will let you go." He gave her a sloppy smile.

Aimée clenched her hands until her nails entered her palms.

"Take a few minutes. I will hold off Nina. Then I'll return."

She wanted to be sick. She watched Mr. Proctor slip back out. Glancing around the chamber and toward her window, she remembered how high up she was. *I will think of something. Even if I do have to jump!*

She walked to the window but it was locked. She slowly returned to her bed and sat down. There had to be a way out. Every other time, Palmer had come to her rescue somehow. That would be impossible now.

But the envelope! Aunt Beryl had handed it to her when she went up to Pop's chamber before she and Mr. Proctor had had their tea. She had placed it in her bodice to read a short time later.

Gram had thought the letters Palmer wrote when he was in Washington were meant for her until she discovered one of them was directed to Aimée. She had not yet had a chance to read it. Surely it was still there.

In all probability, Palmer had written about his desire to wed Cornelia all along and how he looked forward to her leaving *Pencil Ridge*. Maybe not.

Aimée sat up and leaned back against her pillow then reached down until she found it. Carefully pulling out the envelope, she tore open the flap and slowly drew out the folded page. There was but one sheet.

Off in the distance, she could hear the sound of squeaky wheels along the road, which caused her to glance briefly up towards her window, but her mind was more alert to the words on the page.

My Dearest Amethyst Rose,

When we were together, I not once said what was on my heart. With this letter, I shall have my say knowing it will forever be recorded.

My beloved, I have adored you since first we met, even on that morning, when it was difficult to know what was beneath the mud and mire which covered you. My heart ached for you then. It does this day.

I have watched you carry my name in pretense for your own protection. Yet you have stated your heart rests with another. I have prayed you would forget your man Jonathan, and instead consider me.

More than that, I have prayed you would come to know God and experience true peace and no longer look at me as an enemy who fights against all that graces your heart.

The war is over, Aimée. Take consolation in the fact it was not of my making nor design. I served only as I had to. Allow the flame of hatred that once burned in your heart for me to cease and replace it with the love of God.

Walk the same path I walk, Amethyst Rose. For I must confess my loyalty remains first to my God.

Trust and believe, then accept my proposal to become my true wife and helpmate. I will wait and pray with expectancy.

Palmer

Aimée lay staring at the letter, her eyes burning from tears as she choked through Palmer's words several more times before her light fizzled out and the room became dark.

He did love her.

Palmer Jordan did love her!

Jonathan was not the man for whom she had saved herself all those years. All this time it had been Palmer!

Trust and believe…say you will be mine.

Palmer knew nothing of her recent commitment to God! He knew nothing of the flame going on within her now…that refining of her heart. The troubled life she'd had with her sister.

Aimée's dismay increased.

The two in the room below were more than likely going to attempt to make her sell her body to the buyer of choice. This was it. Thanks to her stupidity to even allow herself to have a cup of tea with Mr. Proctor. This time it *was* too late.

Too late because her Palmer was up in Washington, DC, serving his country, believing she remained in Virginia under the protection of his loving grandparents, while, she, instead, had let down her guard once again.

Fears of what tomorrow would bring cobwebbed her mind as she cried herself nearly to sleep. But in the midst of her sobs her chamber slowly filled with smoke.

Aimée, her eyes burning, became instantly wide awake.

* * * *

Outside the sky looked heavily lit just over the next hill, smothering the fog of night as bright embers shot up amidst the smoke.

Fresh flames soared chaotic, causing havoc all over *The French Quarter* while several neighbors stood outside their homes watching the destruction. The onlookers caught site of the carriage pulling up in front of the burning building, and the man with a slight limp in his gait who ran up towards them.

"Is there still anyone still inside?" he asked.

"Couldn't say to be honest, sir."

"I thought I saw a light in an upstairs window," said someone.

"I thought I noticed a landau in front of the place either this morning or was it yesterday? I try not to keep track of the traffic what comes in and out of the place. The whole place is usually pretty well lit up all the time. I say whatever happened good riddance," another neighbor rambled on.

Palmer did not wait for the rest of their suggestions and his booted feet carried him on towards what was left of the burning building.

Heading for the back of the building where it looked as if the fire had not yet taken its toll, he thought he saw someone wrapped in a coverlet, crying from the sun porch.

He jumped up on the platform and wrapped his arms around the weeping woman. They rolled off the porch and into the garden, just as the racing flames started to take hold of the end piece of her protective covering.

When the flame began moving up the fabric, he hurriedly pulled the material off her and rolled her into the nearest bush until the embers smothered out.

"God help this woman!"

Palmer drew in closer until he saw the woman's eyes.

"Palmer, 'tis you?"

Palmer recognized her seconds before she looked up. Then she fainted in his arms.

* * * *

"Will she live, Dr. Boswell?" asked Tante Fran in a hushed tone outside her niece's room. "It's been two days now."

"She'll be fine. The poor woman has miraculously survived a tremendous tragedy. What's amazing is this'll be the second fire she's had to experience herself or endure because of her family in less than two years, just as you said yesterday, Mrs. Simpson."

Dr. Boswell shook his head. "It'll be difficult for her to get some of the images out of her mind."

Fran peeked in the room one more time before shutting the door where Palmer, who had not left Aimée's side, sat watching over her.

"And what about him?" she asked, directing her head towards the man who saved her niece's life. "He's been here for her more than once, I daresay."

"Come with me." The doctor walked her out of earshot of the major. "That man has a deep investment in the young woman, it would appear. I think God will take care of the details of those two, whatever they might be."

* * * *

Tears poured down Aimée's cheeks when she opened her eyes and saw Palmer sleeping against the chair, his head leaning back, his mouth slightly ajar. When she stirred, he woke up quickly and sat upright. A smile spread across his face.

"I am yet alive?" she asked softly.

"You are very much alive, my beloved, and we are in your room at *Primrose Ivy*. The Paramount is no more."

"You are here...with me?"

"I am here...with you."

"Mr. Proctor, Nina?"

"Perished, I've been told. I arrived just in time to pull you off the porch. I do apologize I didn't arrive in time to avoid your getting hurt, my love. You've a small burn on the back of your leg."

Reaching beneath her covers, Aimée felt down at her leg. "That was already there...a reminder of yesteryear...a time past when I experienced another fire."

"I'm sorry about that, too."

"'Twas not of your doing." Their eyes locked.

"Do you know how it happened...the fire at The Paramount?"

Aimée shook her head. "Perhaps one could say the result of what happens when people choose the wrong path in life. Doesn't it say in scriptures somewhere we must reap what we sow?"

"It does, but all that matters to me, Aimée, is you're alive."

"I no longer have your letter."

"I will write you another."

"Palmer, I read it...several times. It is gone."

He smiled. "It didn't drive you farther from me?"

"I'm here, aren't I?"

"Where else can you go!" He laughed.

* * * *

It felt good to Aimée to walk down the stairs to familiar surroundings—to be at Tante Fran's again, to know Palmer was still nearby.

"Tante Fran, have you heard from Sarah?" she asked, walking in to the drawing room.

"Forgive me please, darlins'," answered Tante. "I never did tell you. Yes I did. I've heard from Sarah. In your delirium, you asked about her. She escaped the fire. Someone saw her going north. A family took her in. Thankfully, there are plenty looking for help these days."

"Do you recall my mentioning the letter from David?" asked Fran.

"I don't," said Aimée.

"Mr. Withers said your brother returned to the states several months ago to reclaim *Shadow Grove*. When Jonathan was here, he told me he had seen David first when he came back, and the folks in Vicksburg filled him in on your sister. David wrote me, thinking you might be here. The letter sits on my bureau if you would like to read it"

Aimée's eyes lit up. "How would he have known I was here?"

"I'll wager that was Jonathan's doing as well," suggested Palmer, when Fran left the room. "When he left *Pencil Ridge* with his new bride, they probably went to Vicksburg before leaving the country. Mr. Dewey might've stopped by your old place."

"It's still hard to believe about Jonathan and Cornelia!" said Aimée.

"I don't suppose his new wife minded much when the truth came out he was never was missing-in-action at all from the service," commented Fran as she walked back into the room and handed Aimée the envelope. "Apparently Mr. Dewey wanted to avoid fighting, so he ran and hid till the troops moved out."

"And the wedding, Tante, he wanted to avoid having to support a wife at all costs." Aimée held up her hand to stop her aunt. "Never mind, I need not listen to the details about the man."

Palmer nudged Fran back out of the room.

"Mr. Withers did some research. You might as well know this. Your father told Mr. Dewey he expected him to prove himself, by showing he would provide for you once the two of you were married. Mr. Lebrún refused to release any of your dowry until he saw evidence of the fact. It frightened Mr. Dewey enough not to go through with it."

Aimée shrugged, "My father always knew best, Palmer. As far as I'm concerned, Cornelia and Jonathan are perfect for each other.

Excuse me a moment while I see what my brother had to say here."

She turned to the envelope in her hand. When Aimée pulled out the section David intended for her, she read slowly. Suddenly so much of his life and her sister's life became clear for the first time.

"It was I who ruined your older sister's life and taught her to develop a hatred for men, for me. She will always hate me.

Papa was right in sending me away. He was protecting you. It is too late for Florette, but I hope it is not too late to seek amends with you."

Aimée closed her eyes. She didn't want to read anymore. Now she understood why Florette gained her hatred for men, and why she had treated her the way she had while growing up.

Aimée then recalled how Florette forgave her brother only moments before she died. He didn't know it yet. More than anything, she now understood why David must have stayed away so long.

She had to forgive him, too. She needed to get word to him about Florette and what she had asked her to tell him.

She looked up to see Palmer watching her. "I must see my brother right away, Palmer. Will you help me?"

"You know I will."

Epilogue

I praise you because I am fearfully and wonderfully made;
Your works are wonderful, I know that full well.
Psalm 139:14 NIV

August 1865

Aimée gave him Captain Moreau a kiss on the cheek. "I cannot thank you enough for doing this for me!"

"'Twould be an *honneur* to give zee *jeune* bride away," he declared. "*Dites-juste moi quand* – Just tell me when. *Pardonner*…I hope I shall not slip into my lazy French!"

"It won't matter to me," replied Aimée. "I'm only happy you can be there. Mother and Papa would wish it."

"Your brother, David, he won't mind?"

"No. He is busy rebuilding home and his life, as it should be. I am happy for him and truly blessed *Shadow Grove* will once again be a reality."

After waving goodbye to her aunt and the captain, she hurried down the front steps to meet Palmer, where he helped her up and in the carriage and ordered the driver on their way. On any other day, listening to the rhythmic sound of the horses' hooves along the dry, dust-ridden roads of Southern Louisiana, Aimée would have easily fallen asleep, but this particular afternoon was different.

"Ready to get fitted for your dress, Aimée?"

She nodded. "More than ready."

"You're sure this is what you want?"

"More certain than I've been about anything in my life. I only wish I still had my letter. Maybe it isn't necessary. I memorized the important part."

"And you don't hold anything against me?"

Aimée smiled. "How could I? It's always been you, Palmer Jordan." Tears welled within her eyes. "Even in my bitterness it was you."

"Eventually, I think I knew."

"You knew?"

"Maybe I tried not to."

"Why did we fight each other so?"

"I kept waiting to know where you were in you heart, Aimée."

But are you sure I am what *you* want?"

Leaning across the seat, Palmer took her face between both his hands and caressed her cheeks, as he stared longingly into her eyes. "If you memorized my letter then you know the answer to that. What more is there to say?"

Aimée's eyes searched his. "You're making it difficult for me to breathe right now."

"Wait a minute," he said huskily "How about if I say the important words again. I love you!"

She felt a warm glow. "And I you, Major!" Lifting her chin, Aimée closed her eyes and then opened one eye back up. I've been waiting forever for the real thing."

"Have you?" Palmer brushed a gentle kiss across Aimée's forehead.

"Dreamed of it to be honest with you."

Reaching his arm around her neck, Palmer played with a loose curl and breathed into her ear then pulled her to him and spoke in a ragged whisper. "Do you think you're old enough to handle the real thing? You may be surprised what it can lead to, love."

"Shall I truly? What I'm feeling within right now tells me it's been worth the wait."

"Promise you won't run away from me *this time*."

Aimée smiled at him with her eyes. "I didn't run away before, Palmer. Where would I go? Can I ask you that?" With her dove-soft hand, Aimée reached up and caressed his cheek. "My place is with you."

He pulled her in closer. "No, I guess you didn't, did you? I look forward to welcoming you home for real, Mrs. Jordan."

Acknowledgments

My special thanks to Ruth Logan Herne, formerly of WRP, for her personal advice in some of my earlier drafts

To Barry Denenberg, whose wealth of knowledge in American History helped me to gain a better understanding of such a pivotal time for the people of the South

To the fantastic editorial staff of Vintage Romance Publishing

To God, who's always given me reason to never give up on my dreams.

About the Author

Shirley Kiger Connolly started writing at about age eight, she claims, when a teacher proclaimed her a budding Phyllis McKinley and raised her brow at an avid child's imagination. Shirley's love for historical fiction, literature, and classical poetry only enhances her desire to keep putting her pen to use.

When not in make-believe, she's busy writing light-hearted devotionals, teaching women's group studies, directing her online ministry team, or sharing at ministry retreats. "I use my writing, teaching, and speaking to emphasize God's love for his people; to bring encouragement to women. It's my heart's passion."

Shirley and her husband, Tom, live on the Southern Coast of Oregon. To write to Shirley, feel free to visit her at her website: http://shirleykoinonia.tripod.com.

Coming August 30, 2008
Vintage Spirit
www.vrpublishing.com

Grit for the Oyster: 250 Pearls of Wisdom for Aspiring
Writers
Written by *Suzanne Woods Fisher, Debora M. Coty, Faith*
Tibbetts McDonald, Joanna Bloss
Writing/Non-fiction/Inspirational

A powerful motivator for aspiring writers, *Grit for the*
Oyster offers wit, wisdom, and inspiration to take that
first step and persevere through the writing journey.
More than a how-to, this confidence-building book is
designed to draw readers to a closer relationship with
God, to affirm their calling to write, and to offer pithy
practical guidance from successful writers like Terri
Blackstock, Martha Bolton, James Scott Bell, Liz Curtis
Higgs, Dr. Gary Chapman, and David Kopp.

Including such quotes as:

"In these pages, you'll find a helpful and soul
strengthening community." -David Kopp, best-selling co-
author of *The Prayer of Jabez*

"This is definitely a book you want to keep within close
reach as you work. It's like having your own personal
writer's group and cheering squad right in your own
home!" -Linda Danis, best-selling author of *365 Things Every*
New Mom Should Know

"To those who feel called to write for the glory of God,
Grit for the Oyster is like the 'Writer's Bible.'" -Ruth
Carmichael Ellinger, award-winning author of *The Wild*
Rose of Lancaster

Printed in the United States
116887LV00001B/30/P